Sisterhoods

Linda Regan

Published by Accent Press Ltd 2016

ISBN 9781910939819

Acknowledgements

I would like to thank all the detectives and other police officers who have always helped me and answered my questions, however and whatever they are. I know you don't like being named, so I won't, but my thank you is heartfelt and the sentiment is true: I couldn't have written this without you.

As ever, the street-girls and gangs who kindly spoke frankly to me. I thank you so much.

I would also like to thank Greg Rees for his editing genius, and all at Accent for publishing me.

This book is dedicated to two people who tirelessly encouraged my writing, and whose own talent I will never stop respecting and admiring: my darling husband Brian Murphy, and my very, very special friend Jimmy Perry OBE. Two rare and wonderful human beings.

Chapter One

Tink couldn't see, she could only feel, and the pain felt almost unbearable.

She assured herself that she had endured worse, and soon this would pass. There was nothing this gang of animals could do to her that she hadn't experienced before. She had worked the streets since she was a child, and suffered years of abuse from her drug-addicted mother. If these wimps thought this was going to make her cry out and beg them to stop, tell them everything they asked, and give them everything they wanted, then they were bigger wankers than she already had them down for.

With her face covered, she couldn't see to take a swing back at any of the bastards even if she wanted to, but she had weighed up the pros and cons: there were at least four of them, so it was better to take the beating and get it over and done with. As another blow shook her bony body, she bit into her already bleeding lip. This was just another beating, it would pass, she told herself.

She closed her eyes and dreamed of being the best hairdresser ever, creating new colours and styles, and leading fashion trends. That was going to happen, no matter how many beatings it took, no matter how many buildings on the estate got burned down, and no matter how many rivals thought they could terrorise her gang into giving in. The Alley Cats weren't wimps, they were stronger and better than any of these wankers, they would rebuild all the burnt outbuildings and make a different future for the Aviary Estate.

It wasn't the pain that was the worst bit anyway, it was the humiliation. This gutless gang had caught her off guard, or else she wouldn't be here, locked in this van, with six of them knocking the shit out of her, holding shanks and lighters against her face, threatening they hadn't even started on her yet, and guaranteeing she would soon be begging them to let her hand over the goods that they kept telling her the Alley Cats had stolen from them.

The pain was bearable, just, but the shame – now that was different. She should never have let this happen to her. She was a lieutenant in the Alley Cats, and her gang had respect round here, big time. Respect they had earned. They were looked up to on the Aviary Estate, and Tink had that reputation to keep up. The residents on the Aviary trusted the ACs and depended on them. Even the pensioners weren't afraid to leave their flats these days, knowing that Alley Cats policed the grounds so no muggings happened. The estate kids too, they were all looked out for. No kid from the Aviary went hungry because their parents were too busy sticking needles in their veins or chucking booze down their throats to even remember they had kids – the ACs gave them food and kept a close eye on them. And the Alley Cats did any dealing that happened around the grounds of the estate. No dodgy pushers were getting near the Aviary: the ACs did whatever it took to keep them out and away from the kids. The girls sold drugs, but only to the addicts. They also pimped their own street girls, the ones that still wanted to work the streets around the area, but they took good care of them. They took a cut of the street trade, but the corn they earned from that was used to make the Aviary into a better place for everyone that lived on it.

And, up till now, it had been doing fine. They even

had money to pay for rehab for those residents who wanted to kick their habits, and if any girl wanted off the streets but still needed her fix, then the ACs supported her – though everything came at a price.

They had rebuilt the run-down recreation grounds and the community hall so the kids had places to play and things to do on the estate. No kids were going to suffer the pain of hunger or the feelings of humiliation that all the AC lieutenants had grown up with. The new estate young 'uns wouldn't have to sell drugs or hide firearms or use their young bodies in order to eat.

Tink had been in the process of opening one of the run-down shops at the corner of the estate as a hairdressing and nail salon, since the Alley Cats had invested in her and had sent her to do a beauty and hair course to learn the trade she loved. And she had never been happier, she was going to do hairdressing and pass her skills on to the kids on the estate.

The ACs had plans to rebuild more of the burnt-down shops, to make more to do for the residents; judo was planned, self-defence, different music nights and recording sessions, some gardening for the elderly and cake-making and stuff, but for all these plans the ACs needed to bring in money. So the AC lieutenants, Tink, Panther, Lox and their leader, Queen Alysha, had become snouts for the police. They were on the police payroll, and were making good money from that. It also meant they could keep trouble off the estate with the quiet back-up of the feds, and the feds had promised they would push the council for a second rebuilding grant for the estate.

Being snouts and drug dealers was dangerous, the ACs knew that, but then these four lieutenants had grown up facing danger every day. If any local gangs got wind of what they were up to, though, all the girls knew they would be dead meat. The price of informing was death, on any turf, all of London knew that, but the girls were willing to take the risk. They all wanted kids and they didn't want their offspring having to face the starvation, stealing and prostitution they had all been brought up with. They were all at least sixteen now and feared nothing and no one. Being snouts helped their ambitions. If a dealer or a pimp trespassed on the Aviary and got in their way, then the ACs would simply set them up with the feds. That got dealers off their territory and into prison. But as one gang went down, another one always surfaced, and it was a constant struggle to protect their territory and the new breed of estate kids.

But even after a local gang had burnt down the recently rebuilt community centre, these girls weren't giving up. They were the Alley Cats, and they would find a way to rebuild and keep their dream of a better future alive. However, the powerful East is Best gang, run by the ruthless Zhang family, and the Rifles in Peckham gang from closer to home had now reared their heads again, both determined to take over the Aviary and its rich pickings.

These pricks were RIPs. Some said RIP stood for Rioters in Peckham. Tink didn't give a shit what it stood for, she just knew they were evil bastards who enjoyed inflicting pain. She winced as the ring-adorned fist landed again, and she tasted more blood. Another blow, and her head hit the hard metal of the floor behind her with a painful thud. She of thought the black fed who had assured her police protection was theirs at all times. Police informants were always looked after, that fed Johnson had blabbed to her. So where were they now? Where was anyone when she needed them? The only people who never let her down were her gang, and her sister lieutenants. She knew, only too well, that they would kill these pricks when they found out what had been done to

4

her, and that was the thought that kept her strong, and the fact that she had promised the pensioners on the estate that she would finish making all the cards for their bingo night on Thursday. Even if they didn't have a community centre, they would still have the bingo club: the ACs were running it in their flat on the thirteenth floor of the Sparrow block, with or without the lift working. So she would take this beating, and get through it, she wasn't going to let anyone down. One day a week she did the pensioners' hair too, so she had to protect her hands right now, even if her face was getting messed up. People relied on her, and her fellow lieutenants would get even for this. The arson attacks hadn't stopped them, and this beating wouldn't either. The Aviary Estate was going to change, for the good. This was a mere blip.

The RIP gang were dirt. They didn't like the fact that girls were running the territory and that the young 'uns were listening to them, and not taking the drugs the RIPs dished out, as a way of pulling them into starting the habit. The Alley Cats would have left them alone, they could do what they wanted on their own turf, but now they had trespassed on the Aviary they had to be stopped. Who did they think they were? How did they think they could get away with doing that? They had driven onto the estate, as large as life, in a BMW they had nicked from the East is Best gang, obviously intending to leave it on the Aviary so the EIBs would think the ACs had nicked it and start a war with them. Or else they thought they could fool the ACs into thinking the EIBs were on their territory. Well, the ACs weren't fooled for a moment. They had watched the RIPs drive onto Aviary territory as large as bloody life, so, of course, they had to be taught a lesson.

The girls had immediately been on their phones and summoned their soldiers. They now had a full strength of almost eighty members in the gang, and nearly thirty were there within minutes. They surrounded the BMW and seized the four trespassers inside, and then took them to one of the lock-ups on the Aviary.

Firstly they gave them all a good kicking – that in itself would have been demoralising for those so-called blokes. They would have to go back to their leader, the supposedly formidable Ray Maxted, and admit to being beaten up by a gang of girls. But the girls didn't think a little beating was enough for the crime they had committed, so they took possession of the black BMW that the RIPs were driving, which, as luck would have it, turned out to be housing ten grand's worth of heroin and a consignment of handguns. 'Finders keepers', the girls had told the RIPs, as they unloaded the gear, delighting in the knowledge that by the time they had moved all that gear on in another part of London, they would have enough money to rebuild the community centre *and* help one of their residents who was in deep debt with loan sharks. This woman, Lisa Hardy, was a junkie with two children, and was so deep in debt that she had endured many beatings over it, and now faced being shot if she didn't pay up. The ACs had told her that if they raised the money to pay her debts then it would be on the condition that she went into rehab to get off the stuff before that killed her too.

The girls locked the rival gang members in a garage and made plans. The Alley Cats wanted to send out a message: if you mess with us, you'll pay the price. The rival soldiers had to pay, and the stash of heroin and guns would be the price. It would go a very long way towards rebuilding their estate.

The girls also decided not to return the car to the East is Best gang. It was probably stolen anyway, and if they were seen, which they probably would be, then it would

6

be obvious they had nicked the gear from it. Instead they drove the motor to a back street a few miles away, where Lox set fire to it. The girls knew this would mean East is Best would blame the RIPs for stealing their drugs and firearms, putting them at war with each other, which in turn would keep them busy and out of the Aviary.

After the girls had given the trespassing RIP soldiers a good beating, they had stripped them all naked. Tink then wrote, in bright red nail varnish, across all their backs: *Stay off the Aviary Estate, it aint your territory*. Then the girls tied them up.

Lox called a cab, and gave the driver twenty quid, telling him to take the naked gang boys as far east as the twenty quid went, and then to throw them out into the street. However, the cab driver refused to take them, so they went down to where the street girls solicited, and while Alley Cat soldier Summer was servicing a noisy punter, who conveniently happened to own a 4x4, the girls climbed into the back of the car, held one of the stolen guns to the punter's head, and told him to get out of his car. As they drove off in his car, with the four naked RIP soldiers, they promised the punter they would be back, and told Summer to give him another free trick or two for his trouble.

Tink drove the car as far east as she dared, then turfed the naked RIPs out onto EIB territory, before driving the 4x4 back and returning it to the punter, who was getting a very long, with extras and at no cost, service from Summer. The punter couldn't say anything, as he couldn't admit to the embarrassment of being in that predicament. He got in his car and drove off as fast as he could, and hadn't been seen in the area since.

Tink had been seized from behind as she walked along the street around the estate. A sack had quickly covered her head, a rope was thrown around her neck, then she had been dragged along the road and thrown into the back of this van. She recognised some of the voices. It was definitely Ray Maxted and some of his disgusting gang.

She only knew for certain that there were four or five of them, and that they had all decided to have a go at raping her. Maxted himself, the sadistic Jamaican leader of the Rifles in Peckham gang, was a short-arse. He was five foot four or five, so chances were he had a tiny prick. She had just had one of those up her back passage, and had she not known that this gang would kill at will, she might have laughed when it was pushed inside her. She could hardly feel the fucker, but she knew not to say so. She'd whored for years as a kid, so she knew how to play the game and pretend. She screamed out, as if in pain, as he rode her from behind. Truth was, that bit was merely boring. Being beaten up and raped by this gang wasn't half as demoralising as being caught. How she wished, at this moment, that she had been more on her guard and hadn't let them get her. She had been standing looking at her burnt-down shop when it happened, and was so immersed in sadness she hadn't seen or heard anyone creep up behind her.

After the humiliating gang rape, the sack was removed from her head, but from behind, so she still didn't see faces. A blindfold was quickly tied round her eyes, then she was turned again, to face them, and had taken a severe beating. She was already feeling drowsy from the smacking she had taken, so she knew it wouldn't be long before she lost consciousness. She would be out of it very soon, and then she'd wake up and it all would be over. She lay back, willing herself to pass out.

That was when she heard the flick of the lighter, and then the smell of the gas. She became very awake as her whole body tensed. She hadn't reckoned on being set on

8

fire. Now she was afraid, very afraid.

The blindfold was ripped from her bleeding face and she found herself staring at a flame which was inches away from her face. Everything else was blurred, even the hand that held it. Her swollen black eyes meant she couldn't focus clearly, but she knew she was facing Ray Maxted. The naked flame was now less than an inch from her face. Then the hand moved it away and down, now within inches from the bare skin on her body where all her clothes had been ripped off. And Maxted was grinning, she could see that grin, displaying his gold tooth. She gritted her teeth as he moved the naked flame towards her body, now an inch from her bruised and raw skin. He stopped at her pubic hair. Her body shivered, and then shivered again. She was unable to control herself. He grinned again, and then the flame moved quickly upwards and he dug it into her bare nipple. She screamed out in agony. The pain was like a firework exploding inside her,

'About my brown?' he said, grabbing the back of her hair and moving the flame to in front of her face. 'I think you were about to tell me where you've been keepin' it, since you stole it from my car.'

She spat in his face.

The flame was pressed into her other nipple, and the electrifying pain filled her breast and then her stomach. Then as she screamed again, and gasped for air, she felt the flame catch her ear and hair.

'I asked you a question, bitch.'

She wished with all her might that she would pass out there and then. All the memories of being abused as a frightened child came flooding back to her. She had to fight with all her being not to scream out again in fear and pain.

There was a hammer now, resting against the side of her jaw, which took her terrified attention. Her eyes were too swollen to see which of the RIPs held it. But she recognised the voice.

'Shall I do her skull in, bro?' It was Muscle, Maxted's right-hand man. He had a reputation for brutality and torture.

'Nah, let's burn the witch.'

To her right she was aware that someone held a knife. Christ, she just wished someone would give her one hard bang on the head, and she could pass out. Brave as she knew she was, this pain was just too much to bear. The burning of her nipples was tortuous. She had to keep gasping at mouthfuls of air to tolerate the pain it gave her.

The gang rape had been a joke, she had endured a lot, lot worse, and the beating had hurt a lot, but she'd had loads of those over the years. But this, this was different. She was going to have scars, permanent scars! If she lived, that was. How she could have a hair and beauty school and be disfigured? Just when she had thought life might change for the better, her worst nightmare was happening.

Another stab with the flame, in her stomach again, and this time she threw up.

'Fuckin' bitch! Oi! I'm talking to you, bitch,' Maxted said between his grated teeth. 'Where's my gear, or don't you wanna live?'

Tink could now barely breathe, and she was seeing stars. She had to get through this, she told herself, she had to hope for unconsciousness to come. She'd been glad that she was blindfolded when her knickers and jeans were cut from her, and her bare legs and buttocks pulled into the air, then her legs pulled open as if she was a shopping bag. One after the other, they'd raped her and roughed her up, ripping her top and bra off, then biting hard on her nipples. And then the last one, it was Tip, she knew that 'cos he kept shouting, 'Hey, Man!' as he hammered into

10

her eyes with his fist, the back of her head bouncing against the metal door handle.

'Last time I fucking ask you, bitch!' Maxted shouted at her, as the blurry lighter moved back and forth in front of her face. He didn't give her time to answer. 'Take this as a message to the other cunts,' he continued, his voice now low and threatening. 'Tell them if we don't get back the gear you've stolen, then it's gonna get a lot worse than this, for all of you. Got that?'

He moved the flame again against her arm and singed it up and down, like he was painting the ceiling. She felt her skin shrivel from the burning flame, and she screamed out.

Then the flame was against her body and moving around like a metal detector. She closed her eyes, fought for breath, and prayed for darkness. It was all too much.

She hadn't seen it, so she didn't know it was coming, but now she felt the knife. It was like another burn, an agonising sting, and it hurt like hell. She knew she'd been shanked. Blood was pumping from her stomach, but she felt so dizzy …

Just as she lost consciousness she heard the engine of the van start up and the back door fly open.

'Get the message now, do you,' Maxted shouted as she was kicked, still naked, from the van into the street.

But Tink could no longer hear. She hit the ground, unconscious, and bleeding heavily.

Chapter Two

Detective Inspector Georgia Johnson was in her office catching up on paperwork. She had watered and sprayed each leaf on her pot plant, then polished her desk until she could see her own reflection in the shining wood. It didn't matter that the cleaners came in twice a week; nothing was ever up to her own meticulous standards. Then, having flicked the ceilings with a duster, checking carefully for cobwebs, she sat down behind the pile of papers on her desk and started to catch up on reports.

She was still relatively new to this serious crime and murder department. At thirty-three, she was quite young to have reached the position of detective inspector, but she was very ambitious and now had her sights set firmly on getting a DCI post, which meant putting in many extra unpaid, hours, and taking risks to keep catching criminals and keep reaching and surpassing her targets. She came from a family of high achievers: her parents were both doctors, and her siblings too had all gone into medicine in some form or another.

Georgia had set her sights on a career as a detective after she had been raped as a fifteen-year-old. He had never been caught, as she had been too ashamed to report it. She blamed herself. The night it happened, she had disobeyed her parents and walked home, alone, in the dark, across the local common, where she had been jumped on and dragged into bushes and raped on a pile of filthy autumn leaves. It had left its mark in the form of her

OCD, the compulsive washing habit, but also in her determination. Once there was a criminal out there who needed catching, especially one who had committed a crime against women, Georgia would stop at nothing until she had the bastard locked up.

Competition was fierce, as hers was one of the busiest police stations in South London, and a lot was against her. New gangs were springing up weekly, and with that came a sharp rise in stabbings and shootings on her South London patch. Consequently, Georgia often found herself working double her usual hours to get results. But results brought promotion. She was aware that no matter how much the Met bleated about racial and sexual equality and distributed their countless memos about it, being black and a woman was still a disadvantage in the force. Police work was a white male-dominated profession, and anyone else still had to prove themselves many times over.

Georgia had already made a few mistakes since being seconded to this station, but she was also very astute, and had helped to lower crime figures on the infamous Aviary Estate. The powers that be knew that that in itself was nothing short of a miracle. In the past, the Aviary had been responsible for a high percentage of the knife, drug, and gun crime that was rife in the local area, and, up until recently, no resident on the estate spoke to the police – or 'the feds', as they called them – except to say they had seen nothing. The residents were too terrified of the ruling gangs and the consequences of speaking to the police. Anyone known to have talked to 'the feds' was severely punished, and that meant a deep scar or maybe the loss of a finger – and that was if you were lucky.

The problem for the police was breaking the gangs up, which meant arresting the leading gang members and getting them sent down. However, as soon as they rounded up one dangerous gang leader, and got them sentenced and off the South London streets, then another rose up and took over.

By chance, when investigating a murder, Georgia had befriended a few of the street girls on the Aviary estate. She had found them helpful and unafraid of the consequences from their pimps and gang leaders. The girls had been more concerned for the welfare of the estate residents, and future of the estate's children than for themselves. As they had nothing else to look forward to, the kids had been turning to crime from as young as seven or eight. Georgia saw this as an opportunity, a way of getting to the core of the problems on that estate. She offered to help the girls to get a council grant to rebuild the playground and a community centre so the kids had somewhere safe to go, and things to do. In return she wanted information on the gangs that were dealing drugs and firearms and causing criminal damage on the Aviary. The girls had agreed, and immediately gave her solid information which got a gang sent down for operating grass factories in their houses.

Georgia kept her word. Within weeks the council grant came through and the playground was rebuilt, and then the community centre. Things started to go better for everyone. More dealers were arrested and more firearms found. Georgia's four informants were always spot on. Georgia then took her case to DCI Banham, requesting that the girls were put on the payroll, secretly, as legitimate police informants.

The DCI agreed, on the condition that only Georgia and her sergeant, Stephanie Green, were to know about the arrangement. The four girls were all young: none was more than seventeen. Informing for the police could prove very dangerous to their personal welfare, so at all costs they had to be protected. Local gangs had already shown their depth of brutality towards any resident who spoke to the police, so any revelation that the girls were informants would likely prove fatal for them. All four girls had said they were willing to take the risks as long as they were paid well, and so the police promised them protection as well as regular money.

To date, the arrangement was working: criminals were getting caught, and crime figures on the estate had dropped. Indeed, the fact that Georgia had this morning to catch up on her paperwork showed how crime around the area had decreased. The estate had even started to flourish, its new community centre hosting activities like dancing, self-defence and cake-making. The residents were finally being catered for.

Recently, though, the playground and the community centre had been burnt to the ground again. Just a few months after the council had finished rebuilding it. The four girls, who were now effectively running the estate, tried to get another grant from the council, to rebuild again, but the council had refused, saying that investing money in a sink estate like the Aviary was akin to setting fire to the money themselves.

Georgia didn't want to lose the girls as informants. Crime was down and arrests had tripled. She knew this was down to information from these four, and also how their tip-offs had put her in a good position for the next promotion in the department. And not only were crime figures down, but all police raids around the Aviary had proved successful due to precise tip-offs from these four girls. Every month more criminals were being taken off the streets.

The girls had been nicknamed the 'Estate Angels' by the serious crimes department. Georgia thought that a joke; the girls all had very chequered pasts. Alysha Achter had shot someone, and had it not been for Georgia and her sergeant, Stephanie Green, she would have been sent down for murder. Fortunately for Alysha, Georgia and Stephanie had been nearby when it happened, and were able to testify in her favour, saying that she had fired in self-defence. That had kept her out of prison.

Lox and Veronica, who was known as Tink, had both been in trouble for prostitution and aggravated burglary in the past, and Panther was on probation for ABH. However, Georgia trusted, and liked, these girls, especially Alysha, who was brown-skinned like herself and afraid of nothing. Georgia often thought that if she hadn't had to have her own womb removed, then any daughter she might have had, would probably have looked just like Alysha.

The girls had all had very difficult starts to their lives, but they had learned the hard way, they had now changed and were law-abiding citizens. She believed they were doing a good job trying to better themselves and the estate they lived on. They delivered information, and in return the police protected them and paid them. And crime figures had dropped.

Unlike her 'angels', Georgia had been lucky enough to be born into a comfortably off middle-class family. She had been given love as a child and a first-class education. Alysha, Lox, Tink and Panther had all spent parts of their childhood in care, and the rest on the streets living from hand to mouth. Georgia sympathised, but she also admired their strength of survival. She wanted them to achieve their goals, and make the estate a better and safer place to live, and was glad to help them to do it. She was also aware it was helping her on the road to her next promotion.

She opened her computer, clicked on the first of today's emails, and then sat staring at it. It took a minute for it to sink in, and then she looked at the time it was sent. It was now ten thirty. The email had arrived at eight o'clock, while she was busy polishing her office windows. *Shit!*

Stephanie Green was typing up witness statements. She had been accompanying DI Johnson the day before, when they were out at Larry Hardy's school taking statements. Larry, everyone told them, was a quiet boy, didn't make trouble and rarely got into any, but witnesses had seen him with a large knife as they left school, the week before, and then seen him stab Ji Zhang in the back. The knife had punctured Zhang's lung. He had died before the ambulance could get him to hospital. Larry had stood frozen to the spot, everyone said, holding the knife, with blood dripping from his hand, as if in a trance. Larry was arrested, and because of the seriousness of his crime and the fact that the boy he had killed was known to be a prominent member of an East London gang, the judge had refused bail, and Larry had been taken to a young offender institution, and kept on remand for his own safety.

Georgia opened her office door and called out, 'Sergeant Green, my office.' Stephanie immediately obeyed, hurrying along the corridor holding a bacon sandwich.

Stephanie and Georgia were complete opposites in temperament, looks, and world view, and yet their friendship knew no bounds. Stephanie was a Londoner through and through. She had been born in Stepney Green, hence her nickname, 'The Tube' – for just as most Londoners had been in Stepney Green tube station, most of the men in the murder department had been in Stephanie.

Stephanie found it funny. She knew she had been known as the office bike and she was proud of her sexual conquests. Now approaching forty, and with an appetite for chocolate and fried food, she bore even more weight than her chubby younger figure had. These days her conquests were less frequent, but if she fancied someone, then she went all out to bed them – and normally got her way. For her, it was light-hearted and harmless. She had married very young and was now divorced, with her children finally away at university, it was just a way of having a bit of fun while she still could.

She was an excellent detective sergeant, and had passed both her board, and the exam, for the post of DI, but had refused the promotion on many occasions. As a single parent she had chosen to spend more time with her teenage children. Both were now off her hands, but Stephanie was still happy as a DS. Being a DI meant too much work; she liked the time for herself – and her sexual conquests.

Stephanie didn't care about keeping her desk tidy, or getting mud on her shoes. Georgia, on the other hand, was meticulous to the point of annoyance. The brutal rape Georgia had experienced had given rise to her cleanliness obsession, and she washed and cleaned anything and everything around her at every spare moment. Whereas Georgia came from a family of doctors, Stephanie came from a family of detectives. It was in her blood. She had the nose for it, people would say.

Georgia relied on Stephanie, but never said as much. Stephanie was aware of that but never let on, and never let her friend down. Georgia was the senior officer but Stephanie was intelligent enough to know that if she had applied for that DI post, it would have gone to her. The women however made an excellent team. DCI Banham was aware of it, and made a point of keeping them together, knowing they brought in good results.

As soon as Stephanie had closed the door behind her, Georgia lowered her voice, 'Larry Hardy has been found hanging in his cell,' she told Stephanie. 'He was left, only briefly. No one had the slightest suspicion he needed to be on suicide watch.' The two women stared at each other for a second, then Georgia put her fists to her head. 'Fuck. Fuck, fuck. He was put on remand to keep him safe from the Zhangs, and he's killed himself.'

'The boy had no previous, and apparently hardly ever said boo to a goose,' Stephanie said. 'Stabbing Ji Zhang was completely out of character. But there were so many witnesses.' She looked Georgia in the eye. 'He lived on the Aviary Estate.'

Georgia nodded that she was thinking the same. 'Yup. I think it's time our informants earned this month's salary.'

Alysha Achter's flat was on the thirteenth floor of Sparrow block. Alysha and Lox had been sitting, for the last couple of hours, on the old pink sofa that they had bought in a sale at IKEA, going through figures. Lox had an iPad and calculated all their income and outgoings. They all had a salary from the feds for informing, and there was the cut from the street girls' takings, and the drug deals. They needed more money though. Their community hall, and some shops and the play area, had been burnt down, the council weren't giving them any more money, or 'corn' as Alysha constantly referred to it. They had plans which needed money, so they had to work out ways to get it.

The estate was theirs now, they were the ruling gang. They had fought hard for it, and had kept any of the gangs trying to muscle in well at bay. Now, after their knock-back, there was again a lot to do.

They were discussing the council refuse collectors, who rarely turned up, and the residents who still allowed their dogs to foul, or dumped their used nappies over the balconies. The girls had agreed to turn a blind eye to that, for now. They didn't want the residents thinking the ACs were going to bully them like the last gangs that ran the estate. Lox had suggested that the ACs pay some of the residents who were struggling on benefits, to remove the stinking rubbish and the overflowing bins. It could also be offered as a way of earning a bit of extra cash to the addicts, to stop them shoplifting and mugging on the streets. That, she said, made for another step towards building a community.

The Alley Cats kept their drug-dealing and street girl trade very much to themselves. The feds couldn't know. Dealing was a serious crime, and the feds would never get that you couldn't just stop the addicts overnight, or that if the girls dealt the gear to them, then they could be sure that addicts wouldn't get bad stuff, or get into debt – like one of their residents, Lisa Hardy, who was always in constant fear of violence from debt collectors. The girls wanted to help her. They wanted to get her into rehab, but rehab didn't work if you didn't want to be there. You had to want to do it. It wasn't an easy ride. There were still a lot of addicts on the Aviary estate, and for now, the girls were going to keep supplying them. They'd got to know them all this way; it was another step toward building trust and being able to help them. Lox had been on drugs when she was working the streets, but Alysha and Tink had brought her in, and looked after her, and now she was clean. But she wanted to get that way.

The feds would never understand why these girls sold gear and ran the prostitution around the estate. No feds had ever lived on a sink estate, so they didn't have a clue what it was like. Without protection, it was more than tough. So the girls played their double card very carefully. No one on the estate could know they were informants, that would be too dangerous, and no fed could ever know they dealt drugs and ran street girls, or that they used weapons and hurt people when necessary. It was a dangerous game, but the girls had grown up with danger, and it was all for the good of the estate and the benefit of their residents.

They didn't need pimps for their street girls anyway. Panther was in charge of the streets around the estate and the money it made. Panther was the best fighter ever, she could take on eight men and still come out on top, but she also knew if there was anything she couldn't handle, then back-up was just a phone call away.

Tink wasn't good at figures or anything that needed thought. She'd barely had any schooling. She'd been a child prostitute. Her mother had sold her young body to all the local nonces to make money to fund her own drug habit and alcohol debts. When her mother died, she worked the streets with Alysha to make enough to feed themselves and buy trainers. Tink was naturally creatively talented, and the girls were determined to get her hair and beauty shop rebuilt, so she could be happy doing her stuff, and earning money for the estate fund that way.

Tink and Alysha had both had lived on the estate for most of their lives. Alysha had lost a sister, and had had to look after an alcoholic father, who fortunately was never there any more. She had brought herself up. She and Tink had always been there for each other, and their bond was now unbreakable.

Lox was filling in boxes in the audit app on her iPad, and adding figures up, when Alysha's phone rang.

Alysha took the call, then turned to Lox. Her voice was low, but as the reality of what she had just been told sank in, her voice rose as she clicked off and spoke.

'That was Summer,' she told Lox. 'She's gone to work the corner down by Waters Lane, and she sees an ambulance down there, loading in someone. She went to see what was going on, looked in the ambulance, and she saw a mop of pink hair.'

Lox's head shot up, as she gave Alysha her full attention.

Alysha fixed her angry and devastated eyes on Lox's. 'Summer screamed out "Tink", to make sure it was her, and the ambulance woman asks if she knows her. Summer says she does, and the woman tells her to get in touch with Tink's family.' Now angry tears were threatening to fill Alysha's eyes, and she spoke at pace through gritted teeth. 'She got to get her to hospital, woman says. It's an emergency.' Then her voice rose again as she shouted in anger and fear. 'Tink's unconscious, Summer says. She's been shanked and burnt, she's in a bad state.'

For a second Lox was struck dumb. She stared at Alysha and then she slowly said, 'Jesus.'

Alysha had used that second to grab her silver padded puffa jacket, and Lox's matching beige one. She threw Lox's coat to her. 'It's them fuckin' Chinese bastards, I'll fuckin' bet ya. Call Panther, mate,' she told Lox. 'We'll meet her in Waters, and then we're on our way to St Mildred's.'

As the girls hurriedly pushed their arms into their coats, Alysha added, 'And ain't it the fuckin' truth that the EIBs have got death written on their heads for this. I'm gonna rip their heads off, seven fucking times over.'

'Are we gonna get the feds to help us on this?' Lox asked her, stabbing Panther's number into her mobile as she spoke.

Alysha shook her head. 'No. Get the handguns.'

Chapter Three

DCI Banham had a big smile across his face as he replaced the phone in its cradle. He had been agreeing wedding arrangements with his future bride. The grin was unavoidable; he had wanted to marry Alison Grainger since before he had even dated her, back when he was a DI and she was his DS. They had worked closely together, and many times had put their lives in each other's hands, but she always said she wanted it kept on a professional level and he knew her well enough to know she couldn't be pushed.

The friendship had slowly progressed into a love affair. She continually told him it was on a casual basis, that she didn't want an involvement, so he gave her space. Stuff happened, and they both got promoted. She moved to another division and another station and the love affair petered out, but he kept in touch with her. They had the odd drink together, and then she moved back to his station, and his department, and the affair started up again, this time more seriously. She had become pregnant, but then miscarried. The wedding had been booked. They cancelled it after the loss of Alison's pregnancy. And, then it was on again, and then off, but now it was on for sure, and he was happily looking forward to marrying her.

It would be just a small wedding. When he proposed, a look of panic had spread across her face. She didn't say she would, she just asked what kind of a wedding he had in mind. He had said a very small one, knowing only too well that if they got involved in organising anything too complicated she could well change her mind. She was like that. The woman was born under the sign of Pisces, the two fish, each one going in a different direction, and true to her birth sign, she never could make a decision and stick to it. That was probably why her driving was so bad, he thought with a smile; she changed her mind in the middle of the road, indicated right and then turned left, all that sort of thing. Although he'd never dare tell her that, she had one hell of a temper, and he had been on the wrong end of those tempers too often. She had a touch of red in her waist-length brown hair, and Banham felt sure, if they traced her family tree, he would find Celtic blood in her ancestry. When that temper erupted she was like a madwoman, you had to hit the deck. Still, he loved her to distraction, something he never thought possible after the very dark and lonely years since his young wife was murdered with their one-year-old baby. That was now fifteen years in the past, and he was finally feeling able to move on and be happy again.

The department was doing well too, crime figures had dropped. He put that down to the work that DI Georgia Johnson and Sergeant Stephanie Green had achieved on the very troubled Aviary Estate. He was lucky with those two detectives, they were both sharp as knives and together they made a terrific partnership.

As soon as he finished his call to Alison, his internal phone rang. It was the duty sergeant from Traffic. A young girl had been found, unconscious, in the middle of Waters Lane, which was near to the Aviary Estate, but not on it. She had been stabbed, badly beaten, and badly burnt. The traffic police, who had been called to the incident, suspected by the state of undress the girl was in that she had been raped too, and then thrown from a moving vehicle.

Banham screwed up his face, sighed heavily, and then raised his eyes to heaven. Waters Lane was within yards of the Aviary Estate. There was no significant gang rule on that estate since the last gang had dispersed when their leader was shot. Everyone said it was only a matter of time before new gangs started to test the water and fight for the territory. This could be the start of big trouble if this victim was another gang's girl. And then there was the suicide of Larry Hardy last night. That boy had lived on the Aviary. He wondered if these incidents were in any way connected. Something was going on, and they needed to get to the bottom of it before it exploded in their faces. He couldn't risk another riot, certainly not at a time when the powers that be had been congratulating the station on the sharp drop in crime figures. Once again he was grateful that Georgia Johnson had been clever enough to persuade four your girls from the estate to work as informants. It was time to find out if there was gang trouble brewing down there. He quickly called the DI.

'Where are you?'

'On our way to talk to Larry Hardy's' mother, guv,' Georgia told him. 'If she's not away with the fairies, that is. And then we'll talk to –'

'Go via Waters Lane,' he interrupted her. 'A girl's been thrown from a moving car down there. Likely she's a street worker, or possibly a gang girl. From what I hear she's been stabbed and burnt, and is in a bad way.'

'Any witnesses?'

'Not sure. You'll need to talk to our informants and report back. I'll get uniform to the hospital and tell them to stay with her and take a statement when she comes round, if she remembers anything.'

'Do we know which hospital?'

'St Mildred's. That's as much as I know, so we need to

find out what's going on down there. This looks like an attempted murder, which spells trouble erupting down there. We could have a new gang infiltrating the estate.'

'Shit.' She nodded to Steph, who immediately reached under the passenger seat for the battery-operated blue light and switched it to on. She opened her window and placed it onto the roof of their pool car.

'On the way,' Georgia told Banham, accelerating out into the middle lane and speeding through the oncoming traffic.'

Alysha was standing with Lox and Panther in Waters Lane when Georgia and Stephanie pulled up, siren now turned off. They were talking to the crowd of the working street girls who had heard the news and gone to the lane to help. Georgia stared at Alysha. The girl had added plaited extensions to her own mop of black hair. They were pulled tidily to the back of her head and secured with tiny red ribbons. She wore no make-up. Flat trainers adorned her feet, and jeans and a silver padded anorak on her body. Times really had changed, Georgia thought as she looked proudly at her, thinking how lovely her face was without the layers of make-up. So different from a few years back, when Alysha's twelve-year-old face was thick with it, and she wore micro-miniskirts, and stood on street corners, making money from passing motorists. These days she could have been twenty, she was mature well beyond her years, but she looked so much better.

Becoming informants was the best thing that could have happened to all four girls, Georgia thought. Where would they have gone otherwise? Further into crime and prostitution, drug-dealing and using, and no future for any of them. Now they were all clean, none took drugs, and they were making a very good job of turning the estate round and making it work for the better of the residents.

Although it had been burnt down, Georgia felt this was just a blip, and was sure these girls would get it going again. Even if she didn't admit it to anyone else, she had become very fond of these informants, and was extra-protective toward them. She knew that if it ever leaked out that they worked, grassing to the police, in return for financial help and council grants, then all four of them would be in life-threatening danger, and need police protection and then a change of identity. She was prepared for that, whatever the cost, Georgia had promised herself she would take responsibility and would protect them.

So what was all this about, she wondered a little uncomfortably, as she watched Alysha from a distance. Alysha was clearly angry and had started shouting. That was when she noticed Panther and Lox – but no sign of Tink. Then her heart sank.

As Waters Street was crowded with residents, all wanting to find out what was happening, and very young kids from other estates were bicycling around, as usual trying to find out news to sell it on to other gangs for the price of some fried chicken for their hungry bellies, Georgia had decided to watch, for now, but not approach her informants. Within a minute Alysha spotted her. She walked straight over to her, closely followed by Lox and Panther, all looking agitated, angry and distraught.

Before Georgia had time to say that she thought it was better not to have a conversation with them, at this point or place, Alysha spoke.

'It's Tink,' Alysha said, lowering her voice only slightly. There was desperation in her tone as she continued. 'She's been shanked, and burnt, and thrown from a van. It was a green van. Summer saw it.'

Stephanie immediately pulled her notebook and her phone from her pocket. 'Did she get the van's reg? Or any of it?'

Alysha shook her head. Georgia was aware people were watching the three girls talking to feds, but also aware that Alysha didn't seem to care. 'They didn't get the reg,' Alysha told Stephanie with a shake of her head. 'But the Zhangs drive a green van. She knows it was V at the front of the reg, and that's the same as theirs.'

'And she actually saw Tink being thrown from the back of it,' Lox interrupted. 'She said she called 999 as soon as she could.'

Georgia frowned, so Lox explained. 'She was looking out the window of the car. She was upside down at the time,' she explained. 'She was with a punter. As soon as she finished, which was only minutes later, she rang 999 and then rushed over to her, but Tink weren't conscious. The ambulance was here pronto and rushed her off to St Mildred's.'

'I'll talk to her,' Stephanie said. 'Which one is she?'

'The one by the wall. Gold and black, open bodice and a dragon tattoo on her chest,' Panther told her.

Georgia turned to Steph. 'I'll talk to her, you get onto the station to get an ARV check on green V registered vans, and tell uniform to get any available CCTV from around the area.'

Stephanie nodded as she stabbed numbers into her phone.

Georgia had noticed a few of the young kids on bicycles had pushed their way forward and were in hearing distance. She turned to Stephanie, lifted her eyebrows and tilted her head in their direction, but Stephanie had already noticed them.

She immediately called out to two uniformed police standing nearby. 'Keep the crowds well back, will you. This is a crime scene, so move everyone out of the road and get the area cordoned off. Now.'

Georgia turned back to Alysha and lowered her voice.

30

'It's not a good idea to be seen talking to us, seeing what's happened to Tink. It could be that someone's found out you are our snouts. I have to visit someone else on the estate, and then I'll come round to your flat.'

'I don't give a shit *who* hears me,' Alysha said raising her voice, and turning to look at the young 'uns who were being moved down the street by uniformed officers. 'You want some gossip that you lot think you can sell?' she shouted at them. 'Well you go and tell them this. I'm gonna find the fuckers that done this to my sister and I am gonna cut –'

Georgia grabbed her and pulled her back. 'Pack it up,' she told her sternly. 'Making threats is an offence. We will find out who has done this and we will make sure they get punished. So leave it to us. Go home. We'll take it from here.'

Alysha shrugged her off angrily. 'Fucking feds, do fuck all,' she spat angrily at Georgia. Then she turned back to the young kids on bikes. 'Spread the word,' she said. 'We're on this, and we're coming after them. Got that, have you?'

'Alysha, shut it,' Georgia warned her in a raised and angry tone.

But Alysha wasn't listening. She marched over to one of the black kids on a bicycle and moved in to one of them until her face was inches away from the tiny on the bicycle. Lox and Panther had followed and stood closely behind her.

'Whoever you are working for, you tell them …' Alysha threatened, pointing her long painted nails into her own chest. 'That I am –'

She got no more out. Stephanie was over like a shot and had Alysha by the collar and hauled her away from the kids. 'Shut it!' she shouted into Alysha's face. 'We won't tell you again. This is police business, and if you

31

make any more threats we will arrest you.'

'Tink is unconscious, and that makes it *our* business,' Panther stepped in as she struggled with Stephanie's strong hand to release Stephanie's grip on Alysha's collar.

Stephanie let go. Georgia and Stephanie made eye contact.

One of the uniformed sergeants, who was overseeing the cordon they were putting up to close off the area, then turned to Alysha. He had no idea she was an informant, and Georgia thought that at that moment it was just as well. 'You need to move along,' he said to Alysha. 'I've heard all this, and I'll be putting in a report. You're harassing the police and threatening kids.'

'We're shaking in our boots,' Panther said, towering over him and glaring down into his face.

'We know who you are. Anything else happens round here, you'll the first to be arrested. So do as you're told and move along, this is a crime scene and you are obstructing the police in their work.'

Alysha stormed away, closely followed by Lox and Panther. Georgia lowered her voice as Alysha passed her. 'Find out what you can,' she said to her. 'I'll be round later.'

'Fuck off,' Lox snapped back. 'We'll be at the hospital. We ain't gonna leave Tink on 'er own. She's our family.'

Stephanie signalled to a patrol car. 'Can you run these three to the hospital,' she said to her. 'It's their friend who was injured.'

'Our sister,' Lox corrected her angrily. 'And we don't want a lift from you lot, we'll get a cab.'

Georgia shook her head at Stephanie. 'Just leave them be,' she told her.

Lisa Hardy was a middle-aged white woman. She wore no

make-up, and her greasy dyed black hair displayed approximately four inches of grey roots. It hung down to just below her shoulders, giving the impression of a Halloween cartoon character. Her eyes were glassy, and she spoke with a slur. A multitude of thin sharp lines around her upper lip showed she was a heavy smoker and had been for many years. She wore dirty, dark tracksuit bottoms and an oversized man's shirt, and no shoes. She opened the door less than an inch.

Georgia held her ID card up, as Stephanie said gently, 'We need to come in, Mrs Hardy.'

Lisa seemed hardly just capable of pulling the door open to allow the detectives access.

'I'm very sorry for your loss,' Stephanie said to her as they settled in the grubby sofa.

Georgia scratched her forehead and looked away. She wasn't good at sympathy, and she felt uncomfortable sitting in a flat that hadn't been hoovered since the Stone Age. The dirt of Lisa's unkempt toenails was making her want to heave, but the warning look from her sergeant kept her from asking the woman where the hoover was. Georgia knew Lisa's daughter had learning difficulties, and thought that anyone living in this filth should be a social services issue. She said nothing.

'He should never have been there,' the woman said half to Stephanie and half to herself. 'That boy wouldn't hurt a fly.' She reached for her cigarettes.

'He stabbed Ji Zhang,' Georgia told her.

The woman shook her head. 'He wouldn't.'

'There were witnesses,' Georgia tried to say, but Lisa wasn't listening. Her daughter Karen had walked into the room and was looking nervously at the two strangers with her mother. Karen had the same dark hair as her mother; hers, too, was thick with grease and hung to the top of her shoulders. She was as overweight as Sergeant Green, but

33

over twenty years younger, and wearing a flimsy denim miniskirt with only a bodice, displaying a few rolls of flab that spilled over the waistband, and wobbly thick white thighs. The white bodice top clearly hadn't seen washing powder lately. Georgia thought of the hand cleaning gel in her pocket and longed to use it. Karen too was barefooted, with black dirt between each toe.

'What they want?' Karen asked her mother.

'Fucked if I know,' Lisa said. 'Can't fucking bring him back, so he can't argue for 'imself. They say he killed someone.' She half-laughed as she sucked heavily on a cigarette.

'Was Larry involved in a gang, do you know?' Georgia asked.

'How do I know what he fucking does? He's a good son, that's what I know.' Lisa flicked ash nervously. 'He's good to his mum.'

'No. No he weren't,' Karen told them. 'He weren't in a gang.'

'Did he have friends?' Stephanie spoke gently.

'Course. Don't everyone? He had friends at school, but he didn't go out much, out of school. He had a Saturday job at Tesco to help Mum with money, and that. He wanted to be here. He liked it at home, didn't 'e, Mum?' She climbed on the sofa and curled up to her mother, like a puppy might, leaning against her for comfort.

'Get off,' Lisa said, raising her voice and pushing Karen away.

Karen sat up. 'What's happening now?' she asked.

'There'll be an investigation,' Georgia told her, reading through the notes she had in her hand. She looked at Lisa. 'You said in your statement that none of your knives were missing the day of the stabbing,' she asked, even though she knew Lisa wouldn't notice if the whole house was bare, as she was probably high on crystal meth.

'As yet we haven't recovered the weapon. We're still looking, but you are sure you aren't missing any knives, are you, Lisa?'

'I don't know. A knife's a knife, ain't it? But Larry never carried one, did he, Karen?'

Karen shook her head. 'He never carried a knife.' She shook her head again. 'He never 'ad one.'

'Where were you when he stabbed Ji?' Stephanie asked Karen gently.

'I were on my way home from school. I were at the bus stop with my mates.' She started to get excited. 'Dean Wells came runnin' and shoutin', said Ji were stabbed and Larry had a knife. But he didn't have a knife, did he, Mum?'

Lisa shook her head.

'Someone could have given him one, couldn't they?' Georgia said to her.

'When?'

'In your witness statement,' Stephanie explained slowly, 'you said you weren't there, so you didn't see.'

'I weren't. I were at the bus stop. Waiting for the bus.'

'We know he did have a knife,' Stephanie said. 'Because other people who were there saw him use one. We need to find where the weapon came from, where it went, and what provoked him to do it.'

Karen spoke excitedly. 'Dean Wells came runnin' down the road and told me! So I went back and I never saw no knife, there was ambulances, and everyone said, they said, he'd done Ji. Don't mean he did, could have just said though, couldn't they?' She shrugged.

'We'll never know,' Lisa said in her half-dreamy state. 'He shouldn't have been in prison. He's a good boy.'

'You can talk to a solicitor about it,' Stephanie told her. 'The judge decided it was for his own good. The boy he stabbed was in a very dangerous gang. There could have been retribution, and the judge made the decision that, as there were witnesses to the attack, Larry was guilty, and for his own good, he would be safer on remand.'

'Did he ever get into any fights around here?' Georgia asked her.

'Larry got angry when people teased Karen and called her a mad lump,' Lisa said. 'He always stuck up for her, don't know why. She *is* a lump.'

'Who called you names?' Stephanie asked Karen.

'Some of the boys.'

'Can you give us any names?'

She shook her head. 'No, I seen them hangin' around. I dunno who they are. Not local boys, s'all I know.'

Georgia sat up. 'Chinese, were they?' she asked.

Karen shrugged. 'Dunno really, maybe some of them. Larry never 'ad a knife.'

'Larry wouldn't kill anyone. He didn't stab anyone, I know he didn't,' Lisa said again, half to herself. Then she laughed and shook her head.

Chapter Four

After arriving at the hospital and being told Tink had been rushed into emergency surgery, Alysha, Lox and Panther sat in the hospital corridor anxiously waiting for news.

It seemed hours before a young nurse walked over and invited them to follow her into the ward, where, in the corner bed, Tink had just woken up.

'Jesus fucking Christ, just fucking look at her,' Alysha said loudly as she turned horrified to Lox and Panther.

The nurse immediately shushed her.

'I'm gonna kill 'em,' Panther said, also in a raised and angry voice, and completely ignoring the shushing from the nurse.

Lox moved in and took Tink's hand.

Tink was lying on her back. Her head was partly bandaged, as was all the body that was on view. She reminded Alysha of one of those Egyptian mummies. There only seemed to be parts of her face that were not covered in gauze, or crêpe. She stank like a chemist's shop.

Alysha also read the fear in Tink's striking blue eyes.

The anger inside her bubbled, but she held it back, as she stood staring at the friend she had known since the age of four. The two had ferreted in bins for discarded fried chicken cartons, and stolen chips from leftover tables inside the chicken bars to feed themselves, then gone shoplifting for sweets and bread from the local stores. They had whored together, too, and been used as an under-age double act, and then used by gang leaders to mule drugs and firearms. Now, they ran the estate with the help of Lox and Panther, and helped people who were beaten or used by other gangs.

'We'll … get them for you, Tink,' Alysha said, the crack in her voice mirroring her feeling.

'Yeah. We'll make them beg to be killed,' Panther said, backing up Alysha.

Tink could hear them, that was evident, and good. She was now attempting to sit up, but not having the strength, immediately slid down in the bed again. The young nurse quickly moved in and made her comfortable with a pillow behind her, then lifting the back of the bed with a button-press, so Tink could sit up, but still had the bed to rest against.

'Don't tire her too much,' the nurse told the girls.

Alysha was still studying Tink. She could make out her arms, but with the bandaging going on forever, she couldn't work out where her hands joined them. She could only see blisters covered in yellow cream over the edge of her mauve, nail-varnished, fingernails.

'Just fucking look at you,' Panther said tactlessly.

'Have they given you something for the pain?' Lox asked, taking Tink's tiny hand and kissing it.

Alysha was now looking at the blistering that was peeping through the edge of the bandage over the top of Tink's lips.

'I'm a mess,' Tink slurred.

'Ain't gonna scar, Tink,' Alysha quickly assured her, aware that would be worrying for her friend with her passion for hair and make-up. 'Ain't gonna spoil your beautiful face, mate, you're gonna be OK, ain't she? Alysha said turning to the nurse.

The nurse nodded, a little hesitantly. Then she said, 'I'll leave you for a few minutes.'

'Nurse said it ain't gonna scar you,' Alysha repeated.

'You'll have to stay in here and get healed though,' Lox told her in a motherly fashion. 'We'll get you out, really soon, and we'll take good care of you. But you gotta get them to heal them burns first, make sure they don't leave marks. They look really sore. Are they?'

'I'm stinging like a fucking jellyfish,' Tink whispered with difficulty.

'I know you hate these places,' Alysha added, 'but you have to stay for a bit.' She winked at her, and lifted her thumb. 'I ain't having the best hair and beauty lady in South London having marks on her beautiful boat, so stay here and let them get you better, and leave us sort this for you.' She flicked a warning glance at Panther, who was leaning in and examining what she could see under the bandages.

'Who done this to you, mate, do you know?' Alysha then asked Tink.

Tink stared at her, then frowned, as if confused.

'Tink, we're gonna get them, an' we're gonna kill them,' Alysha assured her. 'Summer says it was EIBs. Was it?'

Tink shook her head. 'No. It was RIPs, but if you kill them, you'll get sent down, then who is gonna be …' Her voice was now slurring away to incoherent. It was obvious she was very tired and confused. She struggled on to speak. 'The shops, get them built back up.' Her eyes were opening and closing as she spoke. 'Don't kill no one. Promise?'

'We ain't gonna get caught,' Alysha told her. 'And we're gonna get the estate sorted, but no one's gonna get away with doing this to you,' she told her.

Tink's eyes fluttered. She was falling asleep.

'Shall I ask for painkillers for you, mate?' Lox asked quickly.

39

Tink nodded.

'I'll go,' Alysha said turning to walk down the ward to find the nurse.

'You sure it weren't EIBs?' Panther asked her again.

Tink shook her head. 'RIPs. Maxted,' she said in a voice that was barely audible.

'Think they'll frighten us, do they, 'cos we nicked that gear?' Lox said.

'Well, they was smack fucking bang out of order in the first fucking place, trying to muscle in, walk onto our territory, and give stuff they nicked from the EIBs to our kids,' Panther said, raising her voice. 'We are gonna protect our kids and our Tink, an' if that means killing the Chinese *and* the RIPs, then that's what we're gonna do.' She turned to Lox, who nodded her agreement.

Tink attempted to shake her head.

'We built them play areas and community halls so the kids didn't go off thieving or get taken in by the barons,' Lox said gently to Tink. 'One of them gangs burned them, and now they burned you.' She nodded to Panther. 'They'll have to die, Tink, or our Aviary will never get on track.'

'An', if we kill 'em, then we'll get the respect out there, an' all around London, and all other gangs will leave our estate be.' Panther told Tink.

Tink was shaking her head slowly, and still fighting to keep her eyes open.

'Where did they stab you, babe?' Lox asked her.

'Stomach,' Tink said, speaking in a low, sleepy whisper.

Alysha walked back with the nurse at that moment. 'She's in pain,' Alysha was telling her.

The nurse bent down to look at Tink. 'She's very tired,' the nurse said, tucking the blanket around Tink. 'She needs to rest. I think you should go,' she told them.

40

'Does she have family?'

'Yeah, us,' Lox answered curtly.

'And you are?'

'Her sisters,' Panther told the nurse.

The nurse looked first at Panther, six-foot-plus and black, with amber-coloured hair, then at skinny Lox, with her waist-length black and green hair and her ivory skin, then at Alysha, petite and mixed-race with black afro hair, and finally at Tink. All that was visible of Tink was a few strands of candyfloss-pink hair resting on her forehead and two startling blue eyes peeping through the layers of bandages that covered her face.

'Real sisters?' she asked, with a hint of amusement.

'Yeah, real sisters,' Panther snapped back.

'All of you?'

'Yes. You got a problem with that?'

The nurse hesitated. 'And no parents anywhere?'

'We don't have parents,' Lox told her. 'We've got each other, an' that's it.'

'We're her fam, OK?' Panther said with an accusing air. 'Why you asking?'

The nurse shrugged. 'When we admit a patient, it's usual to have a next of kin, and I need to write that down on my notes, that's all.'

'Christ, she ain't gonna die, is she?' Panther asked, tactlessly raising her voice as she stood next to Tink.

'No.' The nurse shook her head reassuringly. 'No, it's just a formality. But she has just come out of surgery, and she has been stabbed, so she needs a lot of rest, and I need to know who to contact if she needs anything.'

'Yeah, that's us,' Alysha told her. 'Anything she needs, we'll get her. OK? Right now she needs painkillers.'

'I need the patient to tell me,' the nurse said, frowning in disbelief. 'I'll ask her to confirm that you *are* all her

41

sisters, when she wakes.'

'I ain't asleep,' Tink said in a whisper. 'They are all my sisters, and they are in charge of me, and can I have a painkiller, I am stinging like a fucking wasps' nest.'

'I'll have to ask the doctor, he'll be round to see you very soon, and he'll prescribe your medication. Two policewomen have just arrived. They say they need to take a statement from you.'

Alysha lowered her eyes, and almost imperceptibly shook her head at Tink.

'No,' Tink whispered, immediately taking the hint. 'I've already had to have me fanny examined. I don't want no more questions. I'm too tired, and I'm in pain. It can wait, can't it?'

'I'll tell them,' the nurse nodded. 'The doctor will be round very soon. I'll ask him about stronger painkillers for you.' She turned and walked out of the ward.

Alysha watched her go and moved in to Tink. 'That'll be Georgia Johnson and the fat fed, Stephanie Green, they're wanting to know who done it. They interviewed Amber and Summer – they was the ones who found you and rang us, and 999,' she told Tink. 'Feds are tight on this.' She shrugged. 'It's good, in a way, 'cos it means they are looking out for us. Summer told her it was a big green van, and the feds know the EIBs have got one of them. So they'll be on the case.'

'I reckon the EIBs done it 'cos they found out we work as snouts for the feds,' Lox told Tink.'

'*And* we grassed them up about their weed factories.'

Tink's eyes were closed against the pain. 'It *weren't* EIBs. It were Maxted ...' she whispered with difficulty.

She stopped whispering as the nurse walked in again. 'Right time to go, sisters,' she said half-jokingly. 'Come back tomorrow, though, and phone later if you like. We'll let you know how she is.'

Alysha leaned in and planted a kiss on Tink's bandage. As she did, she whispered, 'Def the RIPs?'

'Yeah. Ray were there, Tip, and a few others.'

'We'll get them,' Alysha said quietly.

Tink lifted her hand and waved it as if to tell them to stop.

Lox turned to the nurse. 'We'll be out in another two minutes,' she said.

The young nurse took the hint. She walked away.

'They're gonna get payback,' Alysha told her.

Tink didn't answer. Her head had sunk into the pillow, and she was fast asleep.

Alysha and Panther looked horrified. 'She ain't dead, is she?' Panther said loudly.

Lox shook her head. 'It's the anaesthetic,' she told them. 'It does that to you. She just gotta sleep it off. Nurse is right, she needs her rest.'

Alysha kissed Tink's forehead again.

'The RIPs have started a war, and the Alley Cats don't back down,' Lox said to Alysha and Panther. 'Let's round up the gang. We're going after them fuckers.'

'We'll get 'em,' Panther told the sleeping Tink. 'Cutting their dicks off will be just the start.'

'The feds can't find out about the guns and that gear, even if we didn't admit we stole it. It's worth too much corn to us,' Lox said as they stood in the car park, shivering in the biting February wind, and waiting for the taxi to come to take them back to the estate. 'That haul is worth thousands. EIBs would have fed it to our kids too. We can pass it on to someone who won't come on our territory with it, and we'll get the corn for it, and we'll use that to install the sound system in the community hall, as well as rebuilding it. That way they'll be paying, or starting to, for what they done to our recreation areas.'

'I gotta give all this thought,' Alysha said. 'Lisa Hardy's a junkie. Junkies have got big mouths. It's in her flat under the floorboards. If that comes out, we'll all go down. We ain't selling it, or doing nothing with it yet. It's too dangerous.'

'But we are going after them, ain't we?' Panther argued. 'I ain't worried 'bout selling the gear on. That can wait. But we can't let them think we aren't big enough to man up to them RIPs. She looked at Alysha. 'What you thinking, Queen?'

'I'm thinking that looking at Tink is making me well angry. And I wanna tear their fucking heads off.'

'So let's make a plan,' Lox told her. We don't get angry, we get even.'

'Are we sure it's RIPs?' Alysha said. 'Tink may not be thinking straight; Amber and Summer thinks it was the Zhangs.'

'They've earned an even-up, too,' Panther said. 'They gave Sammy that coke when we banned the under-tens from going anywhere, apart from their flats or the community hall. Little Sammy refused, and went to the community hall like we told him, and that's when they set fire and nearly killed 'im. They deserve a lesson for that.'

'Yeah, and they got one. We stitched them up to feds, remember and blasted their grass factories. No, this is 'bout Tink.'

'Don't matter, does it? We're gonna square them both.' Panther said.

'Don't you think it was more like George Zhang had her shanked,' Lox said. 'To get even for Larry Hardy shanking his brother.'

'I don't reckon on Larry Hardy shanking 'im,' Alysha said.

'There are witnesses, but we don't know why. Some say he was high on some coke that someone gave him.'

'EIBs fed 'im that, I'll bet,' Lox said.

'Yes, so they need sorting for doing that to one of ours,' Panther said. 'We need to let both these gangs know who runs our estate, or we'll lose respect, Queen.'

Alysha took a moment to think. She caught Lox's eye, then she looked at Panther and said, 'Tink is right. We formed Alley Cats to make our estate a better place, and we vowed we'd keep the dealers at bay.'

'And sometimes you 'ave to kill to get the message across,' Panther was getting heated up. 'They nearly killed our Tink; we just told her we'll get the bastards for her. You ain't going back on that, is you?'

'They all fucking deserve to die, I agree on that,' Alysha said evenly. 'But I'm thinking that's too easy. We vowed the Alley Cats would keep the estate clean, whatever it took.'

'Killing's what it takes,' Panther argued.

'She's right, Queen,' Lox said. 'We 'ave to right it, for Tink, She'd do it for you.'

'This *is* for Tink,' Alysha said, an edge of anger in her voice. 'What we'll do is set both gangs up with the feds. We'll make a deal with feds for the information, and then we'll set one 'gainst the other and let them kill each other. We'll tell the feds we want the council to give us another grant to rebuild the community centre an' shops. That way we get Tink her hair shop back, and we can make good corn from it, and that'll give Tink somefing to get better for. If we kill them RIPs, and get caught, then how will that help Tink, and what will she have to look forward to coming out of hospital?

Panther and Lox looked at each other. Lox shrugged and nodded, and then Panther followed suit.

'Good thinking, Queen,' Lox said.

'I'll go with that,' Panther said, taking it in. 'As long as they kill each other, an' we get the shops back.

'But if Tink's face is left scarred, just one tiny fucking scar on it, then I will kill Ray Maxted myself,' Alysha added with a look in her eye that meant business.

Georgia and Stephanie walked out of the hospital a few moments later, and headed over to the girls.

Alysha read their faces. 'They wouldn't let you see her yet, then?' she said to them.

Georgia shook her head. 'No. She was asleep. Did you talk to her?'

Alysha nodded, and shrugged non-committally.

'How is she?'

'Tired. They've given her stuff, so she's sleeping,' Alysha said.

'I need to talk to her,' Georgia said. 'Could you have a word for me?'

Alysha raised her voice, indignantly. 'She's sparko, mate, so no I can't. It'll 'ave to wait. Another day ain't gonna do much.'

'Did she say who did this to her?' Stephanie asked.

'Nah,' Alysha shook her head. 'It's all a bit hazy for her. Best to talk tomorrow, yeah?'

'It'll have to be,' Stephanie said looking suspiciously at Alysha. 'But time is precious.' She looked into Alysha's face. 'You do want us to punish them for her, don't you?'

'Yeah, course,' Alysha said.

'Then the sooner we can talk to her, the easier it'll be to make an arrest,' Stephanie said.

None of the girls answered.

'And we need to have a chat with you all,' Georgia told them. 'The doctor has said we can use his office, for privacy, probably better than being seen on the estate, going into your flat. I'm concerned that that happened because someone knows you are our informants.'

Alysha and Panther and Lox made eye contact.

'We've ordered a cab,' Alysha said.

'Well, send it away,' Stephanie said. 'We've got a car, mine, not a police vehicle. I'll drop you a few roads away from the estate after.'

Alysha nodded and shrugged reluctantly. Lox opened her phone, then cancelled the cab, and they followed Georgia and Stephanie into the doctor's room.

'OK. How bad is she?' Georgia asked looking at the three anxious faces once they sat down inside.

'She's bad,' Alysha said. 'She's been shanked and burnt, and operated on, and she's asleep.'

'Is there a possibility that someone has found out you're our snouts, and decided to teach her a lesson?' Stephanie asked.

Alysha immediately caught Lox's eye and saw the possibility of money coming their way. 'Highly possible,' Lox said.

'We don't know nothing yet, 'cos she ain't making sense,' Panther answered. 'When we do, we'll report back.'

'If that is the case, then that puts you three in danger too,' Stephanie told them. 'So, we want you to go home, and stay there, do not leave the flat, or we can put you all somewhere safe for a while.'

'We ain't leaving the estate,' Alysha said indignantly.

'Then you go home and stay there. You do *not* go out,' Stephanie told her. 'None of you. Got it?'

'We 'ave to go out,' Alysha argued.

'We make the rules, Alysha,' Georgia told her firmly. 'You work for us, remember. Now you cannot leave your flat. I know I can't put police guard on you –'

'No, you can't,' Alysha butted in quickly, and with an air of panic in her voice.

'It's our job to protect you, you are our informants,'

47

Georgia reminded her. 'Remember the agreement we signed with you. It says if we suspect you are in danger, then we can take you away to a safe house. We won't enforce that, if you give us your word you won't leave your flat.'

'We don't know for sure that Tink has got done over 'cos someone finks we're grassers, though,' Alysha pointed out. 'Could be anuvver reason, and if we 'ave to stay in, we can't find out, can we?'

'We're not prepared to take any chances. So you are to do as we say. You are to go home and you don't go out. If you need anything, we'll get it to you,' Stephanie said.

'And if you are worried, you ring my mobile,' Georgia told them.

Alysha and the others looked, in horror, at each other.

'She definitely hasn't said anything to you, anything at all?' Stephanie asked again.

Alysha looked Stephanie straight in the eye. 'No, she ain't. She's hardly conscious.'

'OK. What do you know about Larry Hardy?' Georgia asked.

It took a second, and then Panther answered. 'Ain't he on remand for stabbing Ji Zhang?'

Georgia shook her head. 'Not any more. He hanged himself in prison,' she told her.

The girls made eye contact again.

'Jeez ...' Alysha said, blowing out air. She looked at Georgia. 'I told you at the time he weren't tough enough. Rumour has it he took somefing and then shanked Ji. His mum owed the Chinese. She was in debt up to her ears. I can't believe he killed someone.'

'There were witnesses, and he had a bloody knife in his hands when we arrested him,' Stephanie told her.

'He could have picked up the knife,' Lox pointed out.

'He was covered in blood and there were witnesses.

Are you telling me my job?' Georgia said.

'Did he admit it?' Alysha asked.

The inspector nodded. 'Yes, he did. But he wouldn't say why. In court, he gave his name, and then didn't utter a word.'

'I never 'ad 'im down for a killer,' Alysha said. 'They're all a bit funny that family. Karen is a bit ...' Alysha put her finger to her head to indicate 'mental'.

'People can seem one thing and be another,' Stephanie told her, then shrugged. 'Anyway, he can't tell us anything now, he hanged himself in his cell,' she said with quiet concern.' She looked at Alysha. 'Remand was for his own protection. If we'd left him out there, the Zhang gang would have lynched him.'

'You want us to find out all we can about this?' Alysha said quickly.

Georgia nodded. 'And we'll find the arseholes that have hurt Tink, and we'll make sure they pay very heavily for what they have done to her,' she assured her. 'I've asked the hospital to let me know as soon as she is awake. I believe you have all gone down as next of kin, so please let me know as soon as they let you know.

'No, that ain't enough for them to pay heavy to you,' Lox said, shaking her head. 'If Tink got done like this for informing for you, then as I see it, you more than owe Tink something, as well as making the bastards that did it pay heavy.'

'S'right,' Alysha said. ''Cos now you're 'specting us to put our heads on the block, yet *again*, and help you.'

'We employ you as informants,' Stephanie reminded her. 'You're on the payroll. We expect you to deliver.'

'Whatever,' Alysha shrugged. 'We ain't doing it for free.'

'You get paid,' Georgia said firmly. 'And that makes us your employers, so we tell you what we want, and you deliver. Rule number one: you have to stay in your flat. We want you safe. You can't go out, but you can make calls.'

'What's it worth?' Alysha snapped at her.

Georgia and Stephanie stared at her.

'We want a bonus for this one,' Lox said.

'Get a result and we'll talk about it.'

'We need to get the community hall rebuilt,' Lox pushed.

'That'll cost thousands,' Stephanie told her.

'It'll save thousands too,' Lox argued back. 'Keeping the tinies off the streets, and out of youth offenders, that'll save loads in taxpayers' money. The community hall needs to be rebuilt and then decked out with sound and recording stuff. The tinies will all stay off the streets if they get that back. We've got someone gonna teach free street-dancing, and we got a request for table tennis, and Panther will teach self-defence, so we need loads of equipment, after it's rebuilt.'

'I admire you for what you're doing with your youngsters,' Stephanie said. 'And I agree, it will keep them off the streets, but that is *way* out of our price range and you know that.'

'Yeah 'tis, for police budget,' Lox told her. 'But if you talk to the councillor, or should I say *persuade* the councillor, then we can get that grant. They'll listen to you but they won't listen to us.'

'You've already had a grant from the council,' Georgia argued. 'The playground and halls were built up. They got burned down. You can't expect them to invest in that again, they simply won't.'

'Not for us,' Lox pushed. 'But if *you* ask, they'll do it for you. And estate crime figures will drop like they did before, and you'll benefit. You know it makes sense.'

'And we'll help a lot with Larry Hardy,' Panther

backed her up. 'We'll find the truth about what happened, and talk to his mum and his sister. Let them know it weren't your fault he was locked up. And we'll tip you off when any new gangs and dealers start movin' in on the Aviary.'

'And then that DCI will promote you really quickly,' Lox added, fully knowing Georgia was ambitious.

Georgia glanced at Stephanie, who shook her head and shrugged her shoulders in defeat.

'We'll do what we can,' Georgia said, nodding at Alysha. 'Bring me some information to go on, and then we'll talk about meeting with the council. But we can't make any promises.'

'We'll do what we can,' Alysha answered, half-mimicking Georgia's tone. 'But we can't make any promises neither.'

Chapter Five

DI Alison Grainger was sitting with Banham, in his office, when Georgia and Stephanie arrived back at the station and knocked on his door.

Georgia immediately noticed the wedding cake brochures spread over the DCI's desk, and the travel catalogues. Exotic honeymoons, Georgia thought, normally lasted two weeks or more. Getting some space from Alison Grainger for at least a fortnight seemed paradise enough for her.

It wasn't that she disliked the woman; more that the *I'll just run that past the DCI* phrase that Alison spouted continually when they were working together, Georgia found irritating, if not unsettling. The whole world knew the DCI would agree with DI Alison Grainger, whatever the woman bloody well thought, so why *just run that past the DCI* at all. And Grainger had another irritating little phrase which seriously got up Georgia's nose: *actually, as I have been a DI longer than you, Johnson, I'll be pulling rank on this.* Yes, she had been a DI longer than Georgia, but that didn't mean she was always right. Besides, she had been away on compassionate leave for a year after a fire on a case, and when she came back to work, she went into the Sapphire Unit, to work with rape victims. So, how many murder cases had she headed in the past two years? Georgia found her a pain in the arse, and much preferred working with Stephanie Green. Stephanie was only a sergeant, but that was out of choice – and how lucky was that for Georgia. Stephanie was the best detective around, everyone in the department would agree with that: the woman came from a family of police detectives, and was just the best there was.

Green had been the one to argue over Larry Hardy's arrest after the fatal stabbing of Ji Zhang. She had also disagreed that Larry should go to a youth offenders on remand; Ji Zhang's brother Ade was in there, and his cousin Yin, both doing time for committing GBH with a sword. Stephanie felt strongly that Larry wouldn't be safe. Alison had argued that leaving Larry out would put him in more danger. Georgia and Stephanie had both argued that putting someone on remand, no more guaranteed their safety, than leaving them to walk the streets freely. Gang culture was rife within the prison system, and no one could watch anyone twenty-four hours a day. But, they all finally agreed he could be kept an eye on inside, whereas outside, on bail, he couldn't be monitored full-time.

Larry Hardy had admitted the stabbing. He had blood on his clothes and hands, but as yet the knife that stabbed Ji had not been found, and until it was, this wasn't an open-and-shut case.

The Zhangs were well known to the police. They had been done for growing marijuana plants, thanks to the four young informants from the Aviary Estate. A few of the gang, all family members, had gone down for that, others were on suspended sentences. The Zhangs were a large family and very feared; they had a reputation for supreme violence, and they and their gang called themselves the EIBs. It stood for East is Best, both as a nod to the Zhangs' Chinese roots and to honour the East End, where most of the family's businesses were based, although they now also came south to sell the hard drugs they imported, and to terrorise and injure other dealers.

Larry Hardy was not known to be involved in any

gangs. It was known he looked after his mother's interests, and his sister Karen, who had learning difficulties of some kind. Larry's mother had a drug problem, and was heavily in debt over it. There, maybe, was the link. So, there were ongoing investigations into this.

Phone messages and records retrieved from Larry's mobile didn't associate him into anything illegal – indeed the only calls on his mobile had been from Alysha and Lox, and calls out to his mother and sister, checking on their welfare.

Alison had been the one to charge him. She was first on the scene and saw the evidence all there. He admitted to the stabbing, although he wouldn't say why he did it. Alison was convinced she would find the knife nearby and forensic evidence on the knife would back up his guilt, none of which, up till now, had materialised.

But now the boy had killed himself, and the press would be all over the case. Georgia could just see the headlines: *Fifteen-year-old boy with a special needs sister, a mother he adored, and no father in his life, was wrongly arrested and bullied, and unable to cope, hanged himself in prison.*

Georgia was also concerned this would open a hornet's nest and cause serious unrest on the Aviary Estate.

'Sir, the incident this morning of the girl that was raped, stabbed, and badly burned, then thrown from a green van,' she said.

Banham closed the travel brochure, and gave Georgia and Stephanie his attention.

'It turns out it was Veronica Andrew – Tink – one of our young informants on the Aviary,' Georgia told him. 'You may have heard. She has been taken to St Mildred's. She is in a bad way, too ill to talk, but we do know the Zhang gang have a green van, registration starting with V, same as the one seen driving at speed from Waters Lane, just after Tink ...' she paused and corrected herself, '... that is, Veronica Andrew, was found unconscious and lying in the road. I'm very concerned the EIB gang may have found out she was an informant and have done this to her.'

'Also, the press are outside in their droves, sir,' Stephanie added, flicking a glance at Alison who was sitting behind the DCI's desk, beside Banham, and listening with interest. 'Asking about Larry Hardy, and the girl found nearly naked, and stabbed in Waters Lane.'

'We've arranged a press conference for five thirty this evening,' Alison told Stephanie.

'That's to talk about Larry Hardy,' Banham told them. 'The press have been all over this, this morning. He lifted his hand and dragged it across his face, a habit Georgia had observed many times when he was worried. 'The boy hadn't officially been charged with murder, he was on remand.'

'He had admitted it,' Alison reminded him.

'We'll give them an update then on Larry Hardy, but we'll say nothing about the rape, burning and stabbing of Tink Andrew, sir. We must protect our informants at all costs,' Georgia said pointedly to Alison.

'There's no reason to even mention that we know her identity at the moment,' Alison told her condescendingly. 'If she's unconscious, and presumably heavily bandaged, then how would we?'

Georgia pushed a few of the loose black hairs that had slipped onto her face from her neat ponytail, back behind her ears. She had carefully gelled the ponytail early this morning so it would stay in place, and found it irritating when the hair slid out and became untidy. 'I spoke to the other three informants, sir. At the hospital, when we went to visit Veronica Andrews.'

'I didn't know Veronica was her real name,' Banham said with a small look of amusement. 'She got very shirty with me once, when I asked her why she calls herself Tink.'

Stephanie laughed. 'She always says as she isn't under arrest she'll call herself what she wants. When we pay her enough money, and all the youth activities and shops on the estate are up and running, then she'll pay, she said, and have her real name of Veronica, which she hates, changed legally to Tink.'

'Only costs a few quid,' Georgia said. 'I'll give it to her.'

'No, you won't,' Banham said quickly. 'I've told you before about keeping a professional distance. We pay them for information they give us, and not otherwise.' He fixed his light blue eyes on her. 'They have officially been taken on by the Met now, as informants, and are paid only for what they do. You and Stephanie look after them, and work them. I am responsible for everything else about them. They are still only sixteen and seventeen, so they are under my rule. Nothing for nothing, that's the deal.' He lifted his eyebrows and held her eyes for another second to let her know he meant what he said.

'Sir,' Georgia nodded. 'Anyway, her name, Tink, came about because she loves pink, and Tink is a cross between 'Veronica' and 'pink', apparently.'

'Oh,' Banham nodded, but it was quite clear to Georgia that he was none the wiser, so she brought the conversation back to business.

'We've spoken to Larry Hardy's mother, and we've asked the girls to find out what they can about Larry and his family, and any dealings the mother may have had with the Zhangs.'

'Could be he was wanting to join another gang,

perhaps,' Stephanie offered, 'and this was part of his initiation. Or it could have been a pay-off, because his mother owed money elsewhere and they had been threatening her – in which case who was behind all this?'

'We do know the EIB gang has been seen hanging around the Aviary a lot lately,' Georgia said.

'The girls told us where their cannabis factory was, and Serious Crime moved in and closed it down, about three months ago now. Ade and Yin Zhang are both doing time for GBH,' Stephanie reminded him. 'We have always suspected the Zhangs and their soldiers burnt the recently rebuilt community centre and playground on the Aviary, in revenge.'

'They use fire as a weapon, then,' Banham pointed out.

'There's a whisper that the Chinese are pushing heroin too, which is coming in from Thailand to the continent,' Georgia added. 'Nothing solid on that one, but we have our informants working on it.'

'The tip-off was Holland to Felixstowe,' Alison answered. 'Serious Crime and Drugs have had surveillance on Felixstowe for quite a while, but so far nothing has transpired.'

'We've asked the girls to work on that, as well as Larry Hardy,' Georgia said.

'That'll cost a bit,' Banham said, 'Those informants drive a hard bargain. What are they asking for now?

'They want the community centre rebuilt,' Georgia said watching Banham's reaction. 'That means more talks with the council.' Before anyone could argue against it, she added, 'I believe that in the long run it will pay off for us too. Crime figures will drop. It's for table tennis, music therapy and dance lessons,' she told him. 'They had all that up and going before the community hall was burned to the ground. It did keep the kids off the streets, and out of danger of temptation from boredom,' she added. 'And don't forget crime rates had dropped in this area.' She looked at him. 'And you get the pat on the back for that,' she added with a grin.

'And, if anyone can get to the bottom of Larry Hardy case, it'll be those four girls. They live on the next block,' Stephanie backed her up. 'That youth offenders is full of ... shall we call it *Chinese* whispers? Personally, I'm not convinced that boy committed suicide, or if he did, that it was of his own freewill.'

'Let's keep the press conference short, sharp, and apologetic, and then let's talk about this over supper in The Crown,' Banham said, lifting Alison's cardigan from the back of her chair and placing it round her shoulders as if she were a delicate porcelain doll.

Georgia lifted one of her perfectly groomed eyebrows and eyeballed Stephanie in silent amusement.

Panther could hardly contain her anger as she walked up Air Street to the spot where the Aviary street girls waited for punters.

Amber was standing by a low wall, smoking a joint. She was as thin as a rubber band, her white arms and bare legs like train tracks from all the crack she had injected over the years. She was still only seventeen years old, and already had two babies. The other girls were all spread around the road and the alleyways where the punters knew to come if they wanted a cheap quickie or a daily quota of their drug. As well as being prostitutes, Amber and these girls were also part of the Alley Cats gang. They sold the drugs for them, but only to the addicts on, and around, the estate. Amber may have been thin and tall, looking worn down and lived in, but underneath it she could fight like a warrior. If anyone threatened, or frightened, her kids, or an Alley Cat soldier girl, she was like a champion boxer. Panther had taught her well, and all the street girls, so they could look after themselves if needed. Any, and all, of them could take on a bloke and easily hold their own in a fight, no matter what his strength. Panther, having spent her childhood in and out of care, or on the streets, had learned a lot and passed it all on to help these girls survive.

Amber and the other street girls had never been happier since the Alley Cats had taken over their streets. They no longer felt threatened by their pimps, and had no fear of being beaten and punished. The drugs they couldn't live without were supplied to them, they were never overcharged and always given good stuff, and the offer of help to get off the habit was always there for them. Amber had joined the Alley Cats to fight for the future of the estate and its kids, which included her own. The last thing she wanted was her own children growing up and walking into drugs, or drink problems like she had done, simply because there was no one to help her, or advise her any different.

The play areas and community halls had given the kids somewhere to go and a purpose, and, like the head Alley Cats, she too was devastated they had been burnt to the ground and her kids were once again left with nowhere to play.

She saw Panther storming up the road, heading her way and immediately jumped off the wall. 'How's Tink?' she asked.

'In a bad way. Are we sure it was the EIBs? 'Cos Tink reckons it were RIPs.

'Not definitely sure, mate. Summer and I saw a green van, that's all I can tell you. We was concerned when we saw it were Tink in the road. We was looking more at her, then the motor was gone.'

'Whoever it was, I am gonna kill 'em, every one of

'em,' Panther seethed. 'They've burned her up, and raped her, and if they think they are getting away with that, then they are about to learn what Alley Cats are made of.'

Amber took a deep drag on her roach, then nodded sympathetically. 'We're all with you, mate.' She blew smoke out through her nose. 'I saw the van, but I never saw no faces. It 'appened so quick. The back door opened and a body went flying in the road, then I saw it were Tink. I rang 999, and Summer rang you, and I went and tried to 'elp her, but she was ...' Amber swallowed, shook her head, and became silent.

Panther put her large brown hand on the girl's shoulder. 'We'll get them, I fucking promise you that. We'll get George Zhang first. I'll burn him up and torture him till he spells out which ones of his stinking lot touched our sister. If it ain't EIBs he'll know 'bout it.'

'Yeah, I'm up for that.'

'What we know 'bout Larry Hardy?'

'I heard he's hung himself.'

'Yeah, he 'as. But how was he involved in that sticking? Does his mum owe them EIBs for her shit?'

Amber shrugged. 'Not that I heard.'

'Must do, 'cos he never disrespects no one.'

Amber shrugged. 'You know his wacko sister has been doing punters, don't you?'

'What? No, I didn't. Where? Down here?'

Amber nodded. 'Well, over the other road. We've told her a few times that she can't stand around showing her arse to passing cars, but she ain't the full loaf, you know that, so no one really took no notice of her. She didn't get no punters stopping for her, and we all just thought she was a laugh, kept us amused, so we didn't say nothing.'

'Why didn't I hear about this?'

Amber shrugged and dropped the end of the roach on the frosty ground. She ground it into the pavement with the toe of her worn silver stiletto sandal. 'She weren't taking trade from us. No punter took her. Everyone knows she's a bit,' Amber put her index finger to the side of her head and then shrugged. 'She weren't harming no one, just pissing about really.'

'I wonder if she gone and walked on them EIBs' patch, that's over the other road. And Larry got involved that way.'

'I dunno.'

'Ask around the other girls for me,' Panther told her. 'And ask around a lot about that green van full of fuckers. And keep your phone open, and alert every Alley Cat that you see. We are going after them both, and we are taking them right out of play.'

'They're big gangs, Panth, and they've got serious weapons,' Amber warned her.

'Yeah, and?' Panther snapped.

Amber shook her head and lifted her hands in the air in defence.

'You with the Alley Cats?'

'Yeah, most def, for sure.'

'Then we're stopping all this on our estate. We ain't having no fuckers selling to our kids, you got two of your own. You want tomorrow to be better for them?'

Amber nodded. 'For def.'

'Then hold it together, 'cos there's nearly eighty of us now, and we're gonna win this fight. We'll play as dirty as it gets. No one does that to Tink, and no one fucks with our territory.' She took a breath, calmed down and added, 'If I had a wish, it would be for you to accept our offer to pay for you to go into rehab. Once you're on the road, you can have a better life. Just think on it.'

'Don't worry 'bout me,' Amber said. 'I just want it right for my kids.'

'Yeah, me too,' Panther told her with a knowing nod.

'An' you know what? That starts with you.'

'I'll ask around and report back,' Amber told her as Panther ran her sharp eyes around the road and then turned and walked back toward the estate.

Alysha and Lox were having a fry-up. The smoke in the kitchen was thick, but neither seemed to notice. Lox left the bacon and sausages sizzling in a pan to butter the toast that Alysha had just taken from the pop-up toaster. Tomatoes and mushroom, thick with oil, were cooking under a high grill and Alysha's watchful eye. Meanwhile, she was stirring a saucepan full of scrambling eggs. Lox smothered the two slices of toast with butter and jam. She handed one slice to Alysha, put the other in her mouth and went back to the pan. The sausages and bacon were ready, so she slid them onto a plate and then took the saucepan of eggs from Alysha and spooned them over, adding the mushroom and tomatoes from under the grill.

Both girls sat at the small kitchen table and tucked into their feast.

'I've left Panther's under the grill,' Lox said.

'She don't mind it cold, she says,' Alysha told her. 'Since she's been overseeing them cookery demonstrations with the pensioners, teaching the kids to cook, she said she's got used to cold food and likes it.'

'Shame that had to stop, it was just getting going.'

'Yeah, the kids liked the cooking demos, especially stuff like breakfasts and things they can do for themselves.'

'And the pensioners met other residents and got out,' Lox added quietly. 'Taught me to do this brekky properly too.' She bit into her toast and jam and quickly spooned egg into her mouth. 'We're gonna kill whoever hurt Tink and then get the estate all right again, ain't we?'

Alysha nodded. 'You fucking bet. There's been too much dissing going on.' She looked Lox straight in the eye. 'Two fucking gangs on our backs now, I'm taking that as a compliment.' She looked away and then looked back. 'But for what they done to our Tink, I'm gonna make sure whoever, or however many of 'em are responsible, is gonna die a horrid death,' she said. 'But we gotta be clever 'bout this and do it right, then we'll get both them gangs off our back.'

'I am worried 'bout the community hall, 'cos we promised the older residents some card games and things. We told 'em no more being scared of going out, that we'll make sure they are safe in their homes. We'll get that grant again, won't we'

Alysha nodded her agreement but her mind was elsewhere. She put her fork down and swallowed hard. The emotion was starting to choke her. 'It'll be a long time before Tink can do their hair again, won't it?' she said quietly.

Lox looked at Alysha. She was calm as she shook her head. 'No. That looks worse than it is, I promise. She's gonna be right as rain. Believe it. Meanwhile, we gotta get on wiv building the community hall back. Then we'll have something to tell her as she gets stronger. We'll get the feds the info that they want and then they'll lean on the council for us. We still got the gear in the Hardys' flat, remember. We can sell it.' She nodded and licked the strawberry jam off the edge of her knife. 'We've had a setback. Like the EIBs burned our shops and community centre, we'll build it again. And we'll rebuild Tink.' She looked at her friend. 'Tink will get better,' she said again. 'We'll sell them guns and gear and pay for the best plastic surgeon in the world to build her back her up, if that's what it takes. She's gonna be OK. But you have to stay strong too. She needs you. We're gonna do it.'

'Yeah,' Alysha nodded. 'We'll sell that gear on, 'cos if we give it to the feds and blame the EIBs and RIPs, they'll take the gang leaders off the streets, and then their soldiers will just take over the gang. Then they'll do us again. Like a merry-go-round. So we have to sort them permanently.'

Lox nodded back. 'Good.'

'And I am gonna kill Ray Maxted myself, if he done that to Tink. Prison's too good for 'im.'

'If we're gonna kill 'em all, we'll need a fucking good plan,' Lox told her.

'Panther's finding out what she can from the street-girls and all the uvver Alley Cats are asking around 'bout that green van. When we gather all that in, and also find what really happened with Larry Hardy, then we'll make plans.'

'We gotta be sure which lot done Tink though, that's our priority. Even if both gangs deserve to die.'

'We better go visit Larry's mum, and Karen, see if they need anything from estate help,' Alysha told her. 'And get back the gear from under her boards in her flat at the same time.'

'I'll get his laptop too, before the feds take it,' Lox said. In case there's anything on that. The feds have got one of his phones, but Karen's gonna get the other and give it to us.'

Panther's size nine feet could always be heard from at least a hundred yards away. Lox was always telling her that panthers were hunters, and hunters crept quietly, stalking their prey. Panther hadn't got a clue what she was on about. What mattered most, she told Lox, was that she was the best fighter around and could pass her knowledge on to the street girls. Panther also liked looking after the older folk on the estate, and they loved her dearly. She spent hours playing cards with them. She also offered to teach them to fight, which amused them, as well as the other girls, as some of the pensioners were on Zimmer frames, others on walking sticks, but Panther said that was a plus, she could teach them to use *those* as weapons if they ever got mugged by enemy gangs.

Since the shops and community centre had been burned, Panther was permanently angry and spoiling for a fight. And now that Tink, had been shanked, raped, and burned, she wasn't tiptoeing anywhere, not until justice was done. *Her* justice.

She turned her key in the flat door.

'We've cooked you a fry-up,' Lox shouted as she came in. 'It's still warm, but I can get it hotter.'

'You will *never* guess what I heard,' Panther shouted as she burst into the room, her large bottom only just making it through the door. She pulled a stack of notes from her pocket and put it on the table in front of Lox. 'Commission from the street girls.'

Lox was brilliant at arithmetic, Panther hadn't got a clue; her and Alysha and Tink had hardly ever been to school. Lox hadn't grown up on the estate, she had been to a grammar school and had excelled at maths. At one time she had plans to be an accountant, before she ran away from a father who abused her, and a mother who was never sober. The girls had found her and saved her life, now she would give her life for them. She lifted the wads of notes, without counting or checking. She threw the money in a drawer to be dealt with later. 'Spill,' she said, turning back to Panther.

'Info on Karen Hardy,' Panther said, taking the piece of toast that Alysha had carefully spread with butter and jam and was holding out for her. 'May give us an in as to why Larry shanked the Chink.'

66

Chapter Six

Banham led the police team as they walked into the press conference. Alison Grainger followed directly behind him, and then Georgia. They settled into their seats to a cacophony of whirring cameras, clicking of flashbulbs and the scraping of seats as journalists settled down, recording equipment, or pen and paper, in hand, eagerly awaiting a story. Sound boom operators with muscular outstretched arms reached across the room holding microphones covered in grey nylon fur and aiming above and at the edge of the camera, so as to pick up the voices of the detectives and still keep the microphones out of shot.

'Good afternoon,' Banham said briskly.

A voice then boomed from the back of the room. 'What can you tell us about the boy that hanged himself in prison?'

'Just that,' Alison shot her reply back, in a curt tone. 'A full enquiry is now ongoing.'

'Were you sure he was guilty of the stabbing he was on remand for?' another asked.

'He had admitted it.'

'Have you found the knife to prove it!' a third journalist shouted.

Alison seemed momentarily to stumble at that. Georgia answered for her. 'We were gathering evidence,' she told the woman who was now standing. 'That's all we can tell you on that, at present.'

'So that isn't a yes, then?' the woman persisted. 'You haven't found the knife?'

'An admission is an admission,' Banham told the journalist. 'We are still looking for the knife, but we will find it.'

'How long would he have served in prison?' another asked.

'Only a judge can answer that, and as we hadn't –' Georgia began.

Alison leaned into the microphone and interrupted. 'What kind of a question is that?' she snapped at the grey-haired female reporter who was now standing and clearly enjoying making the detectives uncomfortable. 'He was on remand; he hadn't yet been to trial. He had admitted the stabbing, which we believe is why he took his own life. It is a tragedy, another young life, but unfortunately these things do happen. No one had any reason to believe he should have been on suicide watch, and so he wasn't.'

'What can you tell us about the knife?' another younger local reporter asked breaking the immediate silence that filled the room for a few seconds.

Georgia sensed this reporter may know something she didn't, so she quickly jumped in to answer before Alison had the chance. 'I'm afraid we can't disclose any details of an ongoing enquiry,' she said. 'All we can say is, we had witnesses to the incident, and Larry Hardy had pleaded guilty.'

'How did he kill himself?' someone else asked.

There was a second's silence before Alison answered. 'He hanged himself from the light with the sheets from his bed.'

'Did he have previous convictions?'

'No,' Alison again answered.

'What can you tell us about the girl who was stabbed and burned and thrown from a van this morning?'

Georgia jumped when she heard that. 'This press conference was called to talk about Larry Hardy. As far as we know, the incident this morning bears no connection.'

Keith Hall, the lanky, thin, public school-spoken journalist from the local paper, persisted. 'You are saying there was no connection between these two cases?' He was enjoying his attempt to make them uncomfortable. Georgia knew him from old, he was a pain in the arse, he was always hustling for a national newspaper story, although so far he hadn't managed to ever get one.

'We have no reason to think so,' she told him, making sure to keep her comments neutral. 'Our enquiries, in one case, are ongoing, and in the other, are just beginning. May I remind you, again, this press call is about Larry Hardy only.'

'Are you saying the cases are not connected?'

'We have just said this is about Larry Hardy,' Banham all but snapped at Hall. 'If there is anything to report to you on the other case, then you will be informed. Other than that, I think that is it.' Banham went to stand up, and glanced at Alison and Georgia by way of a hint to bring the meeting to a close.

Keith Hall spoke again. 'They both live on the Aviary Estate, I believe, on adjoining blocks,' he said, his voice now rising in volume.

'A lot of people live on that estate,' Georgia said dismissively. 'The Aviary consists of six high-rise blocks, each thirteen floors high, and each floor housing a dozen flats. Work those figures out, and you'll realise how many people have their homes there.' She glared at him, allowing the rest of the room to take that in, then she added, 'Because two police investigations are centred on residents from there, doesn't mean that they are in any way connected.'

'Oh, but they are, though.'

Now every head in the room was looking Hall's way, watching, as he produced a large photo from the file he was holding in his lap, and held it in the air for all to see.

'This is a picture of the girl who was stabbed this morning, I believe,' he announced. 'Hard not to be sure of that, she has bright pink hair. No matter how many multitudes of residents live there, not a lot of them have cerise-coloured hair.' He held Georgia's furious gaze for at least a few seconds, during which the only sound was the whirr of the live television camera, then he said, 'But correct me if I'm wrong.'

Georgia was now too angry to speak. He was trying to make the police look like fools on national television and in front of the national press. And succeeding.

'Veronica Andrew,' he said turning around in the room as he held the photo of Tink for all to see. 'She goes under the nickname of "Tink",' he added, nodding another knowing nod to Georgia. He then turned the picture to make sure the television camera got a good shot. It was a large colour picture, and Tink's pink hair was unmistakeable. She was standing, with Larry Hardy, in the middle of the Aviary Estate; next to her was Lox. Larry's hand was stretched out, accepting the large wad of notes Lox was handing him.'

'They must know each other,' he repeated victoriously, as Georgia felt the colour draining from her face. He pointed to the wad of notes. 'That looks like a lot of money she is paying him. And what for, I'm sure we'd all be interested to know? Now if I was a detective and not a reporter, I would say this was more than a friendly "have a drink on me" offer.'

Georgia was aware Banham and Alison were as shocked as she was. Keith Hall was lapping up the attention. He had obviously sneaked onto the estate looking for a story, and got a lucky shot as Lox gave

Larry Hardy money. Tink just happened to be in the picture, but Hall had clearly realised it could be an excellent step in his own career. Georgia had no idea what the handing of the money was about, but she suspected it would be to do with the rebuild of the community centre. Larry had obviously helped and been paid with money Lox earned as an informant. Georgia was obliged to guard the privacy of her snouts, which meant she had to remain silent and couldn't admit any knowledge, or defend Tink and Lox. She seriously wanted to slap this ambitious, mouthy, and troublemaking journalist.

'The two incidents are being investigated as separate cases,' Banham told him giving Hall a hard stare. 'As I said before, if there is anything to report we will let you know, but I have no reason to believe that was anything that would link these two cases – which makes me wonder if you have nothing else to do, rather than sneaking around that estate making needle-in-haystack observations?'

'I have plenty to do, DCI Banham!'

'Then what business did you have on that estate taking pictures? If you believe there is anything that is connected with a police investigation, then you have a legal obligation to bring it to us. Otherwise, Mr Hall, you would be breaking the law.'

There was a silence in the room, which Hall broke after a couple of seconds.

'I have another photograph that I suspect may hold some interest to this case.' All eyes were now on him as he dipped into his file and held up a large photo of Karen Hardy, wearing a tiny denim miniskirt with silver stockings and a suspender belt. She was bent over the passenger window of a car, clearly in negotiation with the driver. Most of the flesh on her flabby bottom was in full view, apart from the tiny bit which was covered by a very

71

thin black G-string. It was cleverly photographed. Her head was tilted at an angle so her face was clear. There was no doubting it was Karen Hardy, or that she was on the game.

'I just wondered if your "no reason to believe" that the family was in any way involved in gangs or crime around the estate, had any bearing on the fact that Karen Hardy is a prostitute, or is that something that, in your over-busy schedules, you also had overlooked?' Hall asked with a triumphant air.

The murmurs that spread through the room at that moment resounded like a noisy and unsupervised assembly hall on the last day of junior school of more than a hundred pupils.

Georgia was speechless.

Banham brought the conference to a close.

'You can't have eyes in the back of your head,' Banham told her, opening his office door as an invitation for the three women to join him inside.

Georgia locked eyes with Stephanie as Banham then pulled a chair out for Alison Grainger and lifted her long hair to release it from getting trapped as she lowered herself into her seat. Alison flicked her head irritably at this gesture. That was probably the only thing Georgia and Alison would ever agree on. Too much male attention would drive her insane. But Banham obviously liked smothering his women, or perhaps he had no idea he was doing it.

'That Keith Hall is a troublemaker,' Georgia said. 'He had absolutely no right to pull that one.'

'Little runt is always out to get one over on us,' Stephanie agreed. 'He wants a national story, and doesn't care what case he walks on to get it.'

'Let it go,' Banham told her. 'We need to find out

72

more about Karen Hardy.'

'She's the last person to end up as hooker material,' Georgia said. 'She's not the full set, bless her. I'll bet she was trying to help pay her mum's debts. We'll talk to our informants.'

'I've got the pathologist's report on Ji Zhang here, sir,' Stephanie said, changing the subject. 'It's quite straightforward, the boy died from a knife wound on the right side of his body, at the back. It was one fatal cut. The knife punctured the lung and surrounding tissue, causing internal damage and a haemorrhage. He was pronounced dead on arrival at hospital.

'Must have been a heavy plunge and a deep cut,' Alison said. 'Just the one?'

Stephanie checked the notes, then nodded. 'Just the one. Yes.' She looked up and smiled. 'It went so deep, it left an imprint on the lung.' She looked up. 'Looks like the knife had a double end, two prongs.' She held up a picture of a scan of the wound. It had the two marks side by side. 'Not many knives like that. Each prong was roughly half an inch. So that'll really help in our search for the knife.'

'Sounds like a Chinese-style knife,' Georgia said.

Steph shook her head as she studied the report. 'Not really big enough, each prong roughly half an inch, it says.'

'Find that knife,' Banham said.

'We've had the school grounds combed and there's not a sign,' Georgia said. 'Which is unusual for that school,' Stephanie added. 'There are usually knives buried everywhere.'

'Someone has gathered them up, then,' Alison said.

'If someone dumped it, it couldn't have been far from the incident.'

'So who else wanted Ji Zhang dead, and is clever

enough to help Larry Hardy hide the knife?'

'Rival gang like the RIPs,' Stephanie said. 'But they're Peckham, not this area. None of them would have been within the school grounds.'

'But there are rival gangs,' Georgia said. 'Larry was working with someone.'

Alison turned to Georgia, 'Your informants told us that the family was squeaky clean. They said the boy looked after his sister, who has learning difficulties.'

'That's right,' Georgia said.

'So what was Lox paying him for?' Alison asked.

'Help with the community hall, I expect,' Georgia said.

'You need to pay Karen and Lisa Hardy another visit,' Banham told Georgia.

Georgia nodded thoughtfully. 'Let me talk to my snouts first, sir.'

'Absolutely. That's what we pay them for. If they haven't done their homework thoroughly, then they need to do it again.'

'I'm wondering if the Zhangs have any of the territory around the Aviary streets,' Georgia said. 'I heard they do. Supposing they had Karen working for them? That would be a reason for Larry Hardy to stab him, wouldn't it?'

'The Chinese territory is all East London,' Alison said.

Georgia took a deep breath. The woman had hardly been back in the area more than a few months, yet thought she knew everything. 'Maybe they're setting their sights wider, and that's what's behind this?'

'But I doubt they'd employ Karen Hardy as a tom.'

'If her mother owed them, they would,' Stephanie said.

'Someone runs the girls down around the Aviary,' Alison pushed.

'Our snouts say the girls run themselves,' Georgia told her. 'No pimps around, according to them.'

Alison shook her head. 'So someone wants that territory,' she said. 'Your snouts could be wrong on that score?'

'They've never got anything wrong before,' Georgia said, careful not to snap.

'So why was Lox giving Larry Hardy money then? That could be on the front of tomorrow's paper,' Alison said. 'We need to know the answer, so we can be ten steps ahead.'

'Well, we can't ask Tink,' Georgia said. 'She's unconscious. But we'll talk to Lox.'

'It'll be to do with the estate,' Stephanie said. 'We know Larry was helping with that.'

'We need to know more than just that,' Alison repeated coldly. 'The press will want to know where girls of that age got that big money from. Someone will have to answer that one too.'

'The council gave them a grant and the estate residents clubbed together to get the community hall painted, it's as simple as that,' Georgia said. 'Nothing illegal.' She turned to Stephanie. 'I'm going over there right now,' she told her, tilting her head for her sergeant to take the hint.

'Yep, I'm coming,' Stephanie told her.

'Is Summer and Amber dead sure that it was Karen, on EIB patch, strutting her stuff?' Alysha asked Panther. They sat in the kitchen of Alysha's flat with Lox, sharing a large bottle of Pepsi, dirty plates strewn over the table.

'Yeah,' Panther said. 'And we know she ain't a hundred per cent upstairs, but she must know what she's doin' on that score, she ain't *that* stupid. She knows we run our patch, and if she wants to work the streets, then she has to come to us. It ain't even the money, it's dangerous for her, out there on her own, on EIB territory.'

'Repercussions ain't worth thinking of,' Lox said. 'If it

weren't important, it would be funny. Let's be serious, she's a lump.'

'I reckon she knows we wouldn't take her on,' Alysha said. 'An' in her own mixed-up brain, she wants to help her mum. She's still big in debt to lenders, even with us helping.'

'She must owe a lot less now,' Lox said, standing up and putting the plates in the sink. 'I gave Larry a load of corn, when he hid the gear we stole from the RIPs. An' I told 'im when we sell them on, we'll pay his mum's debt with the profits. But 'e needed to guard them till we could flog them.'

'Yeah, well, we need to get that gear back now,' Alysha said. 'We should move it somewhere else. I ain't gonna go storming in right now, wiv the family in that state, and feds coming and going. But there is one hell of a lot of brown, and them handguns in there, so we gotta hope the feds don't search in Larry's room too much.'

'It's hidden well,' Lox said. 'They won't find it.'

'I still don't get what Karen thinks she's doing,' Panther said. ''Cos she ain't making no corn, no one's picked her up for a job from what I hear.'

'She's on EIB territory,' Alysha said. 'Whether she's making money or not. She could get hurt. She's all Lisa's got right now. We gotta stop that for both their good.'

'We ain't allowed to leave this building, or have you forgot?' Lox said.

'No I ain't,' Alysha told her. She turned to Lox and then Panther. There was fire in her eyes. 'We've got nearly eighty Alley Cats who believe in us and our rule of this estate. A lot of them are street girls. Potty Karen is parading her arse on EIB ground, and Karen is one of ours. We 'ave to look out for 'er, 'cos she's too thick to look out for herself. We already had our community hall burnt down 'cos we 'ad a run in with the

76

EIBs, and they'll def retaliate if one of ours is tomming on their territory. That could be what 'appened to Tink. Have you thought of that? She could be the mug that took the punishment for what we done to EIB gear and their car, and now with Karen on their territory, someone else might be next. We gotta stay on top of all this shit. We can't lose this battle.' She looked at the girls. 'I know the feds promise the earth, but they ain't gotta clue what it's really like surviving around here, let's face it. And if we look soft, then one of them gangs will move on us for sure, and if that happens, then think what happens to this estate and our kids?'

'What you saying? Panther frowned at her. 'Are you saying that we're losing control of our territory?'

'I'm saying that we lost a bit when they got Tink, and we gotta make sure it don't happen to anyone else. And we gotta get even for Tink, don't we?'

Lox and Panther both nodded their agreement.

'We was doing good. We had the community hall running, and the residents and kids loved it. Tink went on that hair and nail course. Then Jason came back and was teaching street dance in the community. It was going so good. And now look what we let 'em do to us. They burnt our territory and they burnt our Tink.'

'So two fucking gangs think we're soft,' Panther said angrily.

'We showed the RIPs what they were up against,' Lox argued. 'We nicked that gear and handguns that they nicked from the EIBs, and tied them naked and dumped them.'

Alysha nodded. 'And now Larry's hung himself and Tink been shanked and burnt, 'cos we done that.'

Lox and Panther looked at each other. 'We are gonna get them though, ain't we, Queen?' Panther said, her forehead creasing with worry.

Alysha nodded. 'Oh yeah, we are. Whoever hurt Tink is gonna die, and ain't that the truth. But we gonna get it right this time and that ain't gonna be easy. It just ain't gonna be that fucking easy.' She turned her head away as she felt emotion beginning to choke her, then she said, 'But we have to sort Karen.'

'And we'll go after whoever hurt our Tink, and we'll burn them like they did our estate and Tink, and then we'll build our estate up again,' Lox said, taking over and being strong for Alysha. ''Cos we're the ACs. Fuck with us, and you'll pay the price.'

'There'll always be someone out there wants to dirty up what we've cleaned up,' Panther said sensing Alysha's distress and rubbing her shoulder gently. 'You're sore, Queen, 'cos of our Tink. I understand that. So we gonna do this for Tink. I'll happily kill Maxted, if you don't, for what he done to her. Just say the word, Queen, and I'll go and cut him up.'

'I just wish I could have been there to help her,' Alysha said.

Panther and Lox made eye contact. 'We're gonna get them,' Panther said. 'And we'll build her shop back up, so when she's ready she can do her hair and stuff.'

'If no one burns it down again first.'

'Think what we've already done, Queen.' Lox said as she looked at Alysha's desperate face. 'When we have kids, we'll have given them chances. They won't have to sell their bodies like we did, or go and steal to get a bit of food inside them.'

'Yeah, I know,' Alysha nodded. 'But will Tink ever have kids after this? She took a shank to her belly.'

'Who's to say,' Lox answered, flicking a worried glance at Panther. 'But if we give up and let the estate go back to what it was, our old people will never come out, and everyone's kids'll be addicts. They'll all end up dead before they're twenty, or in jail. We promised we wouldn't let that happen. They all rely on us. Come on, Queen, we gotta stay strong.'

'And fucking Jesus, we're working for the feds. If any gangs find that out, they'll kill us, slowly,' Panther said, her big eyes popping at Alysha. 'And I wanna 'ave kids, twenty of 'em! And I don't want them having the shit we 'ad. So it's worth taking big risks, and playing dirty. We know we're taking chances being grasses, and selling stuff, but if no one will help us, then we gotta help ourselves. We know we're risking our lives 'ere. But keep your eyes on the build-up of the estate, and the next lot of kids. Even if they do kill us first, our kids will have chances we never had.'

'They won't kill us, we're gonna make sure that don't 'appen,' Lox said brightly, and shaking her head at Panther.

'But will Tink make it, to see that 'appen,' Alysha's voice broke again.

Lox flicked a concerned glance at Panther again, and then rubbed Alysha's shoulder. For a rare moment Alysha had allowed her own vulnerability to get through, and a big tear fell from her eye. 'I grew up wiv her,' she said wiping away the tear. 'We worked the perverts together so we could buy a bit of food. We've looked out for each other since we were kids, always; an' I should 'ave been there for her.'

'You couldn't have known what was happening,' Lox said gently. 'But she's strong and she's a survivor. She'll get through all this an' we'll take care of her. She'll be the best hairdresser ever, and she'll have a whole football team of kids, you'll see.'

Alysha's sadness changed suddenly back to anger. 'I'm gonna get them for what they done to her. I swear I'm gonna get them fuckers.'

'I'm helping you,' Panther told her. 'I'll rip their heads off.'

Lox put her hands out in front of them. 'We'll make a plan first,' she said, trying to instil some calm. 'C'mon, Queen, let's go sort Karen Hardy first, and then we'll ring the hospital again, and then,' she looked at Panther. 'Then … we'll burn Maxted and them RIPs.'

Chapter Seven

The sound of a gunshot halted Georgia and Stephanie in their tracks. The scream that followed shook the foundations of the Rook block.

'Jesus! What was that?' Georgia aimed her key to her car to lock it, then broke into a run in the direction of the scream.

Stephanie had moved ahead and was now on the grounds of the Aviary, facing the Rook block, looking up to where the scream came from.

Within seconds Karen Hardy appeared on the walkway, hands on ears and screaming helplessly.

'Stay there, love, we're on our way.' Stephanie shouted, as she followed Georgia who was now ahead and bounding up the stairs, heading for the fourth-floor flat.

Having heard the screaming, Panther, Alysha and Lox were out of their flat and down their stairs and they too were running in the direction of the Rook block.

Then, everywhere around the blocks, doors and windows were opening with residents wanting to see what was happening and who had been shot, for there was no doubting, to anyone that had heard the noise, that someone had fired a gun.

Then, in the distance a motorbike fired up, and roared off. Georgia rushed to look over the edge of the walkway on the first floor, but all she saw was the bike speeding off and the back of the helmeted driver.

Stephanie and Georgia both then dashed up the

remaining stairs, Georgia still ahead of Stephanie, who was struggling, and had turned onto the fourth floor. The front door to the Hardys' flat was open so Georgia ran straight past Karen, who was still outside on the walkway, still screaming. Georgia would let Stephanie deal with the hysterics; she couldn't cope with even a small amount of emotion, and Karen was beyond delirious.

Georgia ran straight into the flat. The sight of Lisa stopped her in her tracks. The bullet had gone straight through the woman's eye. The evidence of blood, splinters of skull and the watery, jelly-like substance of her brain had cannoned through to the back of her head, adhering itself to the grubby beige wall behind her. Lisa's body was sliding, slowly, down the wall. It landed with a thud by the side of Georgia.

The DI was on her mobile in a second, calling for immediate back-up. They urgently needed officers to surround the area, others to try and pick up a motorbike that had sped out of the Aviary, and a forensic team was needed ASAP on the Rook block, fourth floor. She turned to shout to Stephanie, but before she could get a word out she came face-to-face with Alysha Panther and Lox, who were standing in the doorway staring at the sight of the dead Lisa Karen's wails still shook the building.

'Out. Out! Wait outside, please.' Georgia shouted into the stunned faces of the three girls.

She checked for a pulse through force of habit. She looked up. Alysha and Lox and Panther all still stood, as if glued to the spot, staring at Lisa. Georgia raised her voice at them. 'Clear. Now,' she ordered.

Back-up was there within minutes, along with Banham and Alison Grainger. Georgia left Stephanie trying to get some sense out of Karen, while she told Banham exactly what she and Stephanie had seen and heard.

'Why did you touch her? Alison asked Georgia.

82

'I checked for a pulse, it's force of habit.'

Alison shook her head crossly, but before Georgia had time to snap back, Banham spoke.

'OK,' he said holding his hands up to Georgia. 'You and Stephanie take the daughter's statement. Alison and I will talk to the neighbours.'

'Good luck with that,' Georgia said sarcastically.

'And talk to those three girls outside,' Alison told Georgia without mentioning Alysha, Panther, or Lox by name. 'See what they have to say.'

Karen was dressed in the get-up she had been described as wearing earlier: the denim miniskirt with the silver stockings and suspender belt.

Stephanie got her inside the flat and into the kitchen, sitting her on a tatty plastic stool in the corner. Stephanie immediately turned the oven off. Lisa had obviously been cooking, therefore, Stephanie thought, hadn't been expecting anyone. She suggested Karen put something warm around her. Karen didn't answer; she just sat on the stool and howled.

Georgia threw an uncomfortable glance at Stephanie as she leaned back against the grubby draining board. She thought briefly of her bathtub at home and how she longed to be in it, washing away the grime of this flat. But first she had a murder to sort.

'I'll get you something warm to put round you, you're shivering,' Stephanie said to Karen, speaking in a motherly tone. While her sergeant left the room, Georgia studied Karen silently. Stephanie returned shortly after with a grubby blue candlewick dressing gown from Karen's bedroom. She was wearing forensic gloves and as she carefully undressed Karen, she put her clothes in a forensic bag before wrapping Karen in the dressing gown and doing up the buttons to keep her warm.

She then handed the see-through forensic evidence bag to the forensic team, who had just arrived and were busying themselves in the hallway.

'OK. Tell us what happened,' Georgia said to Karen, when Stephanie had finished dressing her.

Karen looked up. Her eyes and her complexion were red, blotchy and swollen. 'My mum,' she said as she started to cry again.

'Take deep breaths,' Stephanie told her.

Karen gulped, but said nothing.

'Did someone knock on the door?' Georgia asked.

Karen gulped again, then nodded.

'Take your time,' Stephanie encouraged her gently.

'Mum opened the door, and then there was a shot.' She looked at Georgia, eyes fearful. 'I ran to Mum. She was ...' She stopped speaking and started to fight for her breath. Stephanie and Georgia had both seen victims having panic attacks on numerous occasions. Stephanie rubbed her back. She started to breathe again.

'I'll make tea,' Stephanie said. 'Would you drink some?'

Karen nodded and gulped, and then started howling again.

Stephanie started to attempt to make Karen sweet tea, but she couldn't see any teabags, only milk, so she stirred sugar into a grubby mug of hot water and milk. 'Sip this,' she said handing Karen the drink.

'Did you go near the door?' Georgia asked. 'The front door? Did you see anyone, Karen? Did you see who was at the door?'

Karen wasn't drinking the milk. She was drawing noisy intakes of breath and sobbing. 'I saw ... someone in black,' she said.

'Anyone you recognised?'

She dropped her voice in tone and volume. ''E 'ad a

84

hat on, but I think it were the Chinese man. Mum owes 'im money, you know. He scares me.'

Stephanie and Georgia made eye contact. 'Which one, can you remember his name. Which one? Did you see him, Karen?'

'Didn't see his face. He were in black and wore a hat over his face,' Karen said.'

Georgia looked at Stephanie.

'You mean his face was covered?'

Karen nodded.

Stephanie was writing away, furiously, now.

'Did you see anyone around at any time in the last couple of hours?' Georgia asked. 'This is very important, Karen, please think. 'How long had you been in before that knock on the door?'

'I'd been to the shop … I was in a few minutes. I don't know.' She was wringing her hands in an exaggerated manner.

'OK,' Stephanie said putting her hand over the girl's hands to keep her from becoming any more hysterical.

Georgia was now reminded of Lady Macbeth and the famous sleepwalking scene. She dismissed the thought from her mind.

'Did you see anyone? Anyone at all as you came home across the estate, from the shop?'

'I saw Panther.'

Stephanie looked at Georgia. Georgia lifted her eyebrows at her sergeant to push harder.

'Anyone else?'

Karen shook her head. 'No.'

'Are you sure? Any cars in the car park that you might have noticed as unfamiliar?'

Karen shook her head again.

'What about a motorbike?'

'No.'

'Any idea which Chinese man threatened your mum, Karen?' Georgia asked.

'George Zhang. He's been telling Mum that he'd kill her.'

'Because she owed him money?' Stephanie asked.

'Yes. She owed him lots and lots for her drugs.'

'What did you get in the shop?' Georgia asked her.

Karen looked at Georgia and then at Stephanie and then shook her head. 'I can't tell you,' she said quietly.

'You didn't go the shops, did you?' Stephanie said.

Karen hung her head guiltily as she shook it.

'Were you down in the streets?' Stephanie questioned gently.

Now she nodded.

'How long were you down there?' Georgia asked her.

'Leave me alone,' Karen yelled. 'I ain't telling you nothing. I don't like you.' She glared at Georgia.

Georgia stood up straight. 'Karen, I'm sorry, but you still need to answer my questions. I am trying to …'

Stephanie raised her hand to hush Georgia and the inspector knew that in this sensitive case, her sergeant was right. The girl was unstable at the best of times, and certainly very low on intelligence. Georgia couldn't deal with that, but they both knew Stephanie could. Georgia walked out into the hallway, and went to talk to the forensic team, who were now going about their business around Lisa's corpse.

One was down on her knees, head to toe in bluebell-coloured forensic overalls, scouring the floor tiles with a tweezers for any hair or anything she could find. She had a plastic container in one hand and was picking up stray hairs and placing them inside the container.

Another, a member of the murder unit, was taking pictures of the blood patterns and the dead woman. Georgia could hear Karen telling Stephanie that she had been in the streets trying to sell her body to get money for her mum's debt to the Chinese man. She then heard Stephanie telling Karen to have a lie down in her room.

'I'll come back and talk to you in a while, Karen,' she said.

Stephanie then came out to join Georgia by the door to the flat which was now cordoned off with crime scene tape.

Alysha was standing with Panther and Lox by the lift at the end of the walkway. They were talking to Karen's neighbour. Alysha walked over to Georgia and Stephanie when she saw them come out, and the neighbour quickly closed her front door.

'We can talk here, can we?' Georgia asked the girls, and then added quietly. 'Without the neighbours suspecting you are giving us information.'

Alysha merely shrugged. All three girls looked too shocked to comment.

'After all, word is going round that Lisa has been shot,' Georgia said. 'And everyone will be questioned.'

'Yeah, but no one will say anything to your lot,' Lox told her. 'I've just watched this row of flats close the door in the faces of your DCI and his missus. Gangs have been burning down our estate, you lot ain't done nothing helpful to make it better, so the residents aren't gonna help you. They are scared shitless again. And, after all the work we done to try to stop all that and make them safe on this estate.' She shook her head and turned her back on Georgia.

'You ain't gonna get nothing from these residents,' Alysha said.

Georgia ignored that comment. 'We have things we need you to find out for us, so I'll meet you at your flat in ten minutes,' she said, lowering her voice, and addressing

Alysha.

'Make sure she knows it'll cost,' Panther whispered to Alysha.

'What's happening with Karen?' Alysha asked her. 'She only had her mum and brother.'

'Social services will take care of her,' Stephanie said. 'I'm about to get onto that now.'

Panther jogged her wrist up and down in a rude gesture, at the comment of social services intervening.

'Unless you happen to know where her father is?' Georgia asked.

Alysha answered with a shake of the head.

'You mean who the father is?' Lox said.

'Ain't you noticed that Lisa's white, Larry's mixed race and Karen's white,' Alysha said, raising her eyebrows at Georgia.

'And your point?' Georgia said.

'It means no one knows a fuck who either of their dads are. Listen, Karen's sixteen in a month, she don't need social services.'

'I would say her health report will state she isn't fit to live and cope alone,' Stephanie told her. 'She has a very low IQ for starters.'

'She won't be alone. She's coming over to ours,' Alysha said. 'We'll take care of her,' she turned to the other two girls, 'won't we?

'Course,' Lox said as Panther nodded her agreement.

'I'll have to run that past social services,' Stephanie told her. 'I'll tell them she's with you, and give her your address.'

Alysha shrugged. 'They won't give a shit. They'll just be glad they ain't got anything to do.' She turned to Panther. 'Go and get her.'

Stephanie put her hand up. 'You know you can't go in there. It's a crime scene. I'll talk to her first, see if she wants to go home with you. If she does, I'll bring her over to yours. She's understandably in a bad way at the moment. If she doesn't want to go with you, I will take her to the station and wait for social services, who will take her. I'll let you know.'

'She'll want to come wiv us,' Alysha said in the tone of one twice her sixteen years. 'We'll take care of her. Her IQ ain't bad enough not to know that we'll look after her and the social won't.'

Having got nowhere with the residents, Alison and Banham went back to take a good look around the flat with Georgia and Stephanie.

Karen couldn't wait to get away from her mother's body and go to Alysha's flat, so Stephanie took her over, and then came back and joined Georgia, Banham and Alison to help search the flat.

Stephanie and Georgia went into Larry Hardy's room first. They opened the wardrobe doors, then checked the pockets of the few bits of clothing which were still hanging in his wardrobe. 'TIU has his computer,' Stephanie reminded Georgia. 'There was nothing on it. He didn't even have Facebook.'

'Well, he had secrets, that's for sure,' Georgia said. 'Like why were Lox and Tink giving him money?'

'He had been helping paint the shops and the community hall that got burned down,' Stephanie said. 'We already know that. The girls employed the residents to do a lot of that work. I'm not too concerned about that one.'

Georgia was now rooting through a pile of dirty washing on the floor of the wardrobe. She moved a pair of trainers aside and then lifted a few dirty shirts, and then a pile of socks from the floor. As she moved things aside she leaned on a loose board on the floor of the wardrobe. It bounced as she touched it.

'Steph,' she called, as she tried to fiddle with it to see if something was catching in it or why it was loose. It didn't take much fiddling, as all the other boards around it moved. They too were loose. Steph was now kneeling beside her. Together they carefully lifted the wooden boards. Both froze, staring at the contents of the space underneath.

'Shit,' Stephanie said, as they found themselves facing a stack of small handguns, about a half a dozen swords, and a hoard of what looked like heroin.

'Call the DCI,' Georgia said prodding the heroin and lifting one of the guns in her gloved hand.

'My goodness,' Stephanie muttered, struggling to get herself upright, and then turning and heading for the door.

Lox handed Karen a mug of hot sweet tea and put her arm around her. 'We're gonna look after you,' she told her. 'We'll take it one step at a time.

Karen was shaking her head. 'They've killed my mum.'

'Who? Who shot your mum, Karen?' Alysha asked her.

'Don't know,' Karen shrugged. 'But they did. I know they did.'

Lox wrapped the warm dressing gown around Karen and fastened the belt. 'I'll make you a bed up in here.' she said gently. You can sleep on the sofa for a bit. We'll talk about it when you've had a rest.'

Karen just stared at Lox. 'Mum's been shot. Larry was killed in prison. He wouldn't kill himself, I know he wouldn't. Are they gonna kill me too?'

Alysha knelt down on the floor in front of Karen. She looked up at her. 'Listen to me, Karen,' she said gently. 'No one's gonna hurt you, 'cos we're gonna look after you, but you gotta be straight wiv us. Your mum took

90

drugs, you know that, right?'

Karen nodded. 'Yeah, she was always on summink.'

'Did she take any of that stash? You know the guns and heroin we gave to Larry to look after, we was gonna sell it for her to pay the Chinese with? Did she give them to Zhang to keep him away, or did she tell 'im that she had it?'

Karen shook her head and frowned. 'No, don't think so.'

'And did Larry give that money that we gave 'im to the EIBs for her debt, or toward it, do you know?'

'I don't think it were enough.'

'I know,' Lox said. 'That was just some toward it. Your mum was in big debt.'

'Did she tell the EIBs that she had that gear?' Alysha asked again.

'Larry wouldn't kill himself,' Karen said to Alysha.

'I agree,' Alysha nodded.

'Mum owed them lots of money.'

'Were they threatening her? Is that why Larry stuck Ji Zhang?'

Karen shrugged.

'Panther tells me you been working, alone, on the streets behind the estate,' Alysha said. 'That's EIB territory. So what's all that about?'

There was a pause. Karen looked terrified.

'It's all right, we ain't gonna bollock you,' Alysha said. 'But we've helped you out, wiv money and stuff, and we'll help again; it ain't safe down there, you mustn't go down those lanes.'

'They was pestering Mum!' Karen shouted. 'Larry paid them that money you gave him, but they kept coming round. He gave the money from his job to Mum, and she got more stuff wiv it. Ji Zhang was hassling her big time. Mum was using them drugs you asked Larry to hide. Then

Larry got put in prison. Mum needed money so I went down the lanes.' She looked from one to the other. Her podgy face was still red and swollen. 'I thought no one would know,' she said, putting her thumb in her mouth and frowning.

Alysha and Lox and Panther flicked a worried glance at each other.

'That's EIB territory,' Panther told her. 'You gotta promise us you'll never do that again. You ain't safe down there.'

'Didn't you know George Zhang was running his girls there and selling his gear?' Lox asked her. 'He would hurt you badly for being there.'

Karen shook her head.

'So why didn't you come to me?' Panther said to her.

Karen looked at Panther and frowned. 'You're big and fat, I never knew you were a tom.'

Panther looked surprised. 'That's a bit rude, mate. Anyway, we ain't talking 'bout *me* being a tom. We're talking 'bout you. I don't do punters no more. But, if we're gonna be talking *fat* here ...'

'I was offerin' it cheap,' Karen said, raising her voice.

Alysha shook her head. 'Jesus, Karen, you ain't 'alf stupid. You gotta wise up, mate. You could have got yourself killed. That could be why the Zhangs done your mum. You should 'ave come to us. You know we run this estate an' you know we was 'elping you, and would again.'

'He did know.'

'Who?'

'George Zhang.'

There was a second while they all took that in. 'What you mean? George Zhang knew you was offering cheap blow jobs on his territory?' Panther asked her.

Karen nodded.

'What did he do when he found out?' Lox asked casting a concerned look at Alysha.

'He beat me about a bit, an' then he tells me I owe him loads.'

'Corn?'

'Yeah, lots of corn, and he said Mum already owed him loads. So I told him, I didn't have any money, 'cos no one stops for me.'

'See, what did I say about bein' too fat,' Panther said, half to herself, and with a shake of her head.

'What else did he say?' Alysha interrupted.

'He ain't said nothing.'

'Yet,' Alysha said, looking at the other two.

'But you said you would pay him?' Panther pushed.

She nodded. 'But I won't. He's killed my mum. Will you help me kill him?'

The girls all made eye contact again. Then Alysha spoke. 'OK, Karen, here's the deal. We are gonna look after you. You can join the Alley Cats, but you'll have to prove yourself if you wanna do that.'

'I'll join.'

'Right. Well we are on a mission to get them EIB Chinks and them RIP bastards to back off from our estate. They burnt the community hall and the playground so their cards are marked. We want a safe estate, no drugs and no pimps. Got it?'

Karen nodded. 'Yeah.'

'We've all made mistakes, us four, we all made big fucking mistakes, so don't worry 'bout what you done, just worry about not doing it no more. You're joining the Alley Cats, and you gotta do as you're told, but we got your back at all times. We're gonna fight for this estate, and keep the scum off, and them EIBs are the biggest scum ever. We got nearly eighty in our gang, mainly girls, but some blokes too, and we all can fight as good as any of them fuckers. And we'll get the Zhangs for what they done to your mum and Larry.'

'I can fight.'

'Yeah, good, 'cos you're gonna have to. No gangs are gonna feed our estate kids drugs. It stops here. We want a future. You're like us. You've grown up without no help from no one. Your mum was never there for you, but we will be. Look what's happened to our Tink. She's a diamond, that girl, and that was RIPs that done 'er. Them pricks have really got it coming for that. Tink is our sister. We won't let any of them fuckers move in on this estate, or piss on any of our residents. And that's a promise. Feds are useless, so we do it our way. Two gangs is a lot to take on, but we've got our ways, an' we got a plan. We're gonna get even for you and for your mum and Larry, and for Tink.' She looked at Lox and Panther. 'We are gonna play one off 'gainst the other.'

'And that's where you come in,' Alysha said. ''Cos you are gonna be part of all that. You can fight, so you can be one of us, and we'll be your family. We'll fight, die for you, if we 'ave to. You'll learn what families really do for each other.'

'But you don't knock off no punters to do it,' Panther reminded her.

'So what you say?'

'Yeah,' Karen nodded.

Alysha's phone rang at that second, and she put her hand up as she read the name on the screen.

'What?' She listened as her shocked expression met the concerned looks of Lox and Panther.

Chapter Eight
Evening: 8 p.m.

'Amber's found a knife,' Alysha told them as she cut the call. 'I'm going down to get it before the feds find it.' She grabbed her padded jacket from the back of the lop-sided sofa and checked the pockets. She pulled out a plastic glove then put the coat on. 'Watch from the balcony and call two rings if you see any feds within prying distance.'

'Where did she find it?' Lox asked.

'Near where Tink was shanked and dumped. Amber says there's dried blood on it, so could be prints too. Amber ain't handled it, she says, so with luck, an' if we give it to the feds, we might know which of them bastards actually shanked Tink.' She took an intake of breath, and her voice became cold and hard. 'An' I am gonna kill that bastard myself, a slow and painful death.'

'You ain't going down there on your own,' Panther said to her. 'I'm coming wiv ya. I can keep an eye out for feds.'

'Me too, you need us all,' Lox told her.

Karen stood up.

'No, you stay 'ere, Karen,' Alysha told her. 'Just put your feet up, and we'll back in no time.'

Karen nodded and Panther lifted her feet and put them on the sofa, then tucked the blanket around Karen. 'Won't be long,' she said. 'Don't answer the door. We got keys.'

* * *

While the serious crimes and the CO19 gun unit moved in to the Hardys' flat with a dog unit, intending to turn the flat upside down in a search for any more hidden drugs or weapons, Georgia, Stephanie, Alison and Banham drove to The Horseshoe pub, about two miles outside the estate.

'You are going to bring Karen to the station tonight, to take her full statement?' Banham asked Georgia as he ordered drinks for all of them.

Stephanie had the food blackboard in her hands, and was deciding what to eat. She looked up from it. 'Why don't we take the statement at Alysha's place. Karen's staying there for the time being, and she's traumatised. She'll be easier to talk to her there, the station might frighten her into silence.'

'I don't agree,' Alison said. 'I think she'll tell us more without our informants being nearby or in the next room.'

'You're the boss,' Stephanie said with a shrug, and without taking her eyes off the menu board.

'I'll get a unit car to pick her up and drive her in,' Georgia said to Banham. 'Then Stephanie and I can talk to our informants privately. Someone on that estate saw somebody come to the Hardys' front door. I don't believe no one saw anything. Someone would have seen the bike, and those informants need to find out who. Or the street toms might have seen something.'

'I don't think Karen would have noticed, certainly not if she passed them on her way back from the streets, and she went into hysterical mode after the shooting, so she wouldn't have noticed him leaving,' Stephanie said, handing the barmaid the money for a pie she was ordering. 'She's the last thing from observant, even if she had passed them on her way back from the street or shops. But there would have been a kid, or a dog-walker, someone who saw something, and our informants need to find that person.'

'We also need information from them on Larry Hardy's suicide,' Georgia said to Stephanie.

'No, leave that be for the moment,' Banham said to her. 'The prison will go into that, and when we get their report we'll take it from there. It's a sad state of affairs, I agree, but without parents, and with the workload we have,' he handed a vodka and tonic to Alison, and then turned back to the bar, picked up a St Clements and handed it to Georgia, who was driving, 'let the prison do that work. We need all our manpower to solve this shooting, and find out who has attempted to murder Veronica Andrew.'

'And Larry Hardy's suicide may well speak for itself,' Alison nodded her agreement, 'when we get to the bottom of this case.'

'It seems he really wasn't as squeaky clean as everyone said,' Banham said as he settled himself into the seat beside Alison.

'Which is where our informants come in,' Alison said, looking at Georgia. 'They have to get us the information on where the handguns and heroin came from, or else they don't get paid anything.'

'We have to pay them,' Georgia said sternly. 'They always deliver.'

'We *do* pay them,' Banham said, equally sternly.

'They want us to talk to the council again for them,' Georgia reminded him. 'They're putting in an application for another grant to rebuild the community hall and shops, and play areas, and they want us to help push it for them.'

Banham raised his eyebrows. Georgia noted the sarcasm but carried on. 'It makes sense, guv. When their community centre was rebuilt along with the playground, it kept the kids off the streets, it provided recreation for the residents – everyone was happy, including us. Crime figures dropped, you said that yourself. If we can persuade the council to give them another grant, then we will benefit too.'

'Who's to say it won't get burnt down again?' Alison said.

'It won't if we get these gangs that are trying to muscle onto the estate,' Georgia argued. 'Because that's who burnt it down before. And it's thanks to our informants that we've already rounded up the leaders of the last three gangs working that estate. Oh, come on, admit it, those informants are gold dust for us, and I think we should do everything we can to keep them sweet. You can see yourself no one on the estate will talk to us, they are all too afraid. We can't get information. Yet the girls can, because the residents trust them. If they get another grant, crime will drop again. We all know it will. And they won't get a salary as well as a recommendation for a grant, so our budget can stretch further.'

Alison tutted. 'You know you're being naïve.'

'How do you work that out?'

'You put too much trust in four ex-drug-taking hookers.'

Georgia glared at her.

'We put the last gangs away for very long stretches, for using under-age street girls and carrying firearms, and dealing in Class As,' Stephanie said through a mouthful of pie. 'All thanks to those ex-prossies, as you call them, who were their victims.' She swallowed and looked Alison in the face. 'So I prefer to call them abused teenagers, looking for a way to make good, a way we can help with.'

'It seems we have a big problem with the EIB gang at this moment,' Alison reminded Georgia, ignoring Stephanie's comments. 'The last leaders that we put away, the London Rulers, had a lot of Chinese soldiers, and now look at the Zhangs and their EIBs. They've taken most of those soldiers and the territory, and are pushing drugs and, we suspect, killing, and they seem to be moving south and into this area.'

'We don't know that it was them who stabbed Tink Andrews,' Stephanie said, speaking with another mouthful of pie, and wiping her mouth with her serviette as she spoke.

'We don't know yet,' Banham argued, quickly jumping on Alison's side. 'But Alysha Achter will find out for us, that I am sure of, and then we will haul the Zhangs into court.'

Georgia glanced at Stephanie out of the side of her eye. Stephanie was wiping the bottom of the pie dish with the bread from her plate, but she caught Georgia's eye and raised an eyebrow.

'Our informants are understandably upset and angry at the moment,' Georgia said. 'Tink has been stabbed, probably because someone found out she's a police informant. After we gave them our word that we would protect them. We've let them down, so I think the least we can do now is try and help them get another grant. The council have full power to give it.' She raised her voice and turned to Banham. 'I can't see your objection – it will benefit both the Met and the Aviary Estate and keep our budgets healthy. Crime will drop, because it did last time, and less kids will turn into criminals.'

Banham was listening intently but the stern look on his face told her he didn't like being told what was in his best interest.

'What interests me most,' he said, after a few seconds where he met and held her gaze, 'is the fact that crime figures down there have been excellent recently, but in the last week we have had a stabbing at a school gate – not on the actual estate, I grant you, but not far from it, and involving one of the residents – then a very large haul of heroin and firearms is found in one of the flats on the estate following a fatal shooting, also on the estate. And the death in prison of a resident, and a girl, again from the estate, stabbed and raped just outside it – a girl who just happens to be one of our informants. And yet none of our informants had a clue anything was brewing. And I would *also* like to know why two of our informants were photographed paying money to the boy who stabbed Ji Zhang.'

Georgia shook her head. 'Nothing in that, sir. He was helping with the rebuilding work, that's it. I would say this is something that has grown from one drug-addicted woman who didn't know how far in she had gone, and her daughter, who has special needs, turning to the streets and causing more trouble. Possibly because of that, her son stabs someone. Someone who has been supplying his mother with drugs. She got shot because she couldn't pay her dealers.'

'So where does all the heroin and firearms found in the flat fit into this? Banham asked. 'Why was she so in debt if all that was there?'

'Because Lisa didn't know it was there?'

'So, it was Larry?'

'Had to be,' Georgia nodded.

'Why didn't our informants know anything about this?'

'They can't know everything. They don't have any involvement in drugs any more, so why would they?' Georgia said defensively.

'Are you sure of that?' Alison asked.

'Completely. Which is why I think we should speak to the council for them.' She looked at Stephanie. Stephanie didn't say a word. She lifted her glass and drained the remains of her half-pint of Guinness.

'I think you may be getting too close to our

informants,' Alison said to Georgia.

'Excuse me?'

'OK. Stephanie can bring Karen back to the station, and I'll talk to the informants,' Alison suggested, looking to the DCI for assurance.

Banham immediately nodded his agreement.

Georgia shook her head. 'No.'

'Sorry?' Alison said, irritably.

'No,' Georgia repeated. 'Because they don't trust you, they trust me, so I'll get more from them. They trust Steph too. And I know what I'm doing.'

Alison stared at her for a couple of seconds and then said. 'Make sure they know if they want favours from the council, we want information. We want info on Lisa Hardy's killer, and we want to know for sure who stabbed Veronica Andrew.'

'And we want to know who brought those drugs and firearms into that flat, as well as why Tink and Lox paid Larry in a brown envelope,' added Banham.

'It would have been for work done, I agree on that,' Stephanie said.

'Ask them,' Alison repeated raising her voice. 'I'll be back at the station, and I'll interview Karen Hardy. Then, we'll think about talking to the council.'

Chapter Nine
Evening: 10 p.m.

It was now ten o'clock at night, the rain biting into Georgia's face like tiny needles, making police crowd control on the estate even harder. Harsh weather conditions didn't stop the residents coming out when the word had gone round that a murder had taken place. In good weather, if the feds were there in force and a serious crime had taken place, the grounds of the estate would be full of residents. The older ones even brought put-up seats, and filled flasks with tea, glad to have something to watch other than their predictable television programmes. The estate was full of unemployment and kids who didn't go to school, and a lot of them knew they could photograph the proceedings and then sell the pictures to gang members in neighbouring postcodes, or even bent journalists, who would drop to any level for their story.

Word had gone round that Lisa Hardy's body was being taken down, so the crowd watched with interest as the black coroner's van drew up and the cadaver, zipped safely inside a black body bag to protect it from the elements or anyone nosy enough to peek too closely, was placed safely inside it. A lot of kids were moving in trying to get photos. Alysha had previously told the estate kids that if she caught them doing anything for other gangs, they would have their privileges taken from them. She made strict estate rules, but now that the community centre and playground were burnt, the kids didn't worry about being banned from their favourite dance or self-defence classes, as there weren't any to be banned from.

Having twelve flats on each floor complicated proceedings for all concerned. The Hardys' flat in the Rook block had to be sealed off and no access allowed, leaving the fire exit as the only way some residents could get to their own front doors. Today many of the neighbours were standing solemnly at the end of that walkway, watching the goings-on and having heard the news of both Larry's and Lisa's deaths.

'Did you see anyone come along this way earlier?' Stephanie asked the young Indian woman with black hair that fell to her bottom. The woman had a baby under each arm and wore a small ring in the end of her nose. She was staring with terrified eyes as the body bag was carried from her neighbour's flat by two uniformed officers.

The woman didn't answer.

Stephanie asked again, in a gentle and compassionate tone, 'Did you see anyone approach this door earlier? Or did you hear any voices?'

The terrified woman shook her head.

'But you must have heard the shot?'

The woman turned and was back inside her flat, quickly banging her front door in Stephanie's face.

'As we said to Banham, it's a waste of time, door-knocking on this estate,' Stephanie muttered to Georgia. 'Only Alison, of course, thought different.'

Georgia shook her head with irritation. 'She's getting more like a headmistress every day.'

'Thinks 'cos she's marrying the DCI that she runs the joint,' Stephanie added, rolling her eyes to heaven. 'She's got such a lot to learn.'

'Wish you would seduce him for the hell of it,' Georgia said with a grin.

'Wish I could,' Steph told her. 'While I was eating my

pie, I was wondering what kind of underpants he wears,' she said, her eyes twinkling at the thought.

Even with the wet, windy weather conditions, Alysha knew the knife was still going to be sound. Amber had been back with bubble wrap and it was now safely covered up.

Amber took them straight to it. She walked them down the road by the estate, through the territory that belonged to AC street girls and over to a brick wall that surrounded a small area in front of a block of garages. She leaned over the wall, quickly moving a few large stones that surrounded a bush, retrieved the knife in its bubble wrap, and handed it to Alysha. She quickly and carefully placed it inside her big silver puffa jacket. She then pulled the matching silver hood further over her head and turned to go back. 'Thanks, mate,' she said to Amber. 'You def ain't fingered it, have you?'

Amber shook her head. 'No, Queen, it was raining so I got tha' wrap to protect it.'

Alysha nodded and stuck her thumb up to her soldier. 'I'll call you. Can you find out from your brother all the info you can get on Larry? Does he know who actually killed 'im? Was it the EIBs in there, or did they lean on 'im to do it 'imself?'

'Yeah. I'll get a call in, probs tomorrow, maybe even afford a visit if I can get two more punters in this pissing rain.'

'Just do one, mate,' Panther told her. 'And keep the commission from it. Use that for your fare. If you don't even get one, give me a bell. We'll give you the fare to the prison, so you'll def see your bro. OK?'

Amber smiled happily, and then her phone rang. She winked and pointed at the phone. It could be a punter, a nice regular with a warm car.

105

* * *

'Let's hope we don't get stopped by any uniformed fed on the way back,' Alysha said as she hurried back toward the estate with the knife tucked inside her coat. 'I'll be done for carrying, and before we can get a look at this ourselves I'll prob be done for hurting our Tink wiv it.'

'Any sign of any fed, we'll leg it, hard and fast,' Lox said.

'I 'ope there are fingerprints on it?' Panther said quickening her pace. 'I want to get him so badly it hurts. I'm gonna cut 'im up, first 'is cock, then his face.'

Alysha flicked a quick glance at Lox and then back to Panther. 'We'll get them,' she said as they hurried down the alleyway. 'And that's a promise, mate. Even if this don't tell us enough, we'll hunt them down. We'll go back to the hospital tonight and see Tink after the feds have been round and taken Karen to the nick to give her statement, I don't want Karen wiv us at the hospital.'

They'd only walked about fifty yards along the road when Panther's mobile rang. It was Amber again. She needed to speak to them, she said, she had important info.

'Talk away,' Panther told her, looking at Alysha and pointing to the phone to let her know there was info.

'Needs to be face-to-face,' Amber whispered back down the phone.

'You go on,' Panther told Alysha. 'You got that shank inside your coat. Lox, go wiv her. I'll catch you up. She needs to tell me more.'

Panther wasn't called Panther for nothing. In an instant her long legs stepped out into an athlete sprint and a few minutes later she was back in the street with Amber.

'Spill,' she said to the AC soldier.

'That call was from one of the girls. Apparently she visited her fella in nick today,' she said. 'She asked him about Larry Hardy 'cos I'd said to. Word is, he was done in by the Chinese who are in there. He def didn't kill himself, an' he weren't pushed into it. EIBs physically hung him up.'

''Cos he done Ji Zhang?'

'Yeah, and 'cos his mum's an addict, and she's been stealing from them.'

'She's been stealing from them? The EIBs?'

'No. Lisa owed a lot of money to RIPs, they was supplying her too, and she couldn't pay what she owed, so was told by the RIPs that she could clear her debt by shanking Ji Zhang. So Larry did it for her, and now the Chinese got him.'

'Thanks, mate,' Panther told her, digging in her pocket and handing her forty quid. 'Go home, and use this to go see your bro tomorrow.'

Panther turned and legged it through the rain and caught up with Alysha and Lox just as they entered the back of Sparrow block.

'Can we use any of the money we make to get driving lessons and a motor once we're all seventeen?' Panther asked Lox. 'Only, if one of us drove, we could get around legally, and so much easier.'

Lox shook her head. 'That's a no, mate,' she said. 'Not for a good while anyway. We've got so much money to find to rebuild that community centre, but first we are gonna get Tink's hair shop up and running, so she got something to look forward to when she comes out of hospital. She was doing so good doing hair and nails in that shop, and the kids loved going to day classes with her, and learning to do it too, and that was making us good paper and building up our funds. We gotta get that going again, top of our list.'

'Then they'll just burn it down again,' Alysha said flatly, her hand against her chest where the knife was, and

107

holding it so tenderly it could have been a baby.

Panther and Lox made eye contact. 'We ain't gonna let them beat us,' Panther said putting her big arm around Alysha's shoulder. 'And they won't burn it down again 'cos we gonna get them first. Both of them gangs. Apparently, Lisa owed to both EIBs and RIPs. RIPs asked her to stick Ji Zhang as payment for what she owes them. So Larry done it for 'is mum. That's the word I just got.

'Then the RIPs done her too, in case she squeaks?' Alysha said brightening her mood instantly. 'And they'd know the Chinks would get Larry in prison, so they would be in the clear.'

Panther nodded. 'I'd reckon.'

'And the RIPs done Tink, 'cos we nicked their gear, which they nicked from EIBs?'

'Amber never said that, but yeah, we know that's true.'

'RIPs are dead meat, Alysha said. 'I got the knife now, we gotta decide if we give it to the feds, or use it to shank all them RIP cunts.'

They all jumped in unison, as they turned onto the walkway to the thirteenth floor of the Sparrow block. Georgia and Stephanie were standing outside the flat, waiting for them.

'If the Chinese gang are moving south of the river, then that's going to cause us even bigger problems,' Banham said as he handed Alison another vodka and tonic.

'The Chinese were growing pot,' Alison said. 'I find it hard to believe they're involved in heroin.'

'Why?'

She blew on a forkful of her steak and kidney pie before putting it in her mouth. 'Because they're behind all the grass factories that we seized, and that in itself is a big business. I can't see it; if they were making big money growing grass, why move to Class A?'

'They're greedy and they are expanding,' Banham told her. 'Lisa Hardy was an addict. She had track marks all over her to prove it. So who supplied her? Larry was apparently a nice boy, and yet he stabs Ji Zhang, and then gets killed, or kills himself. Ade Zhang is in that young offenders', along with his cousin Yin. Ade's the second eldest of the Zhang brothers. There's your link.'

'What are you saying? That there's no way Larry committed suicide?'

Banham nodded. 'Yes, I am. I don't think for a moment he did. I suspect an inter-gang war, and that the Hardys were right in the middle of things, through Lisa's addiction. They were victims really, being used, and then their use ran out.'

'If the prison says it was suicide, which they will, there will be nothing to prove otherwise, you and I both know that.'

Banham nodded his head. He sipped his lager and then put it back on the table. 'There had been such a drop in crime on that estate. Georgia's right about that, it was down to our informants.' He looked at Alison. 'Suddenly, it accelerates.'

'I'm concerned that Georgia's getting too close to those informants. She treats them like friends,' Alison said, munching on her pie. 'I think we need get tough with them.'

'I would think what has happened to Tink Andrew will have knocked the stuffing out of them. We must remember they're still only teenagers.'

'Teenagers going on forty! They were on the streets at eight. Nothing frightens them. Alysha killed someone once, if you remember. She got off, as it was self-defence, defending a police officer, but I still think they need someone to come down hard on them. I'm going to interview Karen Hardy tonight, and if Georgia brings us nothing decent back from those informants, then I'll go and give them a very hard time,' she told her fiancé.

Banham leaned over and picked up Alison's serviette, wiping sauce from the side of her mouth. She grimaced. 'Yes, do that,' he said. 'But don't forget they have helped us a lot and we need them. It's quite an undertaking building a row of shops and getting community classes up and running, especially when you're still officially a child.'

'Like I said, nothing frightens them,' Alison answered. 'Perhaps it's time we did.'

Chapter Ten

'I told you not to go out. Where have you been?'

Georgia's tone was curt. Alysha felt the knife jammed inside her puffa jacket, and tightened her arm around it.

'You're supposed to be taking care of Karen. There's no answer at your flat. Where is she?'

Alysha hesitated before she answered. She had fully intended to give the shank to the feds. She needed them to find out who inflicted the knife wound on Tink, and she couldn't test DNA herself, but she had to know first, because whoever did that to Tink was going to die a very painful death, and if the feds got there first, Alysha, Panther and Lox wouldn't be able to get them.

'Where have you been?' Stephanie pushed, as the girls stood facing them.

Alysha's brain was now racing. She couldn't just say the three of them had to wander down to the street, leaving Karen in the flat alone, and just happened to stumble across a knife, that was too obviously a lie. She also couldn't say she was tipped off by Amber. Not only would that put Amber in an awkward position, but it would also give away the fact that the street girls were under her control. It was an offence to make money from pimping. She knew as well as Georgia did that she would be arrested.

The feds arriving had completely thrown her. She needed to discuss the matter with Panther and Lox before she said a word. They needed to stay squeaky clean if they were to get that council grant. The feds would be in debt to them, big time, over this shank. But she had to make it look like they found it, as it stood it was obvious they had gone out on a purpose, and no way would she involve Amber. It was just a fucker that that Georgia Johnson was standing there with the fat sergeant, both with faces like headmistresses.

Alysha decided quickly that this wasn't the time to start bargaining. She pushed the knife tighter into her armpit and turned, key in hand, towards her front door.

'Don't follow us,' was all she said as she passed Georgia. 'Too many prying eyes. 'Give us five or ten minutes and then knock on the front door.'

'I asked where you've all been. And where is Karen?' Georgia asked her again.

'We were looking for you, as it happens,' Lox answered brightly, making Alysha smile at that brainwave. 'We wanted to know what was happening. We wanted to see if something else had happened as loads of feds and dogs had come up on Karen's flat. Don't fret though, Karen's here, she's safe. We told her not to answer the door.'

Alysha had now reached the front door of her flat, but before she had time to fiddle with the key, whilst still making sure she could hold the knife securely inside her jacket, Karen had opened the front door, and Stephanie was standing behind Alysha.

'We need you to come to the station with us, love,' Stephanie said to Karen.

Karen looked terrified.

'Nothing to worry about. We just need to ask you some more questions.'

'What questions?' Karen squealed. 'You ain't gonna take me away.'

'Won't she need a responsible adult?' Lox said, immediately trying to stall for time.

'We've got a duty solicitor there,' Stephanie told her. 'It's all right, Karen, love. You aren't in trouble, we just need to take your statement. Remember we talked about this before?'

'I wanna stay here. I wanna be wiv the girls. They said I could stay here, didn't you?' One side of her cheek was twitching nervously as she looked pleadingly at Alysha.

Alysha reached out and put her free arm around Karen's shoulder. 'They ain't gonna take you for long,' she told her. She felt the knife under her other arm slip slightly, so she quickly pulled away from Karen, and wriggled the knife back under her armpit. She flicked a quick glance to see if Georgia had noticed. No, she hadn't, she was looking at Karen.

'Just go to the station and answer the questions,' Alysha told Karen. 'You'll be back here in no time, and we'll be waiting for you.'

'That's true,' Georgia nodded.

'Excuse me, I'm dying for a pee,' Alysha said, pushing past Karen. She rushed into the bathroom and immediately hid the knife under the box of toilet rolls by the loo, then waited a few seconds before flushing and coming out again.

'We'll be here waiting,' Lox was saying as Stephanie guided Karen out the front door.

'Yeah, we will,' Panther told her as she rubbed Karen's back. 'We'll see you real soon.'

Alysha noticed Georgia had stepped into the flat. She opened the lounge door and turned to Alysha. 'In there,' she told them. 'I have more questions.'

Panther looked at Alysha. Lox looked away. Alysha smiled.

'Sure, and I 'ope you've asked your DCI 'bout the grant from the council,' she said as she sat on the arm of the lopsided sofa and flapped her arms freely to let Lox

113

and Panther know she had hidden the knife.

Lox settled on the floor, and Panther sat back in the armchair nearest the door. Her over-long legs were stretched out, one crossed over the other.

'If you were wondering what the dog team is doing on the Rook block,' Georgia said, looking from one of the girls to the other, 'it's because we have found a very large supply of heroin in the Hardys' flat. Handguns, too.'

Alysha sat bolt upright. 'Where?' she asked, her heart hitting her boots.

'Hidden, under the floorboards of a wardrobe. That's why the dog team is there. The team are turning the flat upside down as we speak. Question is, are we going to find any more?'

Alysha, Lox and Panther all kept completely blank expressions. They showed no sign of surprise, nor did they look at each other. They were masters at playing innocent, they had done it all their lives.

Alysha gave it a few seconds, allowing Georgia to wait, before she spoke.

'You think Larry Hardy was working for one of the gangs around here?' she asked Georgia, shaking her head and pulling a concerned frown.

'That's what I need you to find out,' Georgia said sharply. 'I'm very surprised you heard nothing of this. We pay you to keep your eyes and ears open to what's going on, on this estate. This hasn't gone down well for you all with DCI Banham.' Her tone hardened. 'You know I stand up for you, but you keep asking for help with another grant – that is a huge ask. We need answers. It's not going to be an easy thing to pull off, and all we –'

Alysha saw red. She thought of Tink, lying burnt, stabbed and raped in a hospital bed. She raised her voice. 'Listen, we well put our arses on the line for you lot. I shouldn't 'ave to remind you that Tink is lying in an 'ospital bed, 'cos she nearly got herself killed, so don't come all that arsey attitude in 'ere. We've always got you the info you ask for, and we always risk ourselves to do that. Right now, I don't know what's going on. I don't know if Larry killed himself, and I don't know who done Lisa. But –'

'But we will do our bit and find out,' Lox interrupted, seeing Alysha would blow everything if she really lost her temper.

'I fully expect you to,' Georgia spoke curtly. 'We pay you to do it.'

Panther sat up. 'You don't pay loads, not for what we do for you.'

'You knew Lisa was a user?'

Alysha raised her eyebrows and looked Georgia in the face. 'The whole world did.'

'So Karen would know too?'

Alysha nodded. 'Course. That's why she was trying to get money, to help her.'

'Then Karen would know everyone who Lisa owed money to?'

Alysha shrugged. 'I'm not sure.'

'Not sure isn't good enough, Alysha,' Georgia told her. 'I've got the borough commander on my back wanting to know why you four are on the payroll. We want answers. We want all Lisa's dealers, and we want to know exactly why Larry killed Ji Zhang. And we want to know where all those handguns and heroin came from, and why they were in that flat. And you are going to find that out.' She took a sharp breath. 'If you want us to have a word with the council …' She kept eye contact with Alysha. 'We'll interview Karen and find out what we can from her. So far all we know is that someone in a helmet came to the door. Someone else on this estate saw that person in a helmet, and we want a clear description.'

115

'Then you should have had our CCTV fixed when it got broke,' Lox said sarcastically.

Georgia stared angrily at her. 'Someone on the estate is bound to have seen them. We want to know about it.'

'You won't get anything out of Karen,' Panther said to her. 'She lives in cloud-cuckoo-land at the best o' times.'

'We'll be the judge of that,' Georgia told her. 'Did you know she was on the game?'

Another second's pause before Alysha said, 'Yeah, I'd heard.' She then shook her head dismissively. 'But, no one took that seriously if you wanna know the truth. I mean she ain't exactly Beyoncé, now is she? She were just playing around. She never done no punters.'

'You still should have told me,' Georgia told her.

'The community centre's been burnt down. Tink's been raped and tortured, and two Aviary residents are dead. Karen Hardy parading her pussy around and getting nowhere, ain't doing no 'arm, and ain't *really* top of my priorities right now,' Alysha snapped back.

'But it means that she was thinking in terms of earning money through prostitution,' Georgia reminded her. 'Her mother was in debt. And yet she had all those firearms and drugs under her roof.'

'She obviously didn't know they were there,' Lox said. 'Karen ain't clever enough to hide them. So looks as though there's your link with Larry and the EIBs.

'I need answers,' Georgia said to Alysha. 'I need them a.s.a.p. The DCI is on my back.'

'And we need to know what you're doing about the people that hurt Tink,' Alysha snapped back.

'We've got a police guard on her. As soon as she comes round and confirms who did that to her, I promise you I'll personally have their balls for a dartboard,' Georgia said. She stood up and turned for the door, then turned back. 'Meanwhile, you find out all you can about everything we've just discussed. I know you can and I know you will. You've got my number.'

'Just like that,' Lox said, lifting her cold eyes and piercing Georgia with them.

'Yes, just like that,' Georgia said.

'It's a big deal, and a dangerous one,' Lox told her. 'You gotta guarantee that grant for us if we deliver.'

Georgia turned to her, then shook her head. 'No, Lox,' she said. 'You don't make the rules. We do. You get me that information, all of it, and then I'll do my best to get the DCI to talk to the Borough Commander, who will talk to the council. I can't make promises because it isn't that easy.'

'And you think risking our lives is,' Panther argued.

'Why were you and Tink giving money to Larry Hardy?' Georgia asked Lox.

Lox shook her head. 'We weren't.'

Georgia looked at her. 'I have a photo of you and Tink giving him cash.'

'Who took it?' Panther said, sitting up.

'That'll just be some cash for the painting he done on the rebuilding project,' Lox said dismissively. 'Nothing wrong with that, 'cept he ain't paid tax. Ah, but then 'e was still a student so he didn't 'ave to, did 'e? So, no crime committed there,' she added sarcastically. She looked Georgia in the eye. 'He helped put the community centre back right, built padlocks on what was left of it, so that the bits of equipment that were left after the first burning were safe and the door couldn't be broken into,' Lox told her.

'Equipment got nicked anyway,' Panther said flatly. 'So that was a waste o' time.'

'Then he 'elped Tink paint her shop when it opened,' Lox said again, before pulling a false smile. 'Nothing illegal.'

117

'I'll leave you to it,' Georgia said making no comment. 'You've got a lot to find out for us,' she said turning for the door. 'And I need this information a.s.a.p. Then, I'll see if anything can be done, but no promises about your grant.' She turned and held Alysha's gaze, then looked from Lox to Panther and back to Alysha. 'I want the thugs that hurt Tink as badly as you all do. I want them behind bars as soon as possible,' she said. 'Truth is, I'm worried for your safety too, all three of you.'

'We can look after ourselves,' Panther told her.

Georgia held her defiant look for a second before nodding. 'I'm sure you can. Still, keep in touch with me, you have my mobile.' She opened the door and then stopped again and looked back. 'And Karen mustn't know that you work as informants for us,' she said. 'Have you got that?'

'Yes.'

As soon as Georgia had left, Panther looked from Alysha to Lox. 'Jeez and shit,' she said, while Lox stuck her middle finger up in the air.

Alysha shook her head. 'No worries there. The feds ain't got a clue what's going down on this estate,' she said. 'They really need us. Knife's in the loo, by the way, under the rolls. We can get Ray Maxted's lot put away wiv that. It'll 'ave one of their prints on it at least. There's blood on it too, bound to be Tink's, and maybe a bit of someone who shanked her. Whoever done Tink held that shank, and let's 'ope it was Maxted. So shall we agree to give that to the feds for starters. Tell 'em we want to know soon as they know, whose prints are on it.

'We gotta get them EIBs too, while we're at it,' Panther added. 'Then if we get the grant, we can build the estate back up, without no one torching it again.'

'Suppose we don't,' Alysha said looking at Lox and Panther with sad eyes.

118

'I'll ask Adam Cambridge to help us rebuild it,' Lox said.

Alysha looked at Panther, and then at Lox. 'What?'

'Never know, he just might.'

'Who is 'e?' Panther and Alysha both said together.

'That clever rich bloke on the telly. He has his own programme, and everyone says he helps people in need,' Lox said. 'He lived round here once.'

Alysha and Panther laughed.

11 p.m. that evening

Tink had been asleep. The painkillers were making her extremely drowsy, but the pain without them was unthinkable, so she had given in and slept most of the day.

As she opened her eyes, she saw the nurse was in her room fiddling with the television. The nurse was called Amy. Tink's befuddled brain vaguely remembered her saying that earlier, and telling Tink to sleep, and that she would be keeping an eye on her all through the night.

'It's good that they give you telly in 'ere,' Tink said to her, as she attempted to prop herself up.

'Careful.' Amy hurried over and put an arm round her to help untwist all the tubes that were starting to wind around each other.

'I thought hospital was all rice pudding and old lady nighties,' Tink said, slurring a little and talking with difficulty.

Amy laughed. 'Not quite, this is the twenty-first century. And the television isn't free. You only get that if you buy a television card from the hospital shop, that's why it's got the slot in the side. Yours has got twenty pounds in there.'

'I didn't put no money in it,' Tink told her.

'No, your boyfriend did,' Amy said with a smile. 'He

bought you a card and gave it to us when he came in earlier. You were asleep. And he brought you beautiful flowers. He said you liked white lilies. Sadly I can't bring them to you, flowers aren't allowed in the rooms or the wards any more, so we put them in the visitor's room for you. When you're a bit better you can go and see them, they're lovely. Massive too, cost a packet I would bet. He must really love you.'

Tink nearly shot out of bed at that remark. 'What did he look like?' she asked wincing with the pain of her sudden movement.

'I don't know,' Amy told her. 'I wasn't here when he brought them in. Can you lie back, Veronica, you've got stitches in your tummy. The consultant will blame me if you pop them.'

'Who saw him?' Tink shouted as loudly as she could.

Stephanie was less than pleased when Banham told her Alison Grainger would be interviewing Karen Hardy with her.

Karen was nervous and frightened with no clear idea what was happening. The girl had lost her brother and her mother all in a couple of days. She had nobody left in the world. She needed coaxing; as clumsy an interviewer as DI Grainger could send the girl into a stunned silence, or worse still, hysterics. Stephanie had called in an experienced female social worker as the appropriate adult, as well as the solicitor from the police duty rota, although she didn't feel confident.

They had all settled in Interview Room B where Karen sat, picking her nails.

'I'm very sorry for your losses,' Stephanie said gently. 'Feel free to take as much time as you need to answer our questions.'

Karen didn't look up.

'What can you tell us about your mum's debts?' Alison asked immediately.

Karen shrugged.

'I'm afraid you need to speak, for the tape,' Alison said to her. 'And the video.'

Karen looked up, the fear was clear in her eyes. 'She had a lot of debts.'

'Who did she owe to?'

'Everyone. Bookies, dealers, all sorts.' She looked at the social worker and solicitor and then added, 'Larry and me wanted to help her 'cos men kept coming round and smacking her about.'

'That must have frightened you,' Stephanie said. 'And Larry too, I would imagine.'

'Larry shanked Ji Zhang,' Karen said. 'But he deserved it.'

'Did you ever see Ji Zhang around your flat, coming to visit your mum?'

'Sometimes. There were lots of men who hurt her. Someone broke her arm. They twisted it behind her back and it snapped.'

'Larry must have been very angry about that,' Stephanie said. 'Do you think that was why he stabbed Ji Zhang?'

Karen shrugged and picked at her nails again, reminding Stephanie of a nervous rabbit. 'I dunno. Larry was a good boy. He wanted to look after Mum.'

'I have a picture here.' Alison laid photo on the desk, the one of Karen leaning into a motorist's window in her tiny denim skirt, G-string in full view. 'What can you tell me about that?'

Karen went dark crimson. She turned to her social worker. 'I … I didn't mean to be bad.'

There was a silence while Stephanie and Alison waited for the girl to say more. After a long few seconds she said,

'They built up the community centre, and there were things to do, but now it's all gone. They helped us then.'

'Who?' Alison questioned. 'Who helped you all?'

'Alysha, and Tink and Panther and Lox. They've done good for everyone, but you ain't allowed to do no drugs or carry no weapons or be a prossie. Please, don't tell them. I was trying to help my mum.'

'No guns and no drugs?' Alison questioned.

Karen looked very nervous, as she shook her head.

'Karen, we have found an assignment of handguns, and a large quantity of drugs in your flat,' Alison told her, watching very carefully for the girl's reaction.

There was a fearful look in Karen's eyes, then she turned and looked away. 'Didn't know,' she said.'

Alison raised her eyebrows. 'I think you did, Karen.'

Karen dropped her gaze and then lifted her face again. 'They gave it to Larry to hide,' she said.

'Who?'

'They mustn't know I said.' She was looking nervously from Stephanie to her social worker and then back to Alison.

Alison leaned forward across the desk and lowered her voice. 'Who, Karen? Who gave it to Larry to hide?'

Chapter Eleven

Georgia arrived back at the station to be told, by Alison, that Karen Hardy had given a statement declaring she knew about the firearms and drugs hidden under the floorboards in Larry's bedroom. Alysha, Panther, Tink and Lox, the statement read, had stolen the drugs and guns from the EIB crew, and had made Lisa and Larry hide them. Karen was told not to tell anyone, and Larry was paid by the girls to do it.

Georgia was then summoned to DCI Banham's office along with Stephanie and Alison. Banham was furious.

'So, now we find out our paid informants are dealing in firearms and drugs,' he said, pointing angrily at Karen's statement. 'These informants that you want me to argue with the council to give them a grant for their estate.'

'I trust those girls,' Georgia argued. 'They have never let us down in all the time we've had them on the payroll. Karen isn't very intelligent, and her mother's dealers could have put the frighteners on her. I'll bet she's the one lying.'

'Her statement tallies with the photo that journalist has of Lox and Tink handing a large amount of cash to Larry,' Alison pointed out.'

'Those four girls are respected on that estate. Drugs and knives are banned, and handguns,' Georgia argued back, shaking her head. 'No, I don't believe it.'

'Well, I do, and I'll bet this was the reason Tink got raped and stabbed by the Chinese gang,' Alison argued.

DCI Banham, of course, was listening to his fiancée. 'Right. I will have to reconsider those four girls' position on my payroll,' he said. 'And I want the releasing of them as informants to be cleared up as quickly and quietly as possible, because if the press got wise to any of this then this department would look like idiots and the Borough Commander would be down on us like a ton of bricks. I have instructed DC Andrew Neville to find a magistrate, and get a search warrant,' he said, pinning angry eyes on Georgia. 'I intend to turn those girls' flat upside down as soon as possible. Georgia, I want you to go home and get some sleep, and in the morning, or sooner, if they find a magistrate who is an insomniac, I want you to bring the three girls in for questioning, while Alison and a team search the flat.

'I'm confident we will find Karen Hardy is, at best, confused,' Georgia said, knowing there was no point in arguing further, 'or at worst, lying.'

'Well, I hope you are right,' Alison said, a sharp edge to her words. 'Or this isn't going to look good when you next apply for a promotion. Your character and judgment will be in question.'

'I stand by what I said,' Georgia snapped. 'I trust Alysha Achter. I have watched her change from a child prostitute, who took drugs to get through the day, to a young, worldly woman who cares enough to take chances, to make changes for the better on the estate, for the good of everyone. I believe she works within the law, and alongside us, to make those changes possible. I also trust Lox, Tink, and Panther. They have all had the same journey through child prostitution and drugs and want to fight for something better.'

Banham stared at her. 'I think you've got too close to them,' he said dismissively. 'They are informants, and ex-prostitutes. That type of girl is never completely trustworthy.

'Previously, the Aviary Estate had the highest crime figures in South London,' Georgia reminded him. 'South London has over fifty gangs, but since these girls have been on the payroll as informants, crime on that estate had dropped to an all-time low. That has to stand for something.'

When neither Banham nor Alison answered, Georgia took her voice up a pitch. 'They rebuilt the community centre, and hosted a youth music club, self-defence classes, dancing, table tennis and cake-making. Tink opened a hair and beauty salon, where she gave free lessons.'

Still Banham said nothing, so she continued. 'And then there was that terrible fire, and the community centre was burnt to the ground. Arson was never proved. And now without that community centre, crime is starting to increase once again. Why can't you see that the answer lies in getting the council to have the place built back up?'

'This isn't about youth clubs and hobbies, DI Johnson,' Banham told her. 'This is about a woman being shot at her front door and a large amount of heroin and a consignment of illegal guns, which our informants have been accused of being responsible for. Now, please do as I say. Go home, and I will call you if I need you to arrest the girls before the morning.'

Georgia walked into her flat, straight into the bathroom, and turned the shower to full. She undressed, places her clothes tidily over the towel rail and reached for soap and hair shampoo among the multitude of cleaning products in her bathroom cupboard. She then stepped into the shower She was worried. Her DCI could be right, the possibility was certainly there, that, with no help from the council, and not enough money coming in from the police, her four young informants could have gone back to drug-running and arms smuggling, hence the attack on Tink. If this was the case, then they were going to end up behind bars for sure this time, and her reputation in the force, would be out the window. She had to hope that her character judgement was sound, and that Karen Hardy did have a vivid imagination. As well as that, it would break her own heart. She had, as Banham had said, become too close to Alysha and the other three.

She stood there a long few minutes allowing the hot water to prickle over her skin. Then she leaned her head back, poured shampoo over her hair and rubbed vigorously. That helped to ease the tension that had been building inside her head. If Karen had made that up, which Georgia wanted so much to believe, then why? Why would she want to drop the girls in very serious trouble? They had assured Karen they were going to look after her and keep her out of care. Anyone in their right mind wouldn't upset that apple-cart. So the answer had to be down to the fact the girl was in shock, and behaving very foolishly, out of a combination of not being in her right mind, her low mental age, and the very serious shock of seeing her mother shot. Certainly, if she was stupid enough to stand in the street, in a skirt up to her knickers with her flabby bottom hanging out, attempting to lure passing motorists into paying to have sex with her – *and* on the patch of a known, vicious pimp – then of course she was stupid enough to make things up about Alysha. So, question still was: why *were* those drugs and guns in her flat? Did Lisa know they were there, and perhaps, had been using them, and that's why she was killed? If not, the only other answer was that Larry was up to his neck in something that no one knew about.

Georgia rinsed the soap from her hair and grabbed a towel, immediately rubbing vigorously to get rid of the excess water. She was concerned, very concerned, about her future promotion. She had made a lot of mistakes since becoming a DI, but if it turned out that the girls *were* behind the drugs and guns, then this would prove to be the costliest one of all. Her career would hit the skids.

And she was devastated about Tink. The girl was just seventeen and had never known a parent who cared for her. Georgia had kept Alysha and Tink and Lox and Panther out of young offenders' in the past. She had encouraged them to make good for themselves and to make those positive changes on the estate, so they could chase their ambitions. She had even put her own head on the line to help them do it. It was through her, and the trust she had built up with them, that they had agreed to become police informants. Had she been too soft with them, she wondered, and would she now pay the price for it? Certainly, this time, if they did have any involvement with those firearms and drugs, she would turn her back on them, and they would all looking at a long spell in youth offenders.

She pushed all of this from her mind and rubbed her long slim body with soothing body cream. She then reached for her white towelling robe from behind the door and slipped it round her. She needed to eat and get a few hours' sleep, if possible. Tomorrow was going to be a difficult day.

It may have been 3 a.m. but Alysha was on a mission. She was on her phone to spread the word: she wanted a meeting of every Alley Cat that could get to their meeting place in the lock-up behind the burnt-down community centre. There were nearly eighty Alley Cats these days, but as a large percentage were women, many had babies and kids and found it difficult to drop everything and come out.

With what had happened to Tink, and Lisa's murder, the estate was an uneasy place, and so the biggest crowd of Alley Cat girls ever, along with the few blokes in the gang, were tooled up with shanks and weapons and on their way to the lock-up where the meeting was to take place. Alysha knew it would be a safe spot for the gang to congregate. If the feds, who were still all around the estate like wasps around a sugar bowl, met any of them on their way to the meeting and asked them what they were doing, they would say they were holding a meeting to discuss building the community centre back up again. It was a good time for them, because their kids were all safely sleeping.

'The fact is,' Alysha told the street girls, estate mums, and young blokes and girls who together made up the Alley Cats and protected the estate. 'We've got a shank. Amber found it. It was hidden down the back of the brick wall by Waters Lane, near where Tink got dumped out of that van. So we're pretty sure it's the one Tink got shanked with. We thought we'd give it to the feds, for the DNA, but then *they* would get the RIPs. Feds'll lock 'em up, though, and send 'em down, and they'll be off our backs and off our territory. Although we would like to kill 'em ourselves for what they done to Tink, we would be risking a lot. We wanted to know what you thought.'

'Or we can go after the EIBs *and* RIPs and beat the shit out of both of them before we hand over the shank,' Panther offered.

'Give it to the feds, and let them catch the fuckers,' shouted Carmel, one of the older women, who lived on the estate with her three sons. She had joined the ACs to keep her boys out of trouble, as well as help with the cake-making and bakery activities. Carmel was an ex-junkie, pencil-thin, and with no teeth on one side of her mouth. They had been punched out by one of her boys'

128

fathers. He was also an addict, and she hadn't seen or heard from him since her baby was born. When social services tried to take her last baby from her, Alysha and the ACs arranged for another mum to have the child. The ACs then sent Carmel into rehab and paid the bill for her to stay there until she was completely clean. She was clean now, and had never stopped being grateful. She would lay down her life for the girls and the changes on the estate that they strived for.

'If it's still got fingerprints for Ray Maxted on it, that'll get 'im sent down, but if it ain't his, then one of his soldiers'll go down, and we still gotta deal wiv Maxted, and the EIBs,' Alysha told them. 'We gotta get both these fucking gangs this time, for good. They're both trying it on wiv our tinies, and they need a lesson to know they gotta back off.'

'You ain't thinking of giving them EIB bluds back their gear are you?' Summer asked.

'They lost the right to that when they trespassed on this estate offering free stuff, like fucking wine gums, to our young 'uns,' Panther told her. 'Anita will tell ya. They offered free brown to her Tyler. We all know where that leads.'

'I'll kill 'em for ya,' shouted Anita Richards, lifting her cricket bat. She was one of the women who had been a part of Panther's self-defence classes. 'It'd be my pleasure.'

'Yeah, well, we might need to kill 'em,' Alysha said addressing the gang. 'We know it was one of them burnt down this community centre. They still won't back off after what we done wiv their motor and gear, so they deserve to be burnt.'

'And feds have got the gear from the Hardys' place now,' Lox told the gang. 'So we ain't got the gear to sell on, we lost the chance to move that gear on to London

Norths, and make all that bread toward the rebuild fund.'

'The feds got the guns too, innit?' Panther added. 'They found it all when Lisa was killed. And they've took mad Karen down to the station, asking her questions.'

'Is she safe?' Melanie, one of the older hookers, asked.

'She don't really know too much, so we're hoping,' Lox nodded. 'She ain't very bright, but she's one of us, an' she knows we wanna get the EIBs, and so does she, 'cos we told her it was them got Larry in the nick'

Alysha's phone burst into a rendition of Bob Marley's 'One Love'. She quickly pulled the phone from her jacket pocket and, seeing Tink's name written across the screen, she put her hand in the air for hush.

'It's Tink,' she shouted to the Alley Cat gang as she pressed the button, and put her phone to her ear. 'How you, sis?' she asked her. 'You're awake.'

The girls all watched and waited as Alysha listened. She took a noisy intake of breath and a look of anger and panic spread across her face. 'Get out of there, now,' she shouted into the phone. 'We'll be at the gates.' She clicked off.

'Tink's in trouble,' she announced, jumping down from the wooden box she'd been standing on and looking at Lox.

Lox hadn't wasted a second. Having heard the conversation, she was dialling a cab. Alysha announced to the gang, 'She reckons Maxted's been around the hospital. Someone said he told the nurse he was her fella, an' that he'll be back.'

'We're gonna go get her,' Panther told the street girls.

'She can stay at mine,' Summer said. 'Bring her over. We'll take it in turns to nurse her.'

'Get that shank to the feds,' Anita told Alysha, then looked around to see if anyone else was agreeing. They were all nodding. 'That'll be Maxted stuffed, and then

130

we'll meet again to talk 'bout the comeback over the EIBs' gear. An if you need any 'elp at the 'ospital just bell us an we'll be there to back you.' Many others added their agreement to that.

Alysha was nodding, but checking her phone, and zipping her jacket up as she hurriedly made her way across the courtyard.

'We'll win this fight. We'll get them off our patch,' Melanie shouted after her.

'For good,' another added. 'Let's burn them, it's what they deserve.'

'We'll give the shank to the feds soon as we get back wiv Tink,' Alysha tuned back to say, as Lox went ahead to go and meet the taxi that was on its way. 'We all agreed on that?

All the Alley Cats had their hands in the air.

'We're on it,' Panther told them, hurrying through the crowd toward the exit to the estate. 'We'll keep you up to date. Keep your eyes, ears and phones out, and look out for EIBs. I reckon their silence means they're planning somefin' else, big.'

'Yeah, and look out for Karen,' Alysha added. 'She'll be back later and she'll need looking after.'

'I'll take Karen in,' Anita told them, following to the edge of the estate to check they were safe, as the three girls piled into the taxi heading for the hospital. 'I'll look out for her, I'll take her into mine and make her hot soup and put her to bed. Don't you worry 'bout nuffin', 'cept Tink.'

Tink was struggling. It seemed to take an age to lift her arms and undo the knot that kept the hospital gown in place, at the back of her neck. Her stomach wound was throbbing so badly she thought she might pass out. She stunk of the pink liquid that was keeping the gauze and bandages adhered to her badly burnt skin. The rest of her torso was heavily bandaged to keep her stitches in place.

She had managed to get herself out of the room and into to the bathroom without the nurse seeing her. She then cupped her burnt and bandaged hands under the tap and poured water over her head. She felt dizzy and weak, but still attempted to lift a leg to get her torn jeans back on. She couldn't stand, even if she leaned against the wall for help, she was so weak she just slid down to the floor. She managed by lying on the floor and putting one leg up and then the other, as it was impossible for her to bend with the stitches in her wounded stomach. The pain felt like a hive of bees were stinging her. It was a long struggle; she gave up on knickers, although Alysha and the girls had brought her some very nice underwear when they visited, but it would have to wait for when she was better, she told herself. For now she just needed to cover herself as best she could, and get the hell out of this place. The thought that Maxted could be creeping around was terrifying her. When she was well, she would get him for this, and really hurt him, but for now, she knew she couldn't fight, so she just had to get out. Alysha and her fam were there, in the grounds of the hospital, ready to take her home. That though kept her going.

Eventually, after what seemed like an eternity, she had her jeans just about covering her. They came almost all the way up her thighs. She pulled her long, thick jumper over her head, and decided she was decent enough. Although her head was spinning, and her legs weren't being very supportive. She knew the wall was there so she walked very slowly, holding herself against it. She had no shoes on her feet, but that was the least of her worries.

She opened the toilet door and looked out. She could see Amy. The nurse was behind the ward reception; her head was down, writing.

Tink had been given a private room at the end of the ward. All she had to do now was get back into the room, get her phone and bag, and get the hell out of the place.

She stood for a few minutes, summoning energy. It was going to be very difficult not to be spotted trying to stumble across the ward.

A few seconds later, luck was with her.

Amy must have heard something, because she looked up, turned her head in the opposite direction, and then she left her seat behind the reception, and much to Tink's delight she walked off.

Tink was in the clear. The patients were all snoring and making sleeping noises, so no problem there, and with no nurse in sight, all she had to do was get the few yards to her bedroom door.

It wasn't as quick as she wanted but she could at least move, even if it meant stopping every two seconds to hang on to the end of someone's bed and get breath.

She managed it. She got to her room, held onto to the door handle, then summoned the energy to open it.

Then she froze, staring at the bed.

Her bag was gone. She had left it on the bed only a few minutes ago. It had her phone in it, she had just rung Alysha on it, so she knew she hadn't imagined it.

She stumbled over to her bedside locker and opened the door. The locker was empty, no bag and no phone, but there was a piece of paper in the locker, that wasn't in there a few minutes ago. She stared at the paper. What was going on?

Just as she was staring at it and trying to work out what was happening, she heard her door open.

She turned immediately to see who was there.

Chapter Twelve
4.30 Tuesday morning

By the time the heavy-footed troop of uniformed police and CID officers, led by DI Alison Grainger, had made their way through the Aviary estate and up the thirteen flights of stairs in Sparrow block, news had gone around the building that the feds were raiding Alysha's flat. As was usual, the estate was never asleep, and word spread quicker than a greyhound on a racing track, when the feds arrived and were about to make an arrest.

Recently, raids had been less frequent. However, with Lisa Hardy's murder and Tink's stabbing, no one was really surprised that feds were back. Lisa's body had only been driven away in the coroner's black van a few hours ago. But this was Alysha Achter's flat they were standing outside. Alysha and her girls helped everyone, they ran the estate, with a no drugs or violence policy, so this raid was of particular interest to everyone. The residents of all blocks were soon out on their balconies, all wanting to know why the flat was having its door broken down.

'Stand back,' Alison shouted as the crowds slyly slid around the corners of the stairway having sneaked up the fire exit, arriving on the balcony of the thirteenth-floor flat, then pushed their way nearer, all keen to get a first-hand view of the goings on.

'Police. Open the door,' was bellowed briefly by the uniformed sergeant, dismissing any thought for the few sleeping residents left on the block. This bellowing was followed by thunderous rapping of the door knocker, with the sergeant's other hand leaning on the doorbell.

There was a few brief seconds' wait before the same rapping and bell-ringing was repeated. 'Police. Open the door or we're coming in,' he bellowed again.

Still no reply.

'Karen Hardy's in there,' one of the residents shouted. 'You'll frighten the child's skin off.'

Alison stood directly behind the bellowing sergeant, and right next to the two uniformed officers who were holding the heavy red enforcer to break down the door. Her hand was in the air, ready to give the signal. She turned briefly. 'No, she's at the station. She's safe with us,' Alison shouted back. A second later she brought her hand swiftly down. 'Go, go, go,' she shouted the command to her officers get the door down.

Without hesitation the enforcer was rammed into the door, which immediately gave way, flying inward with a loud thud against the flowered wallpaper of Alysha's hallway. There was a lot of shouting and complaining from the watching crowds. Anita had now pushed to the front of the residents, phone in hand, and immediately called Alysha to warn her, and the other Alley Cats.

Alison was now inside the flat. 'Police,' she shouted again. In one hand she held her ID card and in the other the newly acquired, and necessary, search warrant.

When no one answered her call, she turned back and nodded to the uniformed sergeant, 'Let's get going,' she told him, 'quick as you can.' She immediately pulled the rubber gloves over her hands and moved into the first bedroom to start the search.

The light was creeping in over the night, but it was still bitterly cold, as well as uncomfortably damp from the light rain that fell around the grounds of the hospital car park and over the three girls' hooded heads.

'She def should be out by now,' Alysha said shaking her head and pulling her forehead into a worried frown.

'Well she ain't hiding anywhere round here,' Panther said, looking around anxiously. 'I done the gang whistle too many times. She ain't answering her phone neither. Somefing's happened, I'm sure.' She shivered and rubbed some light rain from her face. 'Where the fuck could she be?'

'Somefing's up,' Alysha said standing up from the damp patch of earth and the large bush that encompassed it, where Panther and herself had made themselves comfortable while Lox went into the hospital to look round. She pushed her hood down to her shoulders and scratched at the roots where her hair-extensions had been recently taken out. 'I'm seriously worried now.'

'Have you got a plan?' Panther asked.

'We'll wait for Lox to come out again. If she ain't found 'er this time, then we are all of us going in.' She looked at Panther. 'That girl's well sick, Panth, an' needs looking after. An' she told us she thought somefing was up in there.'

'She said she were gonna wait outside in the hospital car park and hide if necessary,' Panther said reminding them of the conversation. 'Lots of activity going on emergency ambulances are in and out all the time. Would be hard to get out of 'ere wivout someone seeing you. So, maybe they did, an' she's 'ad to 'ide somewhere else.'

'So why's she not phoned?'

Panther lifted her large shoulders and shrugged, then blew out air, then her eyes widened as she had an idea. 'That could be it,' she said to Alysha. Maybe she did hide and then passed out. It's fucking cold out here, and she's suffering from first degree burns.'

'I'd rather she passed out than got kidnapped,' Alysha said striding off and looking yet again in all the places she'd checked before.

Lox ran out from the main hospital door within minutes. She pointed to a large car at the back of the hospital entrance and signalled for them to all to congregate there.

'Bedlam's broken out in there,' she said as they all squatted down. 'Tink ain't nowhere. I've looked in the loos, all of them, in Accident and Emergency, an' everywhere.' Her hand went to her mouth and she shook her head. 'She's just disappeared, an' they've all clocked it in there. They are all gathered in a heap shouting at each other and panicking. I heard one say that her boyfriend had come in earlier, looking for her.'

'I'm gonna fucking kill 'im myself,' Alysha said jumping up.

'Jesus,' Panther said. 'Oh my Lord.'

'Well, we ain't standing here and talking 'bout it,' Alysha said. 'We been out here for an hour now. 'I'm going in and asking what they think they are doing letting one of their patients go missing. We 'ave a right; she said we were her next of kin thing. And then I'm phoning Georgia Johnson and getting the feds on it, 'cos we ain't risking anyfing else happening to Tink. We'll need the feds to help.'

Lox and Panther both nodded their agreement. 'Let's go,' Panther said marching ahead. Both Alysha and Panther's phones rang; both ignored the calls when they read it was from Anita.

'That's about Karen,' Panther said clicking the ignore button on her phone.

'I ain't interested in Karen at the mo,' Alysha said. 'Gotta get our sister, then we'll worry 'bout her.'

Alysha stopped just as they were about to enter the

hospital and pointed to a CCTV camera. 'If she's come out this way, that will have seen her,' she said. 'An' if someone did come in, like bastard Maxted, then that'll have him for sure.'

'Just a minute,' Lox said stopping in her tracks. 'Didn't Johnson say there was a police guard outside her room?'

Alysha's eyes widened. 'She did an' all,' she nodded. 'So where's he?'

Inside the Bellamy ward, three nurses, one night doctor and a very tired-looking woman in a suit were standing around the counter as the three girls marched into the ward. The medics were in deep discussion and didn't notice the girls until they stood in front of the reception desk.

'That's how easy it is to get someone out of 'ere,' Alysha said to them, by way of a greeting. 'Not one of yous noticed three of us walking in here.'

'Excuse me?' the woman in the suit said in a cold manner to Alysha.

'Where is my sister, Veronica Andrew?' Alysha answered matching the coldness in the woman's tone.

'I'm sorry, I have to be honest, we have no idea at this moment. We can't find her,' the woman in the suit said to them. 'Staff Nurse Caterly was on duty. She says that the last time she spoke to her she seemed very distressed.'

'We were chatting about flowers,' Nurse Caterly piped up, 'She seemed very put out that her boyfriend had brought some in for her, and bought her a television card,' she told Alysha. 'And then next time I put my head in, she was gone.'

'That's 'cos she ain't gotta a boyfriend,' Panther said, rolling her eyes.

Alysha raised her voice. 'You're supposed to look

after her.' Alysha was doing her best to hold her temper, but losing the battle, as she fought back tears of distress at the thought of Tink being taken again and hurt.

Lox interrupted. 'Where are the flowers?' she asked, flicking a worried glance in Alysha's direction.

'We couldn't let her have them in her room, because of hospital rules, but they are in the patients' day room,' Nurse Caterly said.

'Is there a card with them?' Lox asked.

'That was it,' Nurse Caterly said. 'There was no card delivered with them. That's what made her nervous. As soon as I told her that her boyfriend brought them, she became very agitated.'

'That's 'cos she ain't got a boyfriend,' Panther said spelling out the words again, and tutting loudly.

'What flowers are they?' Lox asked her.

'I don't know, but I'm afraid I'm going to have to call the police,' the suited woman told Alysha.

'I'm gonna have a look in her room,' Alysha told her, hardly listening to what the woman had to say. 'And then we wanna see the flowers.'

Alysha pulled the sheets off the bed while Panther looked along the window sills and under it. Lox opened the locker. There was just a piece of paper in the locker which Lox immediately pulled out and unfolded. She turned to Alysha and Panther, both had stopped what they were doing and were now looking at Lox.

'There's a telephone number on this,' Lox told Alysha. 'Do you think they wanted her to ring the number, or did Tink leave it?'

'That weren't there when we come in earlier,' Panther said. ''Cos I put them liquorice allsorts in there, just so she had some, if she felt like eating.' She looked a little guilty. 'Just thinking that hospital food ain't that good, 'that's all,' she added, then jerked her head at the paper again. 'And it def weren't in there when I done that.'

'And it ain't Tink's writing,' Lox said.

'So he's been in here,' Alysha said.

'Shall I ring it?' Panther asked looking in Alysha's direction.

Alysha shook her head. 'No, it ain't Tink's writing, so it's been left for us to call it. So, don't. Call all the ACs for an emergency meeting. We need to do somefing dead quick.'

The door opened and the suited woman's head came round the door. 'I've rung the police,' she said to them, 'and they are on their way over here.'

'You might wanna get the CCTV out from the car park,' Alysha told her. 'If she's gone out the building, that will tell us who she was with.'

The woman shrugged. 'There are many back ways and side doors to this building,' she said. 'And we don't use the CCTV camera that much, but I will send a message to Security to check it out, and see if any of the cameras had film in them.'

6 a.m.

The morning meeting had started. DCI Banham was at the front of the room, his team of twenty or so detectives were sitting perched on the edge of their desks, slurping coffee from polystyrene cups, or dunking tea bags up and down in lukewarm water and milk. Stephanie Green had a flask of hot chocolate and a bacon sandwich on her desk. Georgia's stomach turned as she watched Stephanie consume the sandwich in three large bites. Stephanie then poured gooey chocolate into a plastic cup and offered it to Georgia. Georgia shook her head and turned away. At the same time, the trainee detective, Hank Peacock, handed her a black coffee from the machine, which she gratefully accepted.

Banham's voice brought her back to the job in hand.

'We have the post-mortem report on Larry Hardy,' Banham announced, handing a large pile of photocopies to Peacock to pass around. Stephanie was first to accept, layering the report with tomato sauce from her fingers.

'Larry Hardy died of asphyxiation,' Banham read from the paper. 'He hanged himself with the cotton sheet from his bed. This report confirms it.

'We already knew he was found hanged, Guv,' Stephanie said. 'This neither confirms suicide nor foul play.'

There was a rumble of voices around the room. Banham held his hand up. 'Without anything to suggest otherwise, we have to presume he took his own life.'

Georgia shook her head. 'Sorry, sir, my informants say he would never do that.'

'Your *informants* may well not be on the level,' Banham told her sternly. 'They may not even be police informants any more.' He turned to address the room. 'As you know, we have information stating Alysha Achter has been handling firearms, and Class A drugs with intention to sell.'

'That information has come from a fifteen-year-old girl with a mental problem, who had just seen her mother murdered,' Georgia argued loudly, accusingly, and a little emotionally. 'Surely you aren't taking her word as gospel. I trust my informants.'

'Alysha's flat is being searched as we speak,' Banham told her. 'Should we find anything to confirm that accusation, then she is off the payroll immediately and permanently. She will be facing a custodial sentence. Right now, she is being treated as a suspect.'

Georgia felt her stomach sink. She just had to hope this

wouldn't prove to be true. She knew that whatever Alison Grainger said, the DCI acted on, so she knew better than to argue the point. She had made enough mistakes lately, and if her informants did turn out to be drug and arms dealers, then she really would lose all her cred in the force, so at the moment she chose to keep schtum. She nodded submissively.

Stephanie's hand was in the air, 'Are we one hundred per cent sure that Larry Hardy stabbed Ji Zhang?' Georgia turned to her to listen and noticed a moustache of hot chocolate around Stephanie's upper lip. Tense though the atmosphere was, she felt a strong urge to burst out laughing.

'Larry had metallic residue on his hands when he was arrested, as well as blood which later proved to be Ji Zhang's on his clothing. He also admitted the killing. Read the report,' Banham told her. 'So, short answer is, yes we are. He also had small cuts on the edge of his fingers, from the force of using the sharp edge. The knife, we now know, from the post-mortem on the right lung of Ji Zhang, had a double blade at the last inch, and the pattern of cuts on his fingertips were a match to an identical weapon. No doubt then. That would most definitely give the CPS enough evidence to take the case into the court.'

'This just doesn't sit right with me,' Stephanie argued. 'He had no previous, and everyone said he was a good boy. He just went to school and did odd jobs to help bring in money to help his mother, and he always took care of his sister.'

'Well, they are the facts,' Banham told her. 'Karen Hardy has told us that he told her he stabbed Ji, because Ji was threatening his mother.'

'She didn't actually say she *saw* him stab Ji,' Stephanie pointed out.

'She was down the road at the bus stop. But there are other witnesses. 'Certainly we have evidence of murder. He stabbed Ji Zhang.'

Stephanie started writing notes on her report.

Banham picked up another pile of papers. He took one from the top and again handed the pile to Hank. Banham then read: 'Lisa Haynes was killed by a bullet that went right through her skull. So far there has been no forensic evidence found in the flat to give us any more. We are waiting on that post-mortem. We know the killer wanted a quick result, and then a quick getaway. We know someone left very shortly before we arrived, down the side fire exit, because one of our officers spotted a figure making his way from the bottom of the fire exit at speed across the front of the estate. We are pretty sure this was her killer. As usual there was no CCTV in that area, but we know the suspect was wearing black top and jeans, and a helmet over his head.'

'Could have been a hired killer,' Hank Peacock offered.

Banham nodded his agreement. 'Could be. We know she owed a lot of money to a lot of people. Her daughter tells us she had run up debts. She gambled, she drank, and she was a heroin user.'

Banham's mobile phone started vibrating across the desk in front of him. He glanced down at the caller ID, and then looked up. 'Excuse me,' 'I have to take this,' he said to his team. 'It's DI Grainger. She's heading up the search of Alysha Achter's flat.'

Georgia glanced at Stephanie and then turned back to listen.

'Send it straight to Forensics,' Banham spoke into the phone. He looked up at Georgia as he added, 'And alert all patrol cars. As soon as she is spotted, arrest her, and her friends, and bring them in.'

As soon as he clicked his phone off, the internal phone on Stephanie's desk rang. Stephanie picked it up, nodded a few times, glanced and Georgia, sighed heavily, and then thanked the caller. As she replaced the receiver she announced loudly, 'That was St Mildred's hospital. Veronica Andrew has gone missing. Apparently she disappeared from her private room just after a man, pretending to be her boyfriend, left a large bunch of flowers, but was refused access to see her.'

'She was under police guard?' Georgia looked questioningly at Banham. 'We had her under police guard.'

'We couldn't spare the manpower, simple as that,' Banham told her. He held her eyes which were glaring with anger. 'There's a warrant out for all four of those informants,' he told her. 'So a patrol car will pick her up very soon.'

'Unless she's been abducted,' Georgia said. 'Which I suspected might happen, and why I requested a police guard.

'Let's hope we're not looking at another murder,' Stephanie added, glancing down at her phone as it started its urgent buzzing again. She picked up, listened for a few moments and then clicked off.

'That was the hospital administrator,' Stephanie told Banham. 'The other three of our informants are at the hospital attempting to get the CCTV down from the hospital grounds.'

Banham put his phone to his ear, pressed a button, and within a second was repeating this information to Alison. 'Send a car over and bring them in,' he said.

'Have they found something, sir, in Alysha Achter's flat?' Georgia asked.

'Yes,' Banham said sternly. 'But not firearms or drugs.'

Georgia held her breath as Banham said, 'They have found a large knife with a double point at the end, and dried blood on the blade. It was wrapped in a bubble wrap cellophane paper, and hidden under rolls of toilet paper in the bathroom.'

Georgia turned to look at Stephanie. She was too shocked to speak.

A paramedic was talking to the girls. 'About an hour earlier,' he told them. 'I was bringing in two victims from a car accident, neither of who had life-threatening injuries. The driver had the ambulance's siren turned on, as a precaution, in case anything was going on internally with the victims that he couldn't check at the scene of the accident. The ambulance sped into the hospital car park, heading toward the accident and emergency entrance, when a green van nearly collided into us. It was going at a hell of a lick,' he added shaking his head angrily. 'It didn't stop, it swerved out of the way and headed off down the road going too fast.'

'Did you catch the number plate?' Lox asked.

He shook his head.

'Any of it,' Alysha pushed.

'I think I might have seen a V at the front or end, but couldn't swear to it,' he said.

Alysha turned to Panther and Lox, all fully aware there was a V in the registration of the green van that Tink had been thrown from. That van belonged to the Zhangs, but Ray Maxted must have taken it, to take Tink in it, and get the Zhangs blamed for what he intended to do to her. Maxted must have found out she was alive, and kidnapped her to take her off and finish the job.

'We need to get Georgia and the feds out to help us find her, and quick,' she said to Lox and Panther as she pulled her phone from her pocket.

Before any of them had time to say or do any more, a car roared into the grounds closely followed by a police patrol car and then another one, and behind that a police wagon. All pulled up abruptly by where the girls stood talking.

Alison Grainger jumped out of the civilian car. At the same time four uniformed police swooped from theirs, and within seconds the girls had their hands pulled behind their backs and were being cuffed, while Grainger told them were being arrested in connection of the murder of Ji Zhang.

'What the fuck?' Alysha shouted, as Panther stamped down hard a few times on the officers foot. Lox, meantime, tried the opposite approach. 'Please,' she begged, putting on a show of tears. 'You are making a mistake.'

'We haven't done anything!' Alysha shouted at Alison. 'Tink's been abducted. She's really ill, she could die!'

Alison ignored her. 'You do not have to say anything, but anything you do say may be taken down and used in evidence.'

Chapter Thirteen

'For Chrissake,' Alysha was on the point of hysteria. 'We ain't fucking done nothing, and Tink's been –'

'Just shut up,' Alison gave her a little shake as she stood her up. 'Keep whatever it is that you want to say until we get to the station,' Alysha struggled while she was manhandled into the back of her car, and Alison dumped her so she landed on top of Panther and Lox, who were both also kicking and shouting.

Alysha calmed down and made a last plea. 'Please don't do this. Tink's in a very bad way. Every second counts finding her, and you're wasting –'

'I told you to shut up.'

'We ain't done nothing. We've been helping you,' Panther shouted leaning her large head out of the back window of the car.

'Not according to my search of your flat.'

As Alison pressed the window closed, the penny dropped with Alysha. She screwed her forehead fretfully, then lowered her eyes and nodded as she rubbed her lips together, then she said, 'We had only just found that knife. Amber Townes and Summer Ripley will back us up. Get them on the blower,' she told Alison. 'They found it, and called us, but Tink called us then. She were in a state. We never had time to –'

'Just shut up, save it for the station,' Alison had the back door open now and was pushing both Panther and Alysha's legs to get them in so she could close the door.

Two burly police came to help.

'We went and got it down near Waters Lane,' Alysha persisted, as Alison pushed at her. 'After Amber rang, and told us there was a knife there. We were gonna talk to Georgia and give it her, but then Tink rang,' she said again. 'Maxted was in the hospital.' She turned her body and offered her pocket to Alison. 'Call Amber, she'll –'

Alison pulled the phone from Alysha's pocket. 'Save it,' she told Alysha.

Alysha shouted again. 'Check the call history. Her number'll come up, 'cos she rang me just before Tink did, like I said, an' told us 'bout the knife. Ring her, and she'll tell you the same.'

Alison walked around to the driver's side, slid in and then scrolled down, and found the number as Alysha said she would. She looked at Alysha, then pressed the green *Go* button against Amber's number.

Amber was silent as Alison reeled off her rank and questions, then she heard Alysha shouting across the car to tell her to tell Alison the truth.

'Yeah, I found the knife. I folded it in bubble wrap an' called Alysha because I didn't know what else to do. Alysha come down a few minutes later and took the knife away.'

Alysha shouted across the car to Amber to go and get Karen from the station, as she, Lox, and Panther would be there a while. 'Give the police your statement, Amber, mate, then get Karen, make sure she gets safe and fed.'

Alison clicked off in the middle of Alysha shouting instructions to Amber. 'Social Services won't allow you to make decisions about Karen's welfare,' she said. 'You have an allegation against you that you've been dealing in drugs and firearms, and in possession of dangerous weapons.'

'What?' Alysha turned to Panther and Lox.

'Where d'you get all that?' Alysha asked, shaking her head. 'Don't tell me Karen said that, 'cos,' Alysha put a finger to the side of her head, 'she ain't the full loaf of bread.'

'Save it,' Alison told her as she started the engine.

Karen had been released by the time the three girls arrived at the station. Anita had arrived with Amber to give her statement. Karen was crying and saying she wanted to go home. She said she wanted to go with Anita, so Georgia arranged for a car to take them both back to the estate. She had then followed it with a call to Social Services, leaving a message informing them where Karen was, and that the police were confident she was safe and being looked after by neighbours.

Karen now sat in Anita's flat slurping soup. She missed her mum, and decided that as soon as Anita left her alone, she would find a sharp knife. Cutting herself always made her feel better. Meanwhile she put her sore and bitten finger in her mouth and ripped at the cuticle till it bled.

Alysha sat opposite Alison Grainger and Georgia in Interview Room A; her face was like thunder. Next to her was the duty solicitor, a woman in a boring dark blue suit and smelling of flowery perfume, a short and shiny brown ponytail swinging at the back of her head.

Alison switched the video and the recording tape to 'on'. 'Tell us about the knife we found in your flat, Alysha.'

Alysha flicked a glance at Georgia. 'I ain't gonna lie,' Alysha said. 'I admit I had that knife in my flat. I was tipped off where it was, by Amber, in Waters Lane, very near where Tink was shanked. I went down there and got it. Didn't you notice it was wrapped in bubble wrap?'

151

'Of course we noticed.'

'Well, if I was using it, or had used it, I'd hardly preserve the DNA with bubble wrap, now would I?'

'Quite the little detective, aren't you,' Alison answered.

Alysha fixed angry eyes on Alison by way of a reply. It was clear this woman didn't like her one little bit. Well, the feeling was mutual, but Alysha had a purpose, and this hoity-toity fed wasn't gonna stop her doing what she had to do. She was sure now that the feds had to be played. It was worth it, for the benefits it would bring everyone on the Aviary.

And what did DI fucking Grainger know about growing up a hungry kid on a high-rise estate, anyway? Alysha thought angrily as she stared at the detective. If you didn't do as the drug barons told you, you would starve, or you got beaten up, whereas if you did as they told you, you got fed and given top-of-the-range trainers and mobiles. And when you were six or seven, you didn't know the difference between right and wrong, you only knew how it felt to be hungry, and that's how the road to drugs started. Alysha had set out to make the changes needed to help the up-and-coming tinies, to stop them making the mistakes she and her Alley Cat lieutenants had made, and save them from going down those dark and frightening roads. The Alley Cat gang had more than halved the muggings around the estate because of policing it twenty-four hours a day. But getting what they needed on the estate meant scheming and lying to the feds, but only because the Alley Cats understood what it took to lower crime figures and keep the kids out of trouble, and drugs off the estate, and these feds didn't have a clue.

'You pay me to find things out for you, right?' Alysha said, mirroring Alison's glare. 'And I'm doing that. And, as I told you before, being a grass goes wiv a lot of risks.

My sister Tink is in a bad way, she's been shanked and burnt, and now she's been abducted. You should be worrying about her 'cos she put her head on the line for you. But you ain't, is you?' She turned to Georgia. 'You broke your word to us. You never kept a police guard on her like you said you would. And you said you'd help us get a grant to rebuild the community centre, and now you say it ain't that easy. Well, neither is the risks we take for you. And Tink's injuries are living fucking proof of that.'

'This is about the knife in your flat, not the restoration of your estate, or your friend's welfare,' Alison said firmly.'

'It has to be 'bout Tink,' Alysha raised her voice, ''cos she's ...'

'The knife you found has two prongs at its end,' Alison interrupted.

Alysha shrugged. 'Yeah, but I've seen knives of all shapes. But I get where you're coming from. The knife that stabbed Ji Zhang was the same shape, is that what you're saying?'Alysha looked at Georgia. She furrowed her brow and then lifted her eyebrows and shook her head in exasperation. Alysha couldn't fall out with the feds, they were her ticket to getting that grant, and, now that they had confiscated the stuff from the Hardys', she'd lost all that money. Without a council grant, all their plans would hit the ground. But the feds could be quite thick sometimes, so she knew she could be underhand, she had to be, this was a desperate situation. Her mind was on Tink.

Alysha knew, as the feds did, that either the EIBs or the RIPs had burnt down the community centre, because both were trying to move in on AC territory. It didn't matter which gang had done it, the feds should have moved in on both of those gangs. They had been tipped off enough, but the feds hadn't moved in on them. So the

153

ACs had to do something in retribution, they took their consignment of illegal drugs and firearms. It was brought onto their territory by the RIPs who had stolen it from the EIBs, so what did they expect? They started the war. And Alysha would have handed the gear and guns to the feds, if the feds had got them that grant then, but they hadn't. The feds had dismissed their pleas yet again. The estate funds desperately needed money after that arson, so the girls had no choice but to keep the gear and use it to make money that way. They had to rebuild the community centre, that's why crime had started again. The feds wouldn't see it though; they wouldn't see it as right for the Alley Cats to hide the gear and sell it on to North London boys. It wouldn't affect South London crime, so it wouldn't affect these feds. It would be the North London lot, so she wasn't doing her own feds a disfavour, in her book, but, course, they wouldn't see it that way. If she hadn't taken the RIPs prisoners when they drove onto the Aviary and confiscated the gear, by now the firearms would be all over South London and gun crime would be rife. So really she had done the South London feds a big favour. But these feds wouldn't understand that, because they weren't street girls and didn't have the nous that the Alley Cats had.

'When, and exactly where, did you find that knife?' Georgia asked her again.

Alysha leaned forward on the table. 'Have I got this wrong? See, I thought we worked with you. My sister has been abducted, and right now I need you to help me.'

'Answer the question,' Alison growled.

Christ, this fed was a pain in the arse. 'I already have, six times I fink,' Alysha snapped back at her. Amber Townes found that knife,' Alysha told her. 'You already talked to her, and she told you the same.'

'For the tape please, Alysha,' Alison told her.

'She found it near Waters Lane, an' she give it to me 'cos she knows I run the estate stuff. I was gonna ring and give it to you, although I didn't know that it might be the one done Ji Zhang. I was about to ring Georgia but Tink rang and –'

'The knife should have been reported immediately, you knew it had the two prongs,' Alison said. 'Never mind anything else. You do not have any authority –'

Alysha was really angry now. No one seemed to care that Tink might get murdered or just die from her wounds. She banged her fist on the table and raised her voice and jumped up. 'I never saw the fucking knife as it was wrapped in bubble wrap, so how would I know it had two prongs? I was gonna do it, but in case you ain't noticed –'

'Sit down,' the duty solicitor told her tugging at Alysha's jacket. 'And stop swearing.'

Alysha pulled her arm away angrily, elbowing the woman as she did so and she raised her voice again. 'My sister could die. I should be out there right now, and so should you. She's sick, and she's been taken –'

The solicitor grabbed Alysha again. 'Sit down –'

'Get your 'ands off of me,' Alysha shouted as she hit out at her.

'Alysha,' Georgia said very firmly. 'A team is out there. They are looking for her as we speak, and they will find her. Now sit down. We need to talk to you.'

'Where are they looking? 'Ave they gone round to Maxted's?'

'Yes, as far as I know. If not, they are on their way. Sit down. The quicker we do this interview, the quicker we can all be out there looking for Veronica.'

'Tink,' Alysha corrected, calming her voice. 'It's *Tink*. She don't like being called Veronica.'

'Just sit down,' Alison raised her voice.

Alysha sat.

'Now answer the questions,' Alison told her. 'Did you pay Larry Hardy to hide a consignment of drugs and firearms in his mother's flat?'

'No.' Alysha shook her head. 'Karen told you that, I suppose,' she said. 'I can't believe you even believe all that. She ain't all there. You know that as well as I do.'

'Karen has given us a statement,' Georgia told her, 'accusing you of stealing the firearms and drugs, and paying Larry to hide them.'

Alysha was furious. Why on earth would Karen drop them in it? She knew they were going to look after her, how could she be that stupid? Alysha would have to lie her way, very cleverly, out of this. Alysha also knew Georgia wouldn't say something that wasn't true, so in her stupidity, Karen had sold the Alley Cats down the river, and all because she wasn't the full loaf. The ACs had looked after the Hardy family really well. They had been giving Larry and Karen money regularly for food, not to Lisa because they knew she would only shoot it up her arm, but they had paid some of her debts, up to a point, to help her keep the loan sharks from hurting her. She was an Aviary Estate resident, she was in trouble, big trouble, and that was what the Alley Cats did. Karen needed the ACs more than ever now. She'd never cope on her own, and she had dropped them right in it.

'Be serious,' Alysha said looking Georgia straight in the face. She was an excellent liar and she knew it. 'Would I steal gear, and put the estate in danger of retribution? You know full well we are against any drugs on the Aviary. We are trying to keep the estate clean and make chances for the residents. All we need is money for a grant to start again.'

'So, did you do it for money?' Alison asked her. 'You sell information to us, to build up the estate, grass up people for money, as you say.' Alison leaned back in her chair.

Alysha could see she was enjoying this. 'Perhaps you thought you would sell the firearms and the drugs. Easy money I'd say, and you'd have the contacts to do it.'

Alysha shrugged. 'Maybe. But I didn't do that.'

'So Karen is lying? Georgia pushed. 'Are you saying you know nothing about the firearms and the drugs we found in the Hardys' flat?'

'Yes, that's exactly what I am saying,' Alysha lied. 'I know nothing. If I had of found firearms and drugs, I'd have told you, wouldn't I? That's what you pay me for, ain't it? We tell you what happens crime-wise, and in return you help keep our estate crime-free, an' pay me to keep me off the streets an' stuff?' She stared defiantly at Georgia. She had to talk herself out of this. The residents depended on her, and most of all she had to help Tink. If she and the Alley Cats went down for this, all their dreams of a new future, for their kids and the Aviary, would be up shit creek. The Aviary would become a den of crime again, and the future for the next generation of kids would be as bleak and dismal as her own, not to mention the pensioners'. She couldn't bear the thought of letting all those people down.

The Alley Cats had spent many months pleading for grants and working with members of their community, sometimes sixteen-hour days, and relying on free help from the residents, some pensioners, to start the rebuilding project. Currently, they were having their territory invaded by the two toughest gangs south and east of the river. How bad was it to steal that gear to sell on to North London gangs, if it kept it off the streets of South London? She had done these feds a favour, although they wouldn't see it that way. She had stopped the Zhangs invading the Aviary and selling their bong to the kids, and she had kept the firearms off the South London streets, for

157

a while anyway. She was determined those two gangs weren't going to stop her doing what the Alley Cats had set out to do. If she got sent down, Panther and Lox would go with her, and who would be there for Tink? The EIBs or RIPs would move in on the Aviary, and the consequences of that, wasn't worth thinking about.

Suddenly she felt as if a dam had burst within her head. These feds were sitting here accusing her of all this shit. She raised her voice.

'I don't know about that,' she lied, raising her voice again. 'Like I don't know why her mum got shot. Maybe her mum had the gear; maybe she stole it, or maybe she was supposed to hide it for someone, but got greedy and nicked some of the gear for herself.' She shook her head. 'I only know I tried to help that family and that's the fucking thanks you get.' She calmed herself again and looked at Georgia. 'Karen don't know what day it is. You can't believe her, and not me.' She stared at Georgia and then said. 'Look, I was gonna bring the knife in. Why would I double-cross you, when we need the money you give us for our projects?' She gave a shifty look at the young solicitor, who hadn't seemed to have caught on that Alysha was admitting that she was a paid grass.'

Alison threw the photos of Lox paying Larry handfuls of money across the desk. 'What do you say to this,' she said coldly. 'Why was Lox giving him all that money?'

'Not all this again,' Alysha said lowering herself in her chair and throwing her eyes to heaven. She spoke quickly, 'We paid Larry to help with the community centre,' she said. 'I told you, we gave Karen and Larry money when they never had no food, and we tried to help Lisa, but she was too far down the line.'

'Who do you think was Lisa's dealer? Georgia asked.

Alysha shrugged. 'How do I know? Everyone and anyone who would sell to her, would be my guess. She

158

was in big trouble with money, but I don't know who with. Larry and Karen were trying to make money to help her, but she were well past that. She owed loads to dealers and loan sharks.' She looked at Georgia. 'See, that's what happens when you fuck people about. They shoot you.'

'If there was all that gear hidden in her flat, and you know what happens on the estate,' Alison said, 'then why didn't you know about this? You've already said the residents respect you, and they look to you to run the estate?'

Alysha shrugged. 'I can't know everything.' She turned to Georgia. 'Can I go and help look for Tink now? If anything happens to her, I swear I'll kill myself too. Please will you bring in Ray Maxted? I know he done it.'

'Yesterday you said you didn't have a clue who hurt Tink,' Georgia pushed. 'You said Tink wasn't talking at the hospital. She was too ill. Now you are sure it was Ray Maxted. What makes you so sure?'

Alysha paused to think before she committed to that one. She knew Panther and Lox were next door being questioned by the other feds. They knew what to say about the knife, but they hadn't had time to discuss what to say about Ray Maxted. If they were all clever enough, this could be a chance to get both gangs put away in one foul swoop and stop them trying to invade AC territory. She needed to think quickly. If she didn't incriminate the Zhang gang, then she would still have them to deal with. But right now Tink was top priority, getting her safely back, and Tink had said RIPs had done her, so Alysha felt sure they had come back to get her and finish the job. And Maxted had the Zhangs' green van. He had stolen it from the Zhangs, and it was seen leaving the hospital car park. He was gonna die for this, Alysha would make sure of that. She and Panther and Lox would cut his balls off for what he had done to their sister, but she might need the

159

feds on side to get him, so she had to tread carefully here. The feds now had the knife that she believed had shanked Tink, but she wasn't sure who that would incriminate. If Ray Maxted's DNA wasn't on it, and she didn't accuse him of abduction and rape, then he could get away with all this, and that wasn't happening. He was gonna get seriously hurt by the girls, and then the feds were gonna put him away, she was making sure of that. The feds had found the brown and firearms, and if she could incriminate the RIPs for that too, *and* Lisa's murder, then that was goodbye to them for a long, long, time.

After a thoughtful few seconds, she said, 'I know 'cos the ambulance guy told us he swerved to miss a V reg green van speedin' from the hospital car park, and Summer Ripley saw that van, and she saw Maxted's gang in it, in Waters Lane, when Tink was attacked.

'We've got a team of police out there looking for Ray Maxted and the van,' Georgia told her.

'It could be in … Germany by now. Will you let me know when there's news?'

Alison looked at Georgia. Georgia nodded, and then Alison said. 'If we have any. Meanwhile, we'll speak to the DCI about releasing you.'

Lox and Panther were both interviewed separately and both said the same about the knife – that Amber Townes had found it and phoned them to tell them. That they all went to Waters Lane and picked it up with the bubble wrap still around it, to preserve any DNA, and they were intending to ring Georgia to come and get it, but then Tink had phoned. That was an emergency in their book, and they had rushed to the hospital to be with her. They both said they knew nothing about the haul found in the Hardys' flat.

The next morning, in the investigation room, the phones were buzzing. Banham had been watching and listening to the interview with Alysha. He also had the videos of the interviews with Lox and Panther.

'The CPS would say no solid evidence, it's all circumstantial,' he told the team.

'I believe them,' Georgia said. 'I really think we should let them go. Veronica Andrew should be our concern at the moment,' she said. 'Those girls are our snouts, and very good ones. If anything happens to Veronica, they'll turn against us; we'll be enemies to them. No one else on that estate talks to us. We'll be back to square one.'

Banham took that in and nodded his agreement. 'I will personally go with Alison and pick up Ray Maxted,' he said. 'Let the girls go. Let's keep them on side. Tell them we want them to find out who brought those handguns and the heroin onto the Aviary. I want those responsible behind bars sooner rather than tomorrow. Oh, and we need a full, written, statement from Amber Townes and Summer Ripley.'

Georgia and Stephanie decided to go and find Amber and Summer themselves. They knew if they sent a patrol car, chances were, the women would hide, but because they had seen Georgia and Stephanie around, and they knew Stephanie was always very chatty with the street girls and didn't threaten them, there was a better chance of them finding them and getting a statement. They offered Alysha and Panther and Lox a lift back to the estate but the girls refused, they didn't want to be seen in a fed car.

'Get on with finding out who Lisa's dealer was, and where the heroin and handguns came from. I'll make sure you're well rewarded.

'The only thing we want right now,' said Alysha, 'is to

find Tink.'

'The DCI is on his way to find Ray Maxted and arrest him.'

Alysha, Panther and Lox walked round the corner from the police station and stood still. They had their phones back, and were ready to go.

'WhatsApp all the Alley Cats,' Alysha told Lox. 'Tell them to round up every single AC, tell them we need as many as can get there. Tell the street girls that we need them. And tell them to get well tooled up. We are going into Peckham, we are going to get Tink, and we are going to make Ray Maxted wish he never laid a finger on our sister.'

Chapter Fourteen
2 p.m.

DCI Banham had agreed that Georgia and Stephanie should interview Amber when they found her. He knew those two, if anyone, would get the street girls to talk about how they came to find the knife. He had thought about arresting Amber, and putting her under caution, frightening her with the threat of obstructing a murder enquiry by not contacting the police when she had discovered the knife, but Georgia had persuaded him that would be of no help at all. Amber would wonder why Alysha had told the police that she had found it, and would, for sure, clam up and say nothing.

Georgia was confident if they mentioned Alysha had given the word to talk, then Amber would. She now had to hope that what Amber said would corroborate the videoed interview that Alysha gave earlier.

Georgia had never believed Karen's story that Alysha had paid Larry to hide the drugs and guns in his mother's flat. For one thing, Alysha had proved time and time again that she was on a mission to clean up the estate and help the addicts get off the stuff, investing in other interests for them, and informing on dealers to keep them away from the Aviary. It was obvious Alysha cared deeply about the residents and would know that if Lisa had got her hands on all that gear, it could have killed her. Georgia believed Alysha would have told the police if she knew anything at all about it being there. Much more likely that Larry had stolen it or that someone else had hid their stash at the Hardys' and killed Lisa because of it. And, as Alysha had hinted, highly likely, that was the Chinese gang. Whatever Alison Grainger said about them being just into grass factories, she was wrong, they had clearly moved into bigger things.

Yet with all this in Georgia's head, there was still a niggle at the back of her mind. Surely, with the position Alysha was in on the estate, someone would have known something about that amount of gear, and would have told her. And yet Alysha was adamant she didn't know anything. Georgia didn't believe Alysha was involved herself, but she found it hard to believe she was naive enough not to know that there were firearms and drugs on the estate.

Georgia had kept Alysha out of prison and away from drugs and firearms. She had cleverly, then, made the deal with her to become a police informant, with the DCI's approval and a very strict code of rules. Top priority was no involvement of any kind in anything illegal, everything that was even slightly dodgy on the estate had to be reported to the police, and in return the police kept the four girls on the payroll and gave them protection.

Alysha was now a completely different person from the child who had been forced to live off prostitution. She was grown-up and streetwise, and her mission to clean up the estate was working well. However, the arson attack on the community centre, the playground and Tink's shop, after all the hard work the girls had put in, had knocked Alysha's confidence.

And now that Tink had gone through this terrible attack and rape … knowing how close Alysha was to Tink, Georgia fully believed that if Alysha found out for sure who had hurt Tink, then the girl wouldn't think twice about breaking the law and killing them, and that knife would fit the bill for the job. She only hoped Alysha hadn't gone that far.

The knife was currently with Forensics and the technicians, one of whom Stephanie had recently had an affair with, had agreed to do Stephanie a favour and make the testing a priority. Georgia had smiled as she overheard Stephanie on the phone, requesting speedy results and promising a favour in return. Stephanie had always been proud of her reputation as the office bicycle, and was even prouder now there wasn't long left until she reached forty.

Georgia raised her eyebrows and managed a small smile as Stephanie replaced the receiver, but made no comment. She told her to get her coat; they needed that statement from Amber, and then they were going to bring Karen back in and try and coax her to tell them more about the consignment of drugs and firearms found in her flat. Then, she told Stephanie, they were going to pay a visit to the Zhangs at their main family business, a restaurant and takeaway with flats above. If the Zhangs were unhelpful, they would get a search warrant and pull the whole place apart, and then the flat above it. All roads pointed to the Zhangs with Tink and Lisa, they had all agreed. If only there had been working CCTV on the estate, and they could have got a sighting of whoever came to the door and shot Lisa. Certainly their restaurant offered home delivery and that was done via motorbike.

Meanwhile, Banham and Alison were taking a team of uniformed officers and heading for Ray Maxted's estate in Peckham. Tink, was a top priority; she had to be found – without medical attention she could die. Officers from the police station nearest to the Nichol Estate had reportedly knocked on Maxted's door, but no one had answered.

Stephanie turned into Waters Lane, drove on and turned into Harper's Lane, onto Bellbrook Road, the small road at the back of the estate, and then into another lane, and then another, but there was no sign of any working girls.

'That's funny,' Stephanie said to Georgia. 'I can't see any toms. These streets are usually heaving with street girls at this time. Best time for punters who have had too much to drink at lunch and are feeling randy. Do you think what happened to Tink has frightened them off?'

Georgia shook her head. 'It's a long time since Tink worked the streets,' she said. 'They'd all know it wasn't a punter.'

'The newer girls might not.'

Georgia shook her head again. 'They'd know she was singled out and taken for a beating. More likely because someone's found out she's been informing for us.'

'The street girls don't know that.'

'No, but they know her as someone, who upset someone, and had her shop burnt down for it. Nothing to do with street work.'

'Well something's scared them off. Have you ever seen these streets so deserted?'

'No, but we've got Amber Townes' address haven't we?'

'Yes. She lives on the ground floor of Crow block on the Aviary.'

'Right. Let's go and ask her why it's so quiet, and if she'd like to accompany us to the station.'

There were nearly eighty Alley Cats walking along the main street, all angry and tooled up and spilling into the road as they headed towards the Peckham estate where Maxted lived.

Word had already gone around the streets down there. The shops were bringing down their shutters and closing up early. Kids and their mums were hurrying along the road desperate to get home and inside, all aware, that any

166

moment, something big was going to erupt, and no one wanted to be caught in the middle of it.

Alysha wasn't leading from the front of the mob. She was taking no chance of being filmed on CCTV. She was clad from head to toe in black, including a balaclava, and walking surrounded by many others. She was very angry with the feds. If they weren't going to help her, then she knew her Alley Cat soldiers would. This, she knew, was a big risk, but she was determined to get Tink away and safely back into hospital. If Maxted was responsible for taking her, then there was no question, she cared nothing for the consequences, she was going to kill him. She intended breaking his jaw first, and had her fingers wrapped tightly around the cricket ball she held in her palm for that very reason.

If she was caught, and picked up and arrested by the feds, she knew this would blow everything they had worked and schemed for, but at this moment none of that mattered. Only Tink's welfare mattered, and she wasn't going to let her down. Tink was the only friend she'd had in those dark years of hunger and abuse. She would happily kill Ray Maxted and spend the rest of her life behind bars if it meant evening the score for Tink. No one messed with the Alley Cats, and Maxted and his puny mates were about to pay a big price, as they had before when they'd trespassed on her territory. No one took the piss out of the Alley Cats. If you tried, you faced the consequences.

And Maxted had committed the biggest offence of all: he had hurt an AC lieutenant.

The other AC members were all well-tooled up, but Alysha just held her cricket ball in the palm of her hand. If any fed approached her, she could lose it without it being noticed, but if she carried a shank and was picked up, then for sure she'd be locked in a cell again, and helping Tink would be out of her hands. If she was going to go to prison then so be it, but not until she had got Tink safely back to hospital and avenged her shanking.

The cricket ball had always been her favourite weapon, anyway. She could swing and punch into an eye with it, temporarily blinding her victim. Or knock someone flying if she hit the front of their face with it. If she smashed it hard into the side of someone's head she could probably knock them unconscious, and thrust hard into an enemy's bollocks – there was no telling the damage that could do. You just had to know how to use it, and Alysha knew very well. She had been trained by the best.

Panther was over six foot and had always wanted to be the best fighter ever. From the age of five she had stood for hours on tiptoe outside judo studios, looking in the windows and watching the teachers giving classes. She had made mental notes and memorised the moves. Gradually she got better and better at fighting, and all the while taller and taller, and gave blow jobs to any bloke who'd teach her any new judo or karate or any fight moves. By the age of fifteen, most people were afraid to take her on.

Panther could fight dirty or clean, but she always came out on top. One of her jobs was to teach anyone who lived on the Aviary Estate self-defence. No resident was going to be bullied any more. If they were, they were taught by Panther, so they could go back and take on that bully, and win. If it was a pensioner that had been mugged or bullied, then Panther took on the job herself, and considered it a pleasure to knock anyone out who bullied an OAP.

One older couple from the estate had been bullied and harassed by a former gang. They were frail, very afraid, and couldn't fight back. In the end it had taken their lives. The Alley Cats swore that would never happen again.

168

They would protect their elderly residents and teach everyone to fight, no matter what age. So, a martial arts studio was set up, in the community hall. Since the burning of the community centre, there had been an abrupt end to the judo and karate lessons that Panther had been giving. But, like the other Alley Cats, Panther was a survivor, and on a mission. She had made her mind up that once they got this sorted, and got Tink back, then the ACs were going for the EIBs. It was payback time for the arson attack.

They intended to kidnap a few of their gang, some of their lily-livered young 'uns, and then make the elders of the Zhang gang spill money to build back up the buildings that the girls were sure they had been responsible for burning down. If the feds and the council wouldn't help them, then the Alley Cats would do things their way. No one was getting the better of this gang, not any more, those days were well over.

Alysha and Lox and Panther were furious that the feds weren't taking Tink's abduction as seriously as they should. Alysha had warned them her life could be in danger, that every minute counted, and yet the feds insisted on arresting them, and grilling them about the knife. Meanwhile Tink could be in a ditch, dying somewhere.

Right now people were running, mobile phones were hot, police sirens were shrieking in the distance, but the scores of girls and half a dozen or so of the boys in the gang, were marching on, and the *"Enter at your own risk"* streets of their rival postcode gang wasn't deterring or scaring them one iota. Tink needed them and they were going to be there for her.

Banham and Alison were in Alison's VW Golf, on their way to Peckham to pick up Ray Maxted. Behind them were three uniformed patrol cars. The first of those cars kept flashing Alison.

'You need to keep further in,' Banham told Alison. 'Sergeant Beck is flashing you. You are right out in the middle of the road.'

'Will you stop telling me how to drive,' she shouted back.

She turned from the main road off into a side road. Banham's phone rang, stopping the argument before it started. It was the voice of Sergeant Beck.

'Guv, we've been informed there's trouble in Peckham. It might be a demonstration or a march. Peckham station's receiving calls from frightened residents. They say they think it also could be gang warfare brewing. Papa 08 sent a uniformed team down there; they said the high street is blocked with a large crowd marching through it. We may have trouble getting through the main streets. Shall we re-route and go in from the side roads?'

Alison looked at Banham.

Banham nodded. 'Yes, and send as much back up as you can. Any sighting of firearms?' he asked. He didn't wait to hear the answer. 'Get the riot squad standing by,' he barked. 'And also warn the CO19 gun unit, tell them to stand by, we might need them out there.'

'Guv.'

He turned to Alison. 'If it kicks off, I want you to promise me you'll be careful. We've got a wedding to attend and I don't want you back in hospital. You need to say, "I do."'

Alison took her eyes off the road as she turned to him.

'I don't,' she said.

As the Alley Cats turned the corner from the main road, into the one that led to Maxted's estate, they stopped.

They had come face-to-face with nearly the same number of RIP gang members, who were now only yards from them and walking purposefully, in the middle of the road, toward them. All were also heavily tooled up.

'You're on our territory,' a tall, bony mixed-race youth shouted at the girls. It was Skinner, one of Maxted's lieutenants.

Alysha speedily moved herself to the front of her crowd. She was small for her age, so, even though she had dressed head to foot in black, it wasn't hard to tell who she was. As soon as she opened her mouth, there was no doubting her. The angry, but vulnerable, shout gave it all away. Her voice silenced both her gang and the RIPs.

'I ain't come for trouble,' she said evenly. 'I've come for my sister. Where's Maxted?'

'Ain't none of your business, innit.'

'Our sister Tink is our business.'

'You on our turf here. That's taking the piss big time, and you're gonna pay for trespassing.'

Alysha wasn't in the mood for small talk. She raised her voice and her temper took a sharp upturn.

'Listen up, and listen good,' she shouted at Skinner and the rest of the gang. 'You snatched my sister, and I want her back. We'll be off your turf as soon as we get 'er. If we don't get her, we ain't going nowhere. We'll burn you all, and anyone else who gets in our way, and we'll keep burning yous, until you give her back. She is our sister, so you hear that, and go tell your cunt of a leader what I say.'

The hundred or so RIP soldiers who were facing the Alley Cats seemed to move apart from around the middle of their crowd like a receding tide, as Ray Maxted walked through them. He carried on walking until he reached the front of his gang and faced her. He wore no balaclava, but was never hard to mistake. He was short and stocky, gold

171

dripped from around his neck and wrists, and over his fingers. The collar of his expensive light leather jacket was turned up. Alysha missed nothing: one glance down his body and she spotted the lump protruding from his side pocket. There was no doubting he was carrying a gun. She knew he always wore one in his sock, and she suspected there would also be a knife about his person. She had to make quick decisions; her girls' lives were on the block here.

The sound of police sirens were getting louder and nearer.

She held her ground. A lump in prison, if she was caught, was on the cards, that she knew, but that wasn't bothering her, at this second. Tink's life was at stake. Alysha would give her own life to save her sister. Tink was in trouble, and that was all that mattered.

'We ain't going nowhere unless –'

'You on a suicide mission or what?' he said, opening his arms and showing his hundred or so soldiers, most of whom held weapons. 'Them feds are coming, otherwise you'd have a bullet in your stupid pussy head right now.'

She squeezed hard on the cricket ball. If she ran at him and socked him hard with it, she knew all her ACs would pile in. This lot had guns, and they'd get massacred, even before the feds stormed in. And still Tink wouldn't get help.

'You've shanked Tink well and good,' she shouted at Maxted. 'And now you pulled her from hospital. You scum fucker.' Her voice suddenly rose with her anger. 'You're just lucky, feds are near and I'm still standing here and asking you, 'cos you started a big fucking war.' She paused and took a breath. 'Give her back, and I'll fink about holding back on burning you up.'

'I ain't got her.'

Panther moved forward to stand next to Alysha. 'Don't

172

fuck with us,' she told him in more than a threatening tone. She then lifted the can of petrol and the cloth she held high in the air and waved it at him.

Ray burst out laughing. 'Listen, fuckhead, you ain't burning nothing, 'cos if you do you'd burn your lieutenant. That's *if* I had her,' he added quickly. 'But, I ain't. Whoever told you I have is havin' a laugh on you. She got her punishment. Sorry she ain't dead, but now I'm done wiv 'er.'

That was enough for Alysha. 'You cunt!' she screamed, running toward him. Panther and Lox followed and held on to her, and then the rest of her gang squared up behind them. Now there was only a foot between the two gangs.

'I'm gonna 'ave you for what you done,' Alysha screamed at Maxted. She took another step nearer so now she was nearly in his face. Skinner's hand flew up and shoved her back. Panther opened the can and tossed petrol at him.

Alysha lifted her right arm that held the cricket ball. In a flash Maxted gripped it above the elbow and was about to bend it back when Panther's leg came up and kicked out and knocked his arm back.

'Your fucking card's marked in blood,' he spat at her, flicking his arm up and down and trying to make light of the pain she had inflicted.

The sound of sirens was almost on them. They were at the back of the crowd of Alley Cats, trying desperately to drive through. The gang stayed blocking their way.

'Where is she?' Alysha said, as Lox flicked a lighter and walked towards Skinner. 'I ain't messing. Tell me, an' we can all split.'

'I ain't got her.'

Ray moved in front of Skinner, to protect him from Lox who had another match in her hand.

173

'The van you stole from the Zhangs is on CCTV driving out the hospital gates,' Alysha shouted. 'It was seen. You was driving it.'

The sirens were screeching and the police cars were trying desperately to edge through the crowds. The ACs at the back of the crowd were still doing their best to block them.

'Move!' A uniformed police officer poked his head out his car window, tooted his horn and shouted from the back of the mob of ACs. 'Move, or you're all under arrest!'

Suddenly Skinner pulled a handgun from his pocket and pointed it at Alysha. 'You've taken the piss. If you give us our gear, we'll talk about your mate.'

Alysha was now nervous. Even with the feds only feet away she knew he was mad enough to use the gun. She needed to think quickly.

'Feds have got the gear,' she said. 'Give us Tink, 'cos I swear if anything 'appens to her, we'll come back an' kill you all.'

'Tell you what,' Ray looked at Skinner and nodded for him to lose the handgun. Skinner obeyed quickly, tucking it into his underpants. 'You got one minute to get off my territory,' he told Alysha. 'Or,' he indicated to the police car with his head, 'as soon as feds have gone, we're gonna shoot any of you left *on* my territory.'

Alysha looked back. The uniformed feds were now fighting with the Alley Cats at the rear of the gang. 'Split,' she shouted to her gang. 'But keep your phones near.'

When she turned back, Maxted and his gang were all hastily retreating. She looked at Panther and Lox. 'Everyone move,' she shouted at the top of her voice.'

Within seconds both gangs had jumped fences, or ran down neighbouring roads. Lox and Panther stayed with her, all hurriedly running in the opposite direction to the feds.

Which meant they were running further into RIP territory.

Chapter Fifteen

As the din of the screaming fed sirens grew louder and nearer, the cars started appearing and shifting to a halt, then door banging as feds alighted, armed with truncheons, and ran toward anyone within catching reach. The Alley Cats were all now running in different directions, and sprinting up and over walls to hide and escape.

Alysha was on top of a fence, but stopped, lifting her balaclava, to get a better view.

'Split!' she shouted again across and down the roads to her gang. 'Hurry, hide!'

She pulled her balaclava down again to cover her face, and nodding to Panther and Lox, who were now beside her on top of the fence, balancing by their hands, waiting for her to give the order to jump. At her nod, all three of them dropped to the other side, and hurriedly legged it, as two feds behind them ran towards at the fence.

Both the AC and RIP gangs were in the same area, jumping walls, running, or ducking behind parked vehicles to avoid a fed reaching out and arresting them. All were carrying weapons and all knew, only too well, if they were caught, they would be searched and they would be done.

There were less ACs in number, compared to the RIPs. But all had been trained by Panther to fight well, and all were prepared to do that, and to be arrested if necessary. They were out to find and help Tink, and the consequences of that were secondary. Their leader had told them to split, and this they did. None went far; they scattered, but hid around the borders of the estate waiting a call to re-group. All were aware they'd entered RIP territory, and if they were caught by any of the rival gang, their punishment would be a shanking or worse. On the other hand, if they were picked up by the feds, it could be a prison sentence for carrying. But every one of them adored Tink, and all were prepared to take the risk. Tink gave her time and her love to teach them, or their kids, or their mums, and those she wasn't teaching, she was giving free hairdos and makeovers to. If you lived on the Aviary Estate then the door to her salon was always open, there was a welcome, and the kettle was on for a cuppa and a catch-up; until it was destroyed.

All the ACs had been feeling that loss, they had all put a lot of work into building the community centre up from nothing. That was something the feds would never understand. The four AC leaders had risked their lives creating a future for the estate, and now Tink was near to losing hers, the gang were here to fight for her, whatever happened.

Alysha, Panther and Lox now found themselves in an alleyway, with the feds still closely at their heels. So they kept running, crossing a small road into another alley on the other side, and stopping to press themselves against the fence so as not to be seen as a police car pulled up at the kerb by that same alley.

The fed car drove off; Alysha stuck her thumb in the air and the girls ran on again. They came through to the other end, then stopped dead, realising they were standing inside the estate where Maxted lived with his brother, along with the majority of the RIPs. Their headquarters were in one of these blocks. The place would be swarming with RIP soldiers, although at the moment none were in sight.

The three girls leaned, panting, against the wall of the first block. Alysha pulled off her balaclava, and the other girls followed suit. All stuffed them down their jeans and into their knickers.

'It'll be worse than being picked up by the feds if we get caught here,' Lox said as she checked at her watch. 'I reckon it's only minutes before Maxted's on our case. Then …' She looked nervously at Panther.

'They gotta catch us first,' Panther said, tapping her mate a few times on the shoulder to give her courage. 'And I sure as hell ain't gonna let that happen. Tink needs us.'

'Let's find her, and fuck off then,' Lox said nervously. 'I don't wanna be cremated alive.'

'Fuck thinking like that,' Alysha snapped at Lox. Then her tone became gentle. She knew that Lox was different. Lox hadn't been brought up on the streets or a sink estate. Lox was an abused middle-class child who had ran away from home and the abuse she continually suffered from her father, with a mother who chose not to care. Lox was a frightened and hungry fourteen year old when Alysha found her. Alysha took her in and made her an Alley Cat. She was loyal, bright and finally happy. Alysha knew Lox would give her life for the good of the ACs. 'They ain't gonna catch us,' she said. 'And we're gonna find Tink.' She lifted her right fist, which still held her cricket ball. 'And I ain't leaving without her.' She turned to Lox. 'We always said we'd give our lives for each other. Right?'

'Right,' Lox said, as Panther joined in, verbalising her own agreement.

'Then right now is the test. We are blood, and we are in this together. Panth and I won't let no one get you, and we gotta do the same for Tink, right?'

'Right,' Panther and Lox both agreed again with a

solemn nod.

Then Panther grinned. 'But let's not any of us get got,' she said with a grin which displayed her missing back teeth. ''Cos we promised our residents, remember? We told them we'd fight to the death for chances for them, so let's get Tink and go home.'

Alysha nodded. 'We've let Maxted fucking get her twice now,' she said as sirens screamed around them. 'We need to show 'im we ain't pussies.'

'Let's show 'im what we're really made of. Let's fucking really hurt him back,' Lox agreed.

'Atta girl,' Panther said.

'Imagine how Tink must be feeling,' Alysha said suddenly, shaking her head to flick a tear that threatened. 'I hope she knows we're coming for her.'

Lox put her arm around Alysha's shoulder. 'We'll get her back.'

'Course we will. But we gotta hold it together,' Panther said, half-scolding. 'If we gonna get her outta here in this fucking bedlam. Yeah?'

'We need a plan of action,' Lox said looking around the empty estate.

'We got our full crew around here somewhere,' Panther reminded them. 'Let's hide till the feds fuck off, then go in hard, aim for Maxted, and take him prisoner. Then do a deal, him for her.'

'Nice one,' Lox agreed nodding back at Alysha.

Alysha moved her head from side to side as if weighing up the situation. She walked towards the stairs to the walkway of the blocks and, ignoring a crowd of older residents, up above who had come out to see what the action was, and what all the sirens were blazing around them for, she pointed to a flat on the first floor. 'I reckon that's where Tink is,' she said looking from Panther to Lox. 'Maxted lives up there. His dad's doing time, so the flat's all his, and that no-brain brother of his. No doubt there's loads of his soldiers in there, so we gotta think of a way to get them out, then we can get in there and get Tink.'

'Phone Georgia Johnson and say we know where he's holding Tink prisoner,' Lox said quickly. 'Get him arrested.'

Alysha shook her head. 'Won't work. We already said it's him, and all the feds said is that they'll follow it up. Tink could be dead by then. They don't fucking get it that Maxted's a killer, and he'll find a way to wriggle out of it.'

'They can prove it's him,' Lox argued. 'If they catch her here. That's kidnap and attempted murder. And they'll get that green van, it'll be around here somewhere, it'll have his and Tink's DNA all over it.'

Alysha shook her head. 'He's probably torched the van by now. 'She looked at Lox. 'And we ain't got time to do it by the book, you know that. He'll have his soldiers out looking for us, soon as the feds have buggered off. And on a sighting of any feds approaching his flat, they'll move Tink, and that's if she's even 'ere. Time's everyfing; Tink is well weak.' She turned to Panther. 'If we fight them head on, he's gonna win.' She didn't give Panther time to argue. 'E's got a 'undred, maybe 'undred 'n' fifty soldiers an' we got 'bout eighty round an' about. They could flatten us.' She shook her head. 'No, that ain't gonna work, but I got an idea that will.'

Banham and Alison were a few roads away from where the two gangs had been gathered. All the traffic had been blocked and nothing was moving. Alison was on the phone to the uniformed sergeant running the operation and already at the Peckham estate.

Sergeant Peter Beck was parked up, watching as the

two gangs were going off in all directions. Beck reported that there had been no violence, as yet, and that the gangs had quickly dispersed on seeing police presence. He asked if Banham still required the CO19 firearm team on standby.

'No, luckily, then, it seems we don't,' Alison told him. 'DCI Banham and I are going on, and into the Nichol Estate. We intend to bring Ray Maxted in for questioning. His van was seen leaving the hospital in the early hours of this morning where our rape victim was abducted. We are being cautious; he is a big noise in the RIP gang that think they rule the streets around here. I don't know who the other gang are, but looks like this is a gang disagreement, so be careful.'

'The other crowd look to me to be mainly girls,' Beck told her. 'But it's all quietened down now, ma'am. As soon as they saw us, they all scattered.'

'Keep a couple of patrol cars around, just in case there's a flare-up. We might well need back-up if Maxted proves difficult. Then once you're sure it's all peaceful down there, let the other patrol cars go.'

'Will do, ma'am. And I'll tell CO19 they can stand down.'

'Thank you.'

Alysha and the girls sneaked out of the alley and into the square on the estate facing Maxted's block. Alysha looked up to the balcony of the first floor of the block which they now faced. A wide smile broke across her face as she pointed to one of Ray Maxted's lieutenants, Muscle. A bald, unshaven and heavily tattooed man in his early twenties, with a large ring through his nose, he was leaning over his balcony on the first floor, his finger shaped in that of a pointing gun, and aiming at the three girls.

'Wanker,' Alysha shouted back at him, adding an imitation wanking gesture.

'Four and a half minutes,' came the reply, as he moved his fingers and pointed two of them, with the thumb bent in.

'Na, heard it only takes you thirty seconds,' Lox shouted back. 'Then your underpants get soaked.

Within seconds another half a dozen of RIPs appeared on their balconies from different blocks around the open area the girls stood in. All now aware there were leading ACs on their territory, and all checking their watches to let them know there were only minutes to go till Maxted gave the word, then there would be a big showdown.

Another of them also shaped his fingers in a gun sign, and followed it by spitting on the ground over his third floor balcony.

'He ain't gonna be taking the piss in a few minutes,' Alysha said to Lox and Panther, as she looked at the globule of spit, then looked up. 'Piss yasself wiv fright did ya, arsehole?' she shouted. ''Cos we're coming up for Tink.'

'What's tha plan, boss?' Panther asked. Her body had started moving from side to side in her well-known ready-to-fight stance. ''Cos I'm getting scratchy here, see, I'm wanting to lift his big arse off that walkway and punch his fucking lights out.'

Alysha shook her head and winked. 'We are gonna go burn Maxted's Porsche.'

'You serious?' Lox said. 'The street's still swarming with feds. If we get caught we'll be pulled in for arson, and we'll lose everything.'

'We ain't gonna get caught,' Alysha told her, 'Anyway, rather that than lose Tink. Bell Kelly and ask her if she got the petrol and cloth, and ask her where she is. Tell 'er where we are, and that she gotta move over 'ere dead quick; tell 'er we're gonna burn Maxted's motor. He'll come running when we do, and his lieutenants and soldiers will go running after him. Panth, you are gonna stay here on lookout, but for fuck's sake hide well, and keep belling me, so I know you're OK. I won't pick up, but just bell me every few minutes. That OK wiv you?'

'Yeah, it's well OK – anything for Tink.'

'Lox, I'll need you wiv me, to break the door open on his lock-up.'

Lox had earned her nickname when it was discovered there wasn't a lock in London she couldn't pick in record time. This had proved a godsend, over and over again, and had helped the girls in and out of many a situation, and saved their bacon, since the forming of their gang.

'Best we don't all stay together anyway 'cos of so many feds about,' Alysha told them, 'And Panth, you're a bit of a giveaway.' She looked up from her five foot two inches to Panther, more than a foot taller, as they all grinned and nodded in agreement. She smacked the flat palm of her hand against Panther's. The tall girl then palmed her large brown hand against Lox's tiny white one and all muttered, 'Good luck.'

Lox made the call to Kelly, then clicked her phone off. 'She's on way to the lock-ups round the back,' she told Alysha.

Alysha nodded and licked her lips nervously. 'Keep belling me, two or three rings,' she told Panther again. 'Let me know you're OK.' She turned her back on Maxted's boys and walked back into the alleyway, then pulled her balaclava from her knickers and pulled it over her head again. 'Lox, get your bala on,' she told her before turning to Panther, 'not you though, you gotta hide well, but Tink gotta see it's you.' She looked at her watch. 'We now got two minutes till their after our blood.

184

Reckon we need another three minutes to get fire to the motor. So that's a full minute to be real fucking careful. As soon as they all go running to the burning garage, you bell us three times to give us the all clear, and then make your way to the flat. Tink'll be in there some place. Lox and me'll be running our way to you. Then we get in quick and get Tink out while he is crying over his burning piece of shit.'

'Sounds like a plan,' Panther said shooing them to move it. 'Let's get going. Muscle's clocking us.'

The girls looked over at Muscle; one hand displayed two fingers in a 'V', and the other still had the two fingers in the shape of a gun pointing in their direction.

Lox made another wanking sign, then moved her hand nearer to her body. 'No, sorry, it's smaller than that, ain't it? I heard your dick was called "The Ant". It likes sugar, but no one can find it to feed it, 'cos it's so fucking little.'

Alysha turned to Panther. 'Be careful,' she said to her. 'You're on your own for a few minutes.'

'It'll be fine,' Panther winked. 'I'll give them the run around,' she said confidently, but it didn't fool Alysha, she knew her lieutenant too well, and it was the first time she had seen just how vulnerable this big, six and a half foot, seventeen-year-old judo expert, really was. Both knew she was being left alone amidst serious killers.

Georgia and Stephanie were walking along the walkway on the Aviary estate, toward the fourth floor flat where Summer Ripley lived with her three kids. Stephanie rapped hard on the knocker.

An older woman answered the door, holding a baby in her arms. Summer's other two toddlers were at her side watching. Georgia and Stephanie flashed their warrant cards.

'She ain't 'ere,' the woman told Georgia and

Stephanie, before either of the detectives had time to speak. 'I'm looking after the kids. She's out, and says she don't know when she'll be back.' The door was then closed quickly before they had time to ask any more.

'Interesting,' Stephanie said, banging on the door with her fist. 'Police, open up.'

The door opened, and the woman now stared angrily at Georgia and Stephanie. Georgia noticed the needle tracks on the woman's arm. She brushed her own angry thoughts aside, and handed the woman a card. 'As soon as she comes back, tell her to ring this number. Tell her it's very important. She isn't in trouble, tell her that, but tell her I have to talk to her. It's about a weapon that was found when Summer was in the vicinity.'

The woman snatched the card with the arm that the baby wasn't sitting on. Georgia got a strong whiff of a nappy that badly needed changing, and then the door was slammed in their faces.

Georgia immediately stabbed Alysha's number into her phone. It went to answer. She did the same with Panther's mobile and then Lox's. She looked up at Stephanie. 'It's very quiet down here,' she said her forehead rumpling into a concerned frown. 'Alysha's not picking up, nor is Panther or Lox. Where is everyone?'

She phoned Banham and asked for an update on Ray Maxted.

'We've had a gang clash down here in Peckham,' Banham told her. 'We're having trouble getting through. Looks as though it's clearing now, and there's been no arrests. We'll be at Maxted's in a few minutes. We are bringing him in for questioning. Has Alysha's statement been corroborated by Amber and Summer, about the finding of the knife?'

'No sign of Summer Ripley down here, unfortunately,' Georgia told him. 'And I can't get Alysha on the phone either. I'll try her flat, and then we are heading back to base. We'll check on forensic results. There's been no sighting from ARPV of the green van as yet.'

'All patrol cars around here have been alerted and are looking for it.' 'We'll meet you back at base.'

'Yes, that's fine, sir.'

The Porsche was kept in a lock-up at the side of the estate. Summer, Kelly, and a few of the other street girls were already there, waiting.

'I'll keep watch this side,' Kelly said, turning to the right of the lock-up and moving down the open alley.

'We gotta move really fast,' Alysha told her. 'Muscle's seen us, and I've left Panther on her own to look round for Tink. We gotta get there to back her up, a.s.a.p.'

Lox was already picking at the garage lock. The ACs had done much worse than this, Alysha told herself, they'd even gone as far as having to kill, but somehow this was different. Tink's life was at stake, and now she'd put Panther in the line of fire too. She became aware her fingers were tapping anxiously against her upper arms. She pulled herself together; the safety of seventy-odd ACs was down to her. She couldn't let any of them get hurt.

As she turned back to check to see how Lox doing, the garage sprung open, and Lox held the piece of wire she always kept about her person high in the air as a sign of victory.

Summer wasted no time; she was inside in an instant, pouring petrol over the shiny red car.

'Under two minutes,' Alysha said anxiously.

No sooner had she said that than Summer's happy voice shouted back to her, 'Hey, the fucking keys are only in the ignition!'

'Don't matter,' Lox shouted back. 'We don't wanna

nick it, just burn it.'

'Sssh, keep your voices down,' Alysha told them, batting her nervous hand in the air to quieten them as she listened to the two rings on her phone. She breathed a sigh of relief at that: less than two minutes till the shit hit the fan but, for now, Panther was safe. 'Get in it, pull your balas back on, reverse the motor out, and then torch the fucker, and then fucking leg it,' she shouted.

Summer slipped into the car and slid behind the wheel, immediately firing the engine. At the same second, two uniformed feds walked up the alley. 'Wait,' Alysha whispered loudly as she whistled to Kelly as a warning to get down behind the car and hide. Alysha and Lox ducked into the inside of the lock-up, speedily pulling the door closed behind them, and the four of them ducked down.

'Shit,' Lox whispered, lifting her head a few seconds later. 'Are they still there?'

Alysha pushed the door a few inches and watched the back of the feds moving down to the end of the alleyway.

'They're moving down,' she said as her phone chirped two rings again and a bead of sweat ran down the side of her face. Summer and Kelly were still holding the petrol and matches.

'Panth's OK,' Alysha said, pushing the lock-up another inch to see out.

Lox checked her watch. 'Time's up,' she said looking anxiously at Alysha. 'Panth won't be OK for long. She's alone on Maxted's block, surrounded by RIPs.'

Alysha's heart was beating like a flapping bird, but she had long learned not to show fear. She said a silent prayer for Panther. 'Panth knows to leg it if she 'as to. Gotta wait just a few secs more, to be sure the feds are gone.'

Lox lifted her watch and they all watched the second hand, very slowly, as it moved another ten seconds. Alysha's phone trilled twice again.

Alysha put her hand up to warn everyone to keep still. As quietly as she could, she pushed the garage door open, then her head peeped though. She could now see the feds, they had paused to check the end of the alleyway. She held her breath. Then they walked on.

Then chants of 'Alley Cat cunts, kill 'em,' rang out. The RIPs' warning time was up; they were moving out and ready to kill any AC that came into view.

'Go, go, do it,' Alysha said, opening the garage door wide so the car could get through.

The noise of the RIPs chanting was getting louder, meaning a gang of them was moving in the direction of the garages.

In an instant the Porsche was out. Lox lit the match and held it to the petrol-doused cloth that Kelly held, then threw into the fuel tank of the car.

'Leg it,' Alysha shouted turning and leading them in the direction of the back of Maxted's estate.

A thunderous sound was followed by the windy roar of angry flames tearing through the car. As Alysha glanced back she saw black smoke climbing up into the air that surrounded the burning car. The girls were through the alleyway and back onto the road and heading to the back of the estate in an instant. They stopped briefly to duck behind a line of parked cars to pull their balaclavas off, stuffing them back in their knickers. Still the sound of crackling flames and a car continually backfiring, as the sight of rising smoke, followed by coloured flames, could be seen coming from the lock-ups, which were now two hundred yards behind them.

Within seconds sirens were again screaming, and then screeching to a halt. Alysha's phone rang three times, as the chanting of 'Kill Alley Cat cunts', stopped abruptly. Ray Maxted and a crowd of his soldiers were then heard cursing; they had obviously spotted the burning motor and were running as fast as they could toward the smoke.

'OK, go,' Alysha shouted to Summer, Kelly and Lox, who were all on their phones, messaging the other ACs to say they were needed back at the RIPs' estate, and on Maxted's block.

Alysha ducked as siren screaming cars skidded toward the lock-ups. Then she saw her soldiers appearing. She stepped out so her soldiers could see her and follow. She legged it to Maxted's flat, taking two steps at a time when she reached the block stairway.

Panther was waiting. Lox had her precious wire in her hand, ready to pick the lock in seconds, or as soon as they heard Tink's voice. It wasn't needed – in his haste to get to his precious car, Maxted hadn't even bothered to close his front door.

The girls were in there, and running through the flat, all the cupboards were opened, every door, every drawer, nothing was left unturned. One after the other they followed, looking under beds, on top of wardrobes, every available space was covered.

Alysha then put her hands in the air. 'Stop,' she shouted. 'She ain't here.' She turned to Panther, fighting to hold herself together.

'No, she ain't here,' Panther confirmed with a shake of her head. 'And she ain't in any nearby flats, neither, I been looking and shouting her name.'

'She could be unconscious,' Summer suggested.

There was a commotion starting outside, and the chanting of 'Alley Cat cunts' was starting again.

'They're back,' Kelly said.

'Out. Quick get out of here, all of you, now,' Alysha told them, 'Just run, and don't stop till you're off their territory neither. Go, go, quick! Or death'll fall on the ACs.'

'Don't use the stairs, use the fire escape,' Panther added, pushing them in the opposite direction.

The girls fled, over walls, in and out of alleyways and side roads, avoiding any RIP soldiers or feds, and rounding up and updating all Alley Cats that the word was to split and get off RIP territory.

Alysha and Panther were at the back, they were making sure there soldiers got away. When they were off the Nichol Estate, Alysha stopped and looked around. Panther stopped with her.

'Where's Lox?' she said looking around. 'She was wiv us two seconds ago.'

'Lox!' she shouted, then turned back to Panther. 'Jesus, where's Lox?'

As Georgia and Stephanie turned onto the walkway on the thirteenth floor flat heading to Alysha's flat, they saw Karen Hardy sitting on the floor outside Alysha's door.

'Karen?' Stephanie said moving to her.

Karen looked surprised to see them. She jumped up quickly. 'Have you come to arrest Alysha?' she asked. 'I only told the truth. I had to, didn't I?'

'Yes, you must always tell the truth, Karen,' Stephanie said. 'But we have spoken to Alysha, and she has said that it's not true. She says she knows nothing about the guns and drugs in your flat. But I think you knew about them.'

'She put them there. I swear she did.' Karen's voice was growing in volume as she spoke. Neighbours, too, obviously could hear, as Georgia noticed curtains started twitching in the flats around the thirteenth floor.

'Why are you sitting there, on the cold floor, Karen?' Stephanie asked her. 'Where's Anita? You're supposed to be with her.'

'She said she'd look after me, but I don't wanna do wrong things. I'm a good girl. I don't wanna get taken away. I won't go into care will I?'

'No, you won't, but you must always tell the truth. Where is Alysha? Stephanie said. 'Do you know?'

'She don't trust you. She's gone to find Ray Maxted. She wants Tink back,' Karen told her.

Georgia looked at Stephanie, then back to Karen. 'How do you know this?' she asked urgently.

Karen shrugged. 'I just do.'

'Is there anything you can tell us, or anything you can show us, that will prove Alysha gave your mum and Larry the gear,' Stephanie asked her.

'Don't know,' Karen said, shrugging again.

'Can you remember anything about the person that came to the door dressed in black with a helmet over their head, and shot your mum?' Georgia asked again.

Karen shook her head, shivered, and turned away.

'Listen, Karen,' Stephanie said taking out her phone. 'I'm going to ring Anita. She is supposed to be looking after you. I am going to take you over to her flat.'

'I don't wanna be there. I wanna live with Alysha.'

Anita picked up the phone at that second. 'I been worried sick about her! I took her in, fed her, but then she climbed out the window and run off. She *was* in a state. Don't ring the social, I'll come and get her now.'

'We're not social workers,' Georgia told Stephanie as they walked hurriedly away from the estate.

'I thought Anita might know if Alysha had gone over to Ray Maxted's estate looking for Tink,' Stephanie said.

'Well she didn't, and Alysha's not answering her phone, so she could be anywhere.' Georgia shook her head. Georgia had asked Anita why the estate was so empty. Anita had replied that she didn't know it was. Her house was full of kids, and that was all she had time to think about.

'Banham and Alison said there was gang fighting

going on in Peckham,' Stephanie said. 'I'm putting two and two together. It's possible Alysha has gone over there, as Karen said.'

'No,' Georgia said shaking her car keys from her pocket. 'I don't believe anything Karen says to be honest.'

'I've left a message for Alysha to contact us urgently,' Stephanie said.

'Good. Back to the station,' Georgia told Stephanie. 'We have to meet DCI Banham there. I'm concerned that we haven't got a statement from Summer Ripley yet, or Amber Townes. That gives Alison Grainger too much rope. She's got it in for Alysha, and I don't believe she would leave heroin and firearms in a drug addict's flat. Do you?'

'I don't know. Can we stop for food on the way?' Stephanie asked.

'Why did I know you were going to say that?' Georgia grinned as she clicked her seat belt into place.

Stephanie was armed with a paper bag containing a double cheeseburger and large fries, and Georgia carried a salad from the local supermarket as they walked back into the investigation room.

'Forensic results are hot off the press,' trainee detective Hank Peacock told Georgia. 'I put them in your office, ma'am. Very efficient those forensic boys,' he added.

'Someone in Forensics is keen to collect that promise they are on,' Georgia winked at Stephanie.

Stephanie grinned. 'I like the sound of that.'

'We'll eat in my office then,' Georgia said. 'But if you are going to stink it out, yet again, with fried onions, then you have to buy the coffees. I don't want a vending machine one, pop next door and get two Starbucks skinny lattes.'

'One skinny, one full-fat,' Stephanie told her. 'I can't drink watered-down anything.'

'You really should think about your weight,' Georgia said tactlessly. 'I would love to see you fit and healthy, much easier for running after criminals.'

'One skinny, one full-fat latte,' Stephanie grinned as she turned toward the door. 'Sounds like you and me.'

'You really don't mind being chubby, do you?' Georgia said affectionately. 'But it's bad for your health.'

'But better for your sex life, men like something to hold on to. Take my word for it.'

Georgia smiled a wide twinkly smile. 'Do you really rate sex above your health?'

'Sex is good for your health! I reckon that's why you take vitamins and why you've always got a cold coming. I keep telling you, I know someone who –'

'Skinny latte, please,' Georgia interrupted. She turned her back and went into her office.

She put her food on the side of her desk, and picked up the pile of papers next to it. The forensic report on the DNA on the knife, was on the top of the pile.

Chapter Sixteen

Lox had been hurrying around the flat telling all the AC soldiers to scarper, warning them that the angry chanting from the RIPs was getting louder, therefore nearer, and they needed to split and get off RIP territory.

'Move it, go, hurry, and be safe,' she urged. 'Get off the estate, or the bastards will catch and hurt you.'

She checked all were heading out the door, and followed, opening a couple of cupboard doors again, in a last attempt to find Tink, then knowing it was fruitless, she too belted out of the front door.

As she neared the fire escape she noticed Tip and Skinner running up the stairs and made a split-second decision that it would be safer to dive back into Maxted's flat and get out the back window. She knew she was thin enough to get through it, and chanced that they weren't. There was another walkway at the back of Maxted's flat, which would lead her out of the block by another route. It would mean a bit of climbing from one balcony to another. They were only one floor up, and she was a dab hand at climbing, so it was her best chance. If she followed the way her AC soldiers had gone, then the RIPs would follow too, and chances were one of the soldiers would get caught.

She turned and ran, at top speed, back in the front door, legging it toward the kitchen, knocking over a couple of stools in her haste, then she upped herself on the draining board, scattering crockery noisily, then opened the small window, turning her body so she was half facing inward and half facing out. Her outside leg could feel for the pipe, which it touched, then she lifted her other leg, and was about to swing that out, and grip either side of the pipe, to slide down it, monkey-like, to the walkway beneath, when she heard Tip and Skinner enter the flat. Just another couple of seconds and she would be out. As she speedily swung her leg, she felt firm hands gripping her foot. She pulled the rest of her body quickly through the window so her leg was out, ready to kick out at whoever had her leg and foot. Then she saw him. It was Muscle, Ray's right-hand man, and he was quicker than her. As she swung her other leg, his hand grabbed it, yanking her, so she landed with a thud on the walkway, and found herself on the floor, at his feet. Then he was on her, grabbing her waist-length, green and dark brown hair, and pulling her to standing as he kneed her hard in her back. She gasped for air and tried kicking back but missed. His firm grip now twisted her round so she was facing into his angry face.

'Think you're clever, do you, cunt,' he said between gritted teeth, dragging her along the walkway. A second later and she had fallen to the ground, immediately splitting her jeans and the skin on her knees. He carried on dragging her. Concrete pebbles embedded themselves in her knees and under the skin on the palms of her hands. She cried out, but received a punch in the face. Blood immediately spurted from her nose, then another punch followed, landing on her eye. She felt her cheek immediately swell, blurring her sight too.

She was trying to check for the shank that she knew he would have about him, she needed to get it. It was her only chance. She knew he wouldn't shoot her, the place was swarming with feds and that would alert them in seconds, but a shanking wouldn't be heard, and where they were, at the back of the block, probably not seen either. They were now at the side stairwell, the rarely used fire exit. He had hold of her hair like a puppy on a lead, as he turned, tightening his grip and pulling her down the stairs behind him. The pain shot through her as her face hit the concrete steps, but he carried on dragging and bumping her, one by one, down the piss-stained and uneven concrete steps. Then she heard the voice of Ray Maxted.

'Nice one, mate. And one of the pussy lieutenants. That's two Alley Cunts in a couple of days. My, my, the scumbags are getting careless.'

Muscle hauled her up, and Lox was now grateful she could see very little, as she found herself face-to-face with the mean dark brown eyes of Ray Maxted. Muscle now held her by the back of her torn puffa jacket. She took a deep breath, knowing she was facing a gang-rape, a beating, and a burning and then being left, as Tink was, to die in the gutter. She wasn't afraid, just very angry at being caught, and letting Tink down. She managed to spit into his face.

Maxted froze as the globule landed on his cheek. One second later he pushed the flat of his hand into her bleeding face and squeezed hard, then pushed her back against Muscle. She couldn't help but cry out in pain.

'Now, the thing here is,' Maxted said in a tone that inferred he was holding back his temper, 'someone's just walked onto my territory and torched my car. And I liked that fucking car.' He put his hand in his pocket and pulled out his gold cigarette lighter, which he flicked to *on*. She stared, terrified, at the flame which was a good two inches high.

He stared into her one eye that was open, and could see. 'How I see it is,' he said, still biting down his anger, 'If someone burns my property, then I have the right to burn theirs.' He stared into her one seeing eye, that was blinking as blood slid from her cut forehead and slowly trickled into her eyebrow. Sirens were screaming all around them. He nudged his head in defiance at them. 'No one'll find you here,' he told her with a grin. 'Clever of you to oblige and go out the back way.'

She had no choice but to squint as she looked at him, and then at the flame, with the working eye. Muscle, and now Coffee, who had just joined them, were gripping her arms behind her back, so she couldn't wipe the blood that was also trickling from her nose. She had to use her tongue. It tasted disgusting, with traces of dog shit from the stairs.

'Oh, but you ain't got a car, have you – no, you ain't,' Maxted said, rubbing a hand in theatrically ham gesture across his chin, ignoring her shaking legs which had started to give way, as she sniffed and blinked away blood. 'No car to burn.' He shook his head. 'I'll have to think of something else to burn then. Oh,' he clicked his gold, ring-adorned fingers and laughed. 'I've just had an idea.'

Stephanie was back with the coffees quite quickly. She recognised the look of confusion written across Georgia's face as she studied the forensic report. She immediately put the coffees down on the desk. 'What does it say?' she asked.

'Forensics on the knife,' Georgia told her, looking up. 'There's DNA confirmed on quite a few people, which is confusing. Amber Townes' prints are on it. But we expected that, she found the knife, and stupidly touched it when she covered it. Also Larry Hardy, which proves he used it. Traces of Ji Zhang's blood, which also figures.' She lifted the report up, 'But where does Martin Baxter come into this? His prints are on it too. He has previous

198

for aggravated burglary and GBH.'

'Martin Baxter?' He's second-in-command to Ray Maxted, in the RIP gang. He goes under the street name of Muscle,' Stephanie reminded her.

'Well, the DCI is on his way to bring in Maxted to question him on the abduction of Tink this morning. But how does Baxter fit into Zhang's stabbing? He lives in Peckham.'

'I'll ring the DCI, shall I, let him know? He's over in Peckham, he can bring in Baxter too, and we'll ask him. No one mentioned him being anywhere near the stabbing of Zhang, so his prints must be on it from another crime. As Alysha said, it was found just where Veronica Andrews was thrown from the car.'

Georgia nodded, picked up her coffee and sipped thoughtfully. She turned back to Stephanie, who was on the phone talking to Banham.

'DCI's going to bring him in too,' Stephanie told her.

'Tink was too drugged up to tell us much about her stabbing and rape,' Georgia said. 'We have a witness statement of the Zhangs' van driving away from the scene of the crime. Alysha did say they could have stolen it.' Georgia looked straight at Stephanie, as the pieces were going together. 'The Aviary was a desert this morning, and even Amber wasn't in. The uniform outside the Hardys' flat, said there were a crowd of women in the grounds this morning ...'

She was about to go on when Stephanie said, 'Gang clashes in Peckham ...'

'Please don't tell me Alysha has gone down there to look for Tink.' She picked up her phone and pressed Alysha's number.

* * *

Bull, the heaviest and youngest member of the RIPs, at nineteen stone and fifteen, was running along the back walkway of the fourth floor flat. His massive jeans were in danger of leaving his hips and taking a journey southwards. 'Feds! Feds are coming,' he was shouting as he held onto his jeans and puffed along the back walkway to the flat.

No sooner had he got the words out than Alison and Banham turned the corner from the fire exit and came face-to-face with them.

Maxted quickly put the lighter away, and Coffee and Muscle let go of Lox's arms.

Lox's legs gave way and she fell on her face.

'Where's the girl?' Banham asked Maxted, as Alison ran over and picked up Lox.

'What girl?'

'Veronica Andrews. I need you to come to come to the station and answer some questions concerning her abduction.'

'Are you 'aving a laugh? I ain't never 'eard of 'er.'

Banham was looking at Lox, and his temper was flaring. He called uniform on his radio to come up to level one, where they were, and bring the paramedics. He then turned back to Maxted.

'I am arresting you in connection with the abduction of Veronica Andrews,' he said to Maxted. Then he turned to Muscle. 'And the same for you, Martin Baxter,' he said.

'Oh, yeah, harassment, that's what this is,' Maxted argued.

Within a minute, uniformed officers had come round the corner to help with the arrests. They were followed by three paramedics who immediately went to Lox, as Banham finished reading the suspects their rights.

Alison bent down with her handkerchief, wiping the blood and snot from Lox's face. Lox opened her eyes.

'I'm OK. Thanks,' she said as Alison helped her to stand. Neither of the women gave anything away by using names.

'We'll take her,' the female paramedic told Alison.

'Where is Veronica Andrew?' Banham asked the now handcuffed Maxted again.

'What the fuck is this?' Maxted looked at Banham and wriggled his chained wrists together. 'You can't do this. I ain't done nothing.'

As Coffee turned to slip away, Banham nodded to the uniform police. 'Where do you think you are going? You are under arrest.'

'What for? I ain't done nothing neither,' Coffee shouted.

'What's happened to this girl's face?' Banham asked him, as Lox was helped down the stairs toward an ambulance.

'She's one of our friends,' Maxted butted in. 'We just got set on by a gang from Brixton. They've burnt me motor and ...'

'I ain't one of your friends,' Lox shouted back, turning her swollen eyes on Banham. 'He's kidnapped my mate Tink. I came to find her, and 'e's hurt me ...'

'That ain't true,' Muscle shouted. 'She was like that. We were helping her.'

'I'll ask you again,' Banham said moving in closer to Maxted. 'Where is Veronica Andrews?'

'I've just said. I don't know what you're talking about. If you've a search warrant help yourself to a look round my gaff, but if you ain't ...' he grinned and shrugged, 'well, I'm afraid I'm a bit of an old-fashioned stickler for keeping to the law.' Then his tone changed to anger. 'I ain't got no one hidden in there. I've got my motor on fire,' he said his tone becoming indignant. 'I ain't the guilty party here, you can't just arrest me; you ain't got

201

nothing to pin on me. So what's the charge?'

'Resisting arrest, for starters,' Banham said sarcastically. 'I have asked you to come with me to the station to answer some questions about the abduction and rape of Veronica Andrew. You refused, so I have arrested you.'

'You're a fucking racist.'

Banham turned to the uniformed officers. 'Please take him out of my sight,' he said to them. 'And these two as well.'

'On what charge?' Muscle said as he too was having his hand pulled behind his back and handcuffed.

'Assault,' Banham said, nodding to the police to put him in one of the waiting vans. 'That girl says you hit her.'

Lox was sitting in the ambulance having her forehead cleaned up. There would be no stitches, they told her, but she would have to go to hospital just for a check. 'I'm OK,' she said, over and over, but Alison asked her to go anyway. She was bruised and cut, and they would at least give her painkillers.

Lox was trying continually to reach Alysha, but the phone was engaged. She leaned back as the paramedic cleaned the faeces from her wounds.

'Does it sting?' he asked Lox.

But Lox had passed out.

Alysha watched the phone bleeping its ring, and looked at Panther.

'Answer it,' Panther told her. 'She's rang about six times. Tell Georgia that we was down there, just having a look around for Tink, and he's got Lox, now too. It's the best way. We got two of us family gone now.

Tiffany, Amber, Karen and a crowd of the other Alley

Cat soldiers were also all gathered and sitting on the floor in the thirteenth floor flat with Alysha and Panther. They all nodded their agreement.

'Do it,' Amber said. 'We need the feds to help Lox.'

Alysha shrugged, but didn't pick up the phone. She was worried that Georgia might say something about being their informants, and she knew she couldn't let Tiffany or Amber, and certainly not Karen, in on that.

'Pick up the phone, Queen,' Panther urged her again. 'She won't bite.'

Alysha did. Panther turned it to speaker so the other women could hear the conversation.

Georgia told her about the DNA results from the forensic report, and the fact that they now suspected that it was, as Alysha had said, Ray Maxted who had stolen the Zhangs' green van, and assaulted and raped Tink.

Then she asked Alysha if she had any news on anything for her, Alysha flicked a nervous glance at Panther and Panther quickly clicked the phone off speaker so that it was just for Alysha's ears. Alysha now knew that her plan to get the Zhangs arrested over the abduction had backfired, as the feds had proof from the knife that Maxted's gang had stabbed Tink. She hardly cared. She was missing Tink. Their attack on Maxted had failed too, and now she was worried sick about Lox, and beginning to feel her Alley Cats had been off their heads to think they could take on every gang in London. And what was the cost? Already the estate's facilities had been burned down, built up, and burnt down again. Now Tink and Lox's lives were on the line. They were her family and if they were in trouble, then that was all she cared about.

'Lox has gone missing now,' she said to Georgia. 'We fink she's been abducted by Maxted an' all.'

It was another second before Georgia answered her. 'DCI Banham is at Maxted's estate as we speak,' she told her. 'And there is a team combing every inch of that estate. I'll speak to the DCI, and tell him to look for Lox, and then I'm on my way round to see you. I need to speak to you again, face-to-face.'

'I ain't got nothing to say,' Alysha told her firmly. 'Find Tink and Lox, and then all of us'll do anyfing we can to 'elp you.'

'We will find them,' Georgia told her in an assured tone.

'Do it quick, or we'll do it ourselves. We ain't afraid of Maxted.'

'Don't be silly,' Georgia told her. 'There have already been riots down there today. Leave us to do our job. Your job is to get information on the consignment of guns and the heroin found in the Hardys' flat. Incidentally, Amber's fingerprints were found on that knife.'

'I'll get back to you on that,' Alysha told her. 'Oh, an' you might wanna wait to come round 'ere,' she looked at Amber. 'Amber's on her way in to the station, to give you that second statement you wanted 'bout where her and Summer found the knife.'

'She's on her way now?'

'Yup.'

'You've seen her.'

'I just said, she's on her way to you.'

'OK, we'll be here waiting. But keep on asking around about that consignment.'

'Let me know when you got news on Tink and Lox,' Alysha said and then hung up.

'We gotta hold this together, Queen,' Panther told her, reading the look of desperation on Alysha's face. 'We are gonna get Tink and Lox back, do you hear me, Queen?'

Alysha nodded half-heartedly. 'Go and give the feds a statement,' she told Amber. 'Tell them where you found the shank, and that you handled it before you wrapped it.

Tell 'em you only gave it to me, and not them, 'cos you know I look out for the estate.'

Alysha then looked at Karen and shook her head. She knew the girl wasn't bright, and she was also aware that she had lost all her family, so she spoke gently. 'Karen, you've got us into a lot of shit by telling the feds that I gave you that gear.'

'Yeah, but you did.'

'Yeah, I know that, darling,' Alysha said, trying to keep calm. 'Your mum was in a lot of trouble and a lot of debt, and we was helping her. If you are gonna be with us, then Alley Cats have to report everything that happens to one of us. An' you *never* talk to the feds, 'less we tell you, and we tell you what to say, have you got that?'

'Yeah. I got that,' Karen said. 'I won't tell them that it was you that burnt Ray Maxted's car.'

Alysha and Panther made eye contact.

'You say nothing 'bout that to no one,' Panther told her sternly. 'You are living wiv us now. Why don't you have a little rest while we all sort this mess out? Bed's made up in our room.'

Karen nodded. 'I don't say nothing,' she repeated.

'That's AC rules,' Alysha repeated. 'You have to do as we say. We look after you, but you must keep it buttoned. Got it?'

'Yeah, I got it,' Karen grinned happily. 'Buttoned.'

Panther turned to Alysha. 'The feds are arresting Maxted, you say.'

Alysha nodded.

'Then we can go back to the estate and look for Tink and Lox.' She looked at Tiffany. 'Round up as many ACs as you can. 'We're going back to those fuckers' territory again tonight, and we're finding our sisters and we're bringing them home. We'll burn the fucking buildings down if we have to. She turned to Amber. 'Go to the station now, but get back by tonight, 'cos we'll need ya,' she told her. 'This is war. No fucking RIPs are gonna get the better of us. Eh, Panth?'

'That's more like it, Queen,' Panther grinned.

'Why they arrested Maxted?' Karen asked after picking up a duvet that was draped on the floor. 'He never 'ung my brother, that were the Chinese. We should kill them, yeah?'

Alysha caught Panther's eye again. 'Yeah, but one gang at a time,' Panther told her. 'First we are gonna get Tink and Lox, and then we're gonna sort out them Chinese. That's a promise.'

'Wayne was in that nick,' Amber told Karen. 'He's my brother. He was in there wiv your brother Larry, and three of the Chinese lot are in there too. An 'e knows it was them in there, that 'ung Larry, but 'e won't grass 'em up, 'cos there're too many of 'em.'

'We'll find a way to get the Chinks,' Alysha told her. 'I promise you,' she told Karen. 'We're gonna get even for you.'

Karen looked around, and then smiled, but her eyes were afraid.

'I know you feel alone,' Alysha told her. 'We've all been there, and it ain't nice. But you ain't alone, 'cos we're 'ere. That's what we formed the Alley Cats for. We are family for anyone on the estate that needs us, and you need us, so we are here for you. We fight to the death for each other. Right?'

'Right, right,' came the plural replies as Karen turned, dragging her duvet, toward Panther's bedroom.

Amber had given her statement and, as instructed, had hurried back. The ACs were once again, on their way to Peckham. They were tooled up, their hoods and bandanas were on, and they all had balaclavas down their knickers and all were ready for another fight, all determined this time they would find Tink and Lox.

Georgia got the news from Banham that Lox was found and had been taken to St Mildred's. She immediately phoned Alysha.

Alysha saw Georgia's name come up on her phone, and ducked into an alleyway off the street as the ACs were approaching Peckham to take the call.

'That's a relief,' Alysha told her trying to keep the phone down and away from the noise of traffic and the police sirens that were passing every second, also on their way to Peckham.

'Where are you?' Georgia asked her.

'In the alley near the estate,' Alysha lied.

'Why can I hear sirens behind you?' Before Alysha had time to think up a lie, Georgia said, 'Jesus, you're in Peckham, aren't you?' she said. 'I told you, you are to go nowhere near Peckham, do you hear me? That is our job.'

'Tink is still missing,' Alysha shouted defiantly. 'You ain't found her yet.'

'Here's what you are going to do,' Georgia told her in a tone that was nothing short of a command. 'You are going to go to St Mildred's and you are going to get Lox and take her home. She needs you too. We pay you for information and I want you to get it for me. I want to know how those firearms came to be on the estate in the Hardys' flat, and I want you to find out if anyone saw and give a description of the man in the helmet that came to the Hardys' door and shot Karen. In return, we will find Tink for you. I have Maxted here at the station, and I promise I will get it out of him. Is that clear?'

'Yes.'

'I am going to speak to the DCI now, and he will be in touch with the team, who are, as we speak, searching the

207

whole of the Nichol Estate. If any of them see you, my instruction will be to arrest you on sight, and any of your friends, and I will charge you with getting in the way of a police operation. I hope I make myself clear.'

'Yes, you do,' Alysha said flatly.

'Incidentally, do you know anything about the damage to Maxted's car earlier today?'

'No. How would I?' She still spoke in a flat tone, as if Georgia was boring her.

'I just wondered if that was anything to do with you.'

'That's criminal damage,' Alysha said, a tone of sarcasm creeping into her voice. 'And criminal damage is a crime, ain't it? You told me I had to uphold the law if I was going to work for you.'

'Yes. So get yourself away from Peckham, and go to the hospital and get Lox. That's an order. And we'll find Tink.'

'Oh, by the way, ma'am,' Alysha said, not being able to stop herself. ''E never 'ad no tax, or no insurance, so it's more than a shame 'bout 'is car.'

There was a silent few seconds while Georgia took that in, then she said, 'I'll be round later. Go and get Lox, she needs you, and so does Karen.'

Chapter Seventeen

Alysha swore at the phone as she rang off, 'We 'ave to call off this attack,' she said, 'for now. Tell the ACs it ain't safe, which it ain't, too many feds around. We'll go get Lox from 'ospital, then get the gang to stay on standby for when the feds move out. If they ain't got Tink, we move in and tear the place down if we 'ave to.'

Panther nodded as she texted, and sent word around. There would be a meeting back at the Aviary Estate in an hour, she told them.

Anita immediately messaged back and offered her brother Dean, who was at home, to go with the girls to get Lox and bring her home in his motor.

'Na, fanks,' Alysha rang back to tell her, as she and Panther hurried down the road looking for a cab. 'We wanna be wiv 'er on our own, we'll bring 'er back. But fanks for the asking. Can you take care of Karen for us while we're gone, though? We're only gonna give them feds another hour or so round Maxted's place. Just while we get Lox, and then we're gonna go back an' we gonna tear the RIP territory up, 'cos we're gotta find Tink.'

Panther was now ringing the cab company. She looked up as she listened to Alysha's conversation. 'She's already in a very bad way,' she shouted out. 'An' the feds don't seem to realise it, or if they do they don't give a fuck.'

Within minutes the cab pulled up by the edge of the main road where the two girls stood. As Alysha opened the back door to climb aboard, she slid her cricket ball into her pocket. It would come out again later. The next time she faced Maxted, she intended to be with Tink, and she would crack Maxted's cheekbone open and leave him screaming in agony for what he had done to her mate. And that was just for starters.

Muscle was thick-skinned and not in the mood to talk. A young female duty solicitor sat beside him, looking stressed.

Anyone addressing him as Martin, or Mr Baxter, was immediately frozen out. Street life had taken him over; he only answered to the name of Muscle. Looking at the red veins on either side of his nose, and the mauve tinge on his young cheeks, it was clear to Georgia that he over-indulged in alcohol. The irritability which he displayed was a clear sign to her that he was a drug-user. His arms, however, showed no signs of track marks, so Georgia suspected cocaine or crystal meth was his chosen recreational drug.

Georgia sat facing him, Stephanie sat beside her. Both were worryingly aware that every minute Tink was not found was a further emergency, and they were now concerned whether she was even alive.

Georgia studied him as he gave his monosyllabic answer of 'No comment,' to every question fired at him. She raised her voice.

'My patience is thin on the ground here,' she almost shouted. 'You need to start talking to us, Martin. I'm not going to beat about the bush. We know you were accessory to the abduction of Veronica Andrew from St Mildred's Hospital earlier today. That girl is badly in need of medical treatment. You are already looking at a custodial sentence here, but there is every probability we could, at any second, be charging you with accessory to murder. However, if you help us, you help yourself.'

'Go fuck yourself.'

The duty solicitor turned and shook her head at him.

He opened his hands wide. 'I ain't done nothing,' he shouted back at her. 'She's accusing me of stuff I ain't done. Wants me to set up my mate, who *also* ain't done nothing.'

'Innocent as a newborn, you,' Stephanie said flatly.

'We have a statement from Alice Baker. She'll be known to you as Lox,' Georgia added quickly. 'The statement accuses you of GBH. You punched her in the face, and your so called *innocent* friend then kicked her in the stomach.'

He shrugged. 'Didn't know who she was. She broke into my mate's flat, so that makes her a burglar, and that was after she torched his car. Law's hardly on our side here, now is it, so can't blame us for defending ourselves, can you?'

'So you admit you hurt her?'

'No. She was already duffed up. We just threw 'er out of the flat, an' she fell over and then fell down the stairs. Nothing to do with us.'

'Why did you rape and burn Veronica Andrew?' Stephanie asked quickly.

'Never touched her.'

Georgia pushed a polythene bag containing the knife with the double pronged end, across the table to him. 'For the convenience of the tape, I'm showing exhibit 913 to Mr Baxter,' she said, 'a knife with Mr Baxter's fingerprints and DNA confirmed as over it.' Then looking back to Muscle she said, 'Can you explain to me then why this knife has your fingerprints and DNA on it?'

Muscle lifted his forefinger to wipe the sweat from the top of his lip, and then the flat of his hand over his shaved head. 'Must be some kind of mistake. I dunno,' he said, now scratching across the back of his other thick hand which displayed a large tattoo of a crown. His leg started twitching.

Stephanie leaned in toward him. 'Forensics don't make mistakes.'

Georgia raised her voice. 'Martin, if anything happens to Veronica, which it will, if you don't cooperate and tell us where she is, you will be facing a murder charge. Now where is she?'

'Go fuck yourself.'

Lox's nose was swollen, she'd had three stitches across the top of one of her eyes, and an X-ray, then her knees and face were cleaned up. The X-ray showed bruising, but no haemorrhaging. The tiny particles of concrete were then carefully, and painfully, removed from her hands, legs and face, with the help of tweezers. She was covered in disinfectant cream, then discharged and told she could go home.

She dialled Alysha's number, and then changed her mind. She knew they were looking for Tink, so quickly decided the belling of a phone might put her mate in danger, she decided to call a cab. As soon as it came, she left the hospital, heading back to the estate and messaging Alysha as she went.

As Alysha and Panther entered the hospital and walked up to the enquiry desk, Alysha's phone rang.

'Sorry, no phones are allowed in here,' the receptionist told her. 'Can you turn it off, please.'

Alysha checked the caller ID. It was a number she didn't recognise. She knew it would be one of the AC soldiers, returning her call, but she had no choice, she turned it off. Lox was what mattered at this second. She gave her information to the receptionist at enquiries, who, after several phone calls, and more wasted time, eventually told Alysha and Panther that Lox had been discharged and had left the building.

Alysha threw her hands in the air irritably, as she was given the news, then she turned and left the building. As soon as she turned her phone back on, the same number came up again as trying to call her, but it was the message from Lox which took her attention.

'Didn't want to bother you, 'cos I'm fine. Keep looking for Tink. I'm on my way back to flat, c u there.' the text read.

She showed it to Panther.

'It's good,' Panther told her. 'Means she's OK, then. I'll call us a cab and we'll get back to the meeting.'

Maxted was playing his police interview completely opposite to Muscle, all butter-wouldn't-melt. His personal solicitor sat beside him, a man who seemed similarly innocuous, but Banham knew his history. Gary Graystone had grown up on the Nichol Estate and, after his sister was accidentally shot in the crossfire between two enemy gangs, suddenly found he had enough money to pay for his much-wanted legal training in full, and he went on to qualify as a solicitor. He represented all the low-lifes around the Nichol, mainly Maxted's gang, and was clearly in the pocket of the gang leader.

Alison had taken the lead in the interview and, as Maxted charmingly denied all her accusations and, indeed, any knowledge of who Tink even was, insisting they should be concentrating on catching the people responsible for torching his car, her famous temper was beginning to brew. She banged her palm on the table to stop him in mid-flow.

'You can cut your crap,' she said in a raised voice. 'Every second of it is a threat to Veronica Andrew's life.

We already have information that you abducted her, so cut the bullshit and tell us where she is.'

'Your information's wrong,' Maxted said, in the same annoyingly polite tone. He narrowed his dark eyes and shook his head. 'I'm sorry to have to disappoint you,' he said, lifting his hands and tapping them together, displaying the array of gold rings, ''cos I know you need your arrest figures an' all that, to get your pat on the back from the borough commander an' all, but I ain't abducted no one. So, sorry, 'fraid I can't help you. But, now, see, I can help with your crime figures, 'cos my car was torched this morning, and my van was nicked yesterday, and you don't seem to give a shit.'

'It's been reported to Traffic,' Banham said speaking in an even tone and keeping his eyes locked on Maxted. 'They'll be dealing with it. I'm only interested in Veronica Andrew's welfare.'

Maxted shook his head. 'It's 'cos I'm black that you don't wanna help, ain't it?'

That was too annoying for Alison. 'No,' she snapped a little too loudly, and then spoke in broken syllables. 'It's because it isn't our job isn't to find how your car went up in flames. Our job, and priority, is to find a girl whose life is in serious danger if she stays out of hospital much longer. We know you've attacked one of her friends –'

'I ain't attacked no one. See, you do this. Yous putting words into my mouth.'

'Mr Maxted has never said he attacked anyone,' the solicitor spoke up. 'What evidence do you have, please?'

'She told us herself before we sent her off to hospital and we also –'

'That girl walked into my flat bleeding everywhere,' Maxted butted in,' and we was trying to help her, when you walked in and arrested us. Not my fault if the tart slipped over.'

'Oh, please,' Alison blew out air, shook her head, and threw her eyes to heaven.

'You were at the hospital yesterday,' Banham said, 'Visiting Veronica Andrew, known as Tink,' he said evenly. 'Now you aren't denying that, are you?'

'Yeah. I ain't been nowhere near the hospital.' He turned to his solicitor. 'What's this about?' he said accusingly. 'Do I really have to listen to this crap?'

'Mr Maxted, it's common knowledge that you are involved in a gang known by the name of the RIPs, who largely come from the Nichol estate,' Banham said to him.

Maxted shook his head, and looked vague. 'Not me.'

'A green van was seen on the hospital CCTV camera, speeding away from the building in the early hours of the morning. You have a green van, don't you? Alison said.

'A lot of people have got green vans.'

'Abduction carries a custodial sentence, but if anything happens to Veronica, you are looking at a murder charge,' she said holding his eyes.

'Only if I done it,' he replied with a smile and a flash of his gold tooth. He shrugged. 'But I ain't.'

'Does the CCTV show the van's registration plate clearly?' Gary Graystone asked, turning to Alison with a smug look across his face. 'Only, if it doesn't, well, I wouldn't like to take a guess at how many green vans there are in this area, so we would be talking circumstantial evidence here, would we not?'

Maxted shook his head and smiled that flash of gold tooth again. 'I am givin' it to you straight; I don't know where my van is. It's been nicked. I was going to report it but then my car got torched, and the van got pushed aside.' He turned to Graystone. 'Someone obviously don't want me to drive.'

'I should think the whole of England,' Alison said. 'As

215

your car wasn't insured.'

Graystone came back quickly. 'It was parked off the street,' he told them, 'in a private garage. The law doesn't require tax and insurance for cars parked off the street and garaged.' He raised his eyebrows and turned his wrist to check the time. 'Now, if you have no further evidence or questions, I would request that you release my client.'

'Yeah, good idea,' Maxted nodded and turned to his solicitor. 'I'm getting 'ungry,'

With no evidence against Ray Maxted and pressure from the solicitor, DCI Banham had to agree to release him. He was able to charge Martin Baxter, as his prints and DNA were on the knife that matched the fatal stab wound to Ji Zhang, and they now knew it was the same knife that stabbed Tink.

As to how it got from Zhang to Larry Hardy to Maxted, they had yet to work that out. The fact that it was found near where Tink was stabbed probably meant it was tossed from the van as the van sped away from the attack, but how had it got in there in the first place? Maxted must had found it in the Zhangs' van, which he had stolen – after reporting his own missing – and cleverly used to shift the blame to the Zhangs.

Anita had made Karen jam sandwiches for her tea. Karen had said they were her favourite, and that her brother used to make them for her. Karen was making gurgling noises with a straw as she sucked her carton of fruit juice and sat, sandwiches on her knee, looking out of the window.

Lox had needed a bit of help getting out of the taxi in the grounds, but as soon as Karen saw her, she put her drink and sandwiches aside, then opened the window and climbed out onto the second floor balcony. She ran along the walkway, and down the fire exit, straight across to the other side, ignoring Anita's shouts to come back, running to Lox and throwing her arms around her.

'It's OK,' Lox told her, pushing her away from her throbbing face and limbs. 'I'm OK, don't worry about me. It's Tink we have to worry about. Is there any news?'

'Alysha's on her way back 'ere. She phoned Anita and told her. Can I come home with you?'

'Yes, course, but make sure Anita knows where you are. We don't want the social poking their nose in our business.'

'No, we don't want the social poking their nose in our business.'

As Ray Maxted stood at the reception checking his personal effects, which the duty sergeant was handing back to him, Amber walked out of an interview room, having given her requested statement. She stopped when she saw Maxted. 'They ain't let you go, have they?' she said to him as her eyes flared in anger and, unable to stop herself, she spat at him.

'Oi, pack that in,' the desk sergeant told her quickly.

'Sorry,' she said sarcastically. 'I thought it would clean up where he's dirtied your floor with his disgusting presence.'

Maxted glared at her and spoke in a threatening tone. 'No one does that to me and don't get payin' back,' he told her. 'I owe you.'

'Oh, what, you gonna rape and burn me too? You disgusting piece of shit.' She turned to Stan the duty sergeant. 'I can't believe you're letting him go. He's raped my mate an' –'

'Shut up,' the sergeant told her, to show he wasn't having any more nonsense.

'An eye for an eye,' Maxted said.

'I'm fucking quivering,' Amber said.

The sergeant raised his voice again. 'I said that's enough!'

'Yeah?' Amber said to Stan. 'An you 'eard all that. He's not denying what he done to Tink, an' he's making threats to me, an' you're telling *me* to shut it.' She shook her head. 'He should be locked up and never let out. I can't believe you're letting 'im go free.' She turned back to Maxted. Graystone was now walking toward them, a takeaway coffee in his hand, which he handed to Maxted. 'Latte, two sugars,' he said.

'Oh and 'ere's the other dickhead,' she said to Graystone, then lowered her voice and added, 'If you got any fucking sense you'll tell 'im to give us Tink back.'

'Are you threatening us?' Graystone answered in his loud and well-enunciated tone.

'You wanna believe it,' came the reply.

'Just get out, all of you,' the sergeant said, all but throwing Maxted's personals at him. 'Get out, or I'll lock up the lot of you up.'

'Excuse me?' Graystone said.

'OUT!'

The phone rang again as Alysha and Panther walked to the end of the long hospital drive. Alysha pulled her phone from the pocket of her jacket and checked the number. It was the same one that had rang before, twice, inside the hospital. She put the phone to her ear.

'Yeah?'

There was no mistaking the voice. 'I am going to make you a very good offer,' George Zhang said in his cold, clipped tone.

'What you want?'

'I want Karen Hardy.'

Alysha immediately put the phone on speaker so Panther could hear the conversation.

'What do you want Karen for?' Alysha asked, staying calm but frowning at Panther.

'That's for me to know, and you to wonder. Now, I suggest you take this offer. It's a good one. I only offer a deal to you because I want Karen. I was going to kill you and your friends, and I still might, but first I offer this deal. I want Karen Hardy enough that I will give your friend Tink in exchange for her, or what's left of your friend Tink.

There was a stunned silence where the two girls stared at each other. After a couple of seconds Alysha said. 'You ain't got Tink, so how can you give her to us?'

'I know where she is.'

'So tell me?'

'First you must give me Karen.'

'You're tricking us. I ain't giving you Karen. Anyway, I don't know much about her, I don't know where she is.'

'I think you do. And you surely don't want to never see your friend Tink again.'

Alysha tried but failed to keep her temper. 'You fucking stinking rat. You're winding me up, and playing me 'cos you fink I'll fall for your shit. You ain't got Tink …'

There was quiet the other end, at first Alysha thought he had hung up, but then she heard the sound of steps, and then a tiny, weak voice.

'Lysh?' There was no doubting it was the voice of her pal. 'Lysh, listen to him. I'm here.'

Alysha swallowed hard. 'Where's here, darling?' Another few seconds quiet during which Panther and Alysha stared at each other, hearts beating wildly.

There was the muffling sound of someone putting their hand over the phone, and speaking in a harsh Chinese accent to her.

'I don't know where "here" is,' Tink said before

pausing again for more breath. 'It ain't the Zhangs' place, and I ain't well, I know that. But EIBs have taken –' There were muffled sounds again and then George Zhang was back on the line.

'As I say, I am willing to give your friend to you in exchange for Karen Hardy. A very fair exchange, I'd say, and very kind of me. Do we have a deal?'

Chapter Eighteen

As soon as the cab drew up outside the Sparrow block, Alysha and Panther hurried out and ran up the stairs to their flat. Lox was waiting at the front door, and, as they all group hugged, Alysha updated her on the situation with the phone call from George Zhang.

Panther ran into the flat heading for the bedroom door. 'I'm gonna kill 'im,' she shouted, as she pulled open a cupboard door.

'No, you ain't thinking right,' Alysha shouted at her, following her in. 'Think of the consequences.'

'I don't give a shit for the consequences, I'm getting the shooter, an' I'm gonna blow his fucking 'ead off.'

Panther was now tossing blankets and sheets from the cupboard as she searched for her gun.

'An' where'll that get Tink?' Alysha demanded. ''Sides, we don't know where they are. He ain't told us yet.'

'I'll find out,' Panther raised her voice, again. 'I ain't waiting for 'im to phone and give us orders. I'm gonna kill 'im anyway. He's done enough harm to our gang.'

'No, you ain't,' Alysha now spoke in an authoritative tone, following Panther out of the room, and blocking the path to the front door.

Panther held the gun in her hand.

Alysha held her hand out for it. 'I'm Queen Cat,' Alysha reminded her, 'and I say no.'

Panther stared at Alysha.

'We need to do what's best for Tink,' Lox jumped in to back Alysha up, while Karen stood at the edge of the door to the lounge, her eyes full of fear.

'Killing that fucker is best for everyone. I'm telling you,' Panther argued.

'You can kill 'im *after* I know Tink is safe,' Alysha said, putting her two hands in the air, palms facing Panther to stop her moving. 'I ain't risking Tink like that.'

'Yous too upset to fink right,' Panther told her.

'Look, cool it, both of yous,' Lox shouted, ushering Karen back down the hall. 'Sweetheart, go in the bedroom for a few minutes. There's biscuits in the tin in there, help yourself. This is a bit of private stuff going on, here. We'll be in in a minute.'

Karen looked from one girl to the other and then obeyed.

Lox waited till the sound of the biscuit tin rattling could be heard from inside the bedroom, then she turned back to Panther, 'Look, Tink has to come first 'ere. And if you go after Zhang with a gun, then Tink, is gonna get badly hurt, and then all of us.'

Panther nodded. 'I agree. We gotta think of Tink. Whatever the cost.' She turned back to Alysha, lowering her voice, she said. 'If you won't let me kill 'im, then we 'ave to give him Karen.'

Alysha shook her head. 'We ain't doing that. The Alley Cats were formed for street kids who 'ad no one but each other. Tink knows what we're about, and she'd agree with me. Karen ain't got no one, only us. We ain't gonna let her down.' She shook her head and then said, 'And we ain't gonna let Tink down neither.'

Lox and Panther both shook their heads.

'We put them firearms and the heroin in Hardy's flat for a safe place to hide it,' Alysha said. 'Admittedly we done it to help Lisa, but also cause we knew we couldn't have it here. We now gotta take responsibility for doing that, and we've gotta look out for Karen, 'cos we're all she's got, and that's what we vowed to do.'

'But what 'bout Tink?' Panther argued.

'I know she'd agree wiv what I am saying.'

'What, let something happen to her 'cos your protecting someone who's just a new Alley Cat soldier?' Lox argued, shaking her head. 'I know Tink would never put no one before you.' She shook her head again, then put her hands to her forehead as pain hit her.

'I'm fucking sure she wouldn't,' Panther added.

'I'd give my life for Tink,' Alysha told them. 'You know I would. And for you Lox, and for Panther. But I won't give someone else's. It ain't fair, and it ain't what the Alley Cats do.' She looked from Lox to Panther, and then she winked. 'So, we are gonna save 'em both,' she said. 'Zhang's gonna ring back ain't 'e? He's giving us time to fink on this one.'

'I really thought this was down to Ray Maxted,' Lox said. 'We wasted all that time on Nichol when we could have been burning down the EIBs. So I hope you got a good plan.'

Alysha nodded. 'I have,' she said. 'Then she grinned a little as the noise of the biscuit tin rattling happened again. She lowered her voice. 'I'm gonna ring the feds. I ain't taking any chances wiv Tink's life. We need help, and a lot of it. If the Zhangs don't fink we're gonna play it their way,' she lowered her voice again, 'and give them Karen, then they'll hurt Tink without a second thought. We know that. They don't know we got the ear of the feds and we'll need them on board this time. Can't take no chances now we know Tink is definitely there.'

'If they even smell feds they'll kill Tink,' Panther argued, shaking her head.

'No, they won't,' Lox said. 'Alysha's right. 'That is

the only card we hold right now. They won't kill 'er wiv feds around, they ain't that stupid. Why do they want Karen though?'

''Cos Larry killed Ji.'

'They've had him hung for that,' Lox argued. 'Karen shouldn't be part of that. They've evened that score.'

'If Zhang wants Karen, it's 'cos he wants to kill 'er, so chances are it was 'im who killed her mum too,' Lox said. 'He obviously wants to wipe out the whole family as a way of getting even.'

'He ain't getting Karen,' Alysha said defiantly. 'We said we'd take care of her, an' we will.'

Alysha's phone rang again. It was a different number from the one Zhang had rang on earlier. She picked up.

'Have you got her?' Zhang said in a tone that told Alysha he wasn't going to be messed with.

'No, but I know where she is. Why d'you want her anyway?'

'Mine's to know, and yours is to do,' came the abrupt answer. 'Ring me when you have her, and I'll tell you where to bring her. And don't take all day about it.' There was a pause before he added, 'Your friend's not getting any better.'

'You fink we're stupid or what?' Alysha snapped. 'No. You give us Tink first, an' then I'll tell you where the other is. Make a place to meet, an' I'll be there with the info. But I wanna see Tink before I tell you anything. I don't trust you.'

There was a pause the other end, then he spoke again, and in a tone that was clipped and threatening. 'If you want to see your friend alive again, you do as I say. Ring this number when you have Karen. And don't fuck me about.'

A second later there was a scream in the background which Alysha recognised immediately as coming from

Tink.

'You cunt, what you doing to my girl,' she screamed at him.

'Letting you know we mean business.' He hung up.

Alysha immediately pressed numbers into her phone. 'I'm ringing Georgia Johnson,' Alysha said before Panther had the chance to argue.

Georgia was in a meeting with Alison and Stephanie and some of the team when her phone buzzed silently on the desk in front of her.

On the whiteboard beside her were the pictures of Tink lying unconscious in the road, with 'Veronica Andrew, known as Tink' written underneath. She was burnt and bleeding, her clothing was torn and she looked in a bad way. Beside that there was the photograph of Lox handing a wad of notes to Larry Hardy, and then a photo of Karen Hardy wearing an ill-fitting miniskirt and leaning over the passenger window of a sports car, and then another of her getting into the same car. There were also pictures of the murdered Lisa Hardy, Ji Zhang, and one of Larry Hardy after he was found hanged.

Georgia addressed her team. 'What we need is the link that ties these deaths,' she said. She pointed to Karen leaning over the sports car. 'We know Lisa owed money to a lot of people, and her children were out trying to earn money to help her pay her debts. We know they had a large consignment of guns and drugs hidden under the floorboards of a wardrobe in Larry's room in their flat, that Lisa hadn't been using. So, as an addict, we have to believe she couldn't have known they were there. So who did? And how did they get there? She pulled the photo of Karen over the car down from the board and handed it to Hank Peacock. 'See if you can get any part of the reg blown up and the owner traced. See what went on, if he was a regular, did he pay her? And how much? Had he seen her around the area a lot? All that and more,' she said.

'We also have a statement from Amber Townes,' Georgia told her team. She glanced down to her desk and noticed her phone was vibrating again. She moved in and saw it was Alysha's number. She decided to ignore it. 'Amber has confirmed that she found the knife near where Veronica was thrown from the moving vehicle. She has told us she covered it in bubble wrap to protect DNA and then informed Alysha Achter about it as Alysha runs the estate residents' society and she didn't know what else to do. Alysha then got an emergency call and rushed to the hospital to her friend Veronica Andrews, leaving the knife in her flat. She has assured us she intended bringing it to the station to us, but her flat was raided first.'

Georgia looked over at Alison.

'I can't say I wholly believe her,' Alison said.

Georgia spoke over her. 'The knife went to Forensics. There have been a variety of prints lifted from it, so far. Martin Baxter's, for one – known as Muscle, he's a member of the RIP gang from Peckham, where the riots took place this morning. He is still in custody. Also Drew Robert, known as Tip, another member of the same gang. We have yet to find and pick him up.'

Georgia's phone started vibrating again. She checked it again and saw Alysha's name was back on her screen.

'Excuse me,' she said to her team. 'I need to take this call.' She picked up. After Alysha had shrieked, panic-stricken, telling Georgia about the Zhangs having Tink, and wanting Karen in exchange, Georgia calmly asked Alysha where she was, then checked she had Karen with her. 'Stay in the flat. Do not go out. I will talk to the DCI and call you back. Have you got an address yet?'

She cut the call. 'Excuse me,' Georgia said to the team. 'I need to talk to the DCI.'

'What's going on?' Alison asked.

'George Zhang has got Tink. He's offered her to Alysha in exchange for Karen Hardy.'

Banham's door was open. He was up and out of his seat. He had heard the conversation. 'Does she know that for sure?'

'Yes,' Georgia told him. 'Alysha has personally spoken to Tink. She said she is very weak and distressed, and being tortured.'

'Do we have an address?'

'We're waiting on that.'

'What does he want?'

'Karen Hardy, in exchange.'

'Why does he want her?'

'Must be to do with the heroin shipment and the firearms. I'll lay money he killed Lisa over it.'

'We need a hostage negotiator,' Banham told her. 'Tell Alysha that under no circumstances is she to do anything. I'll go undercover as a cab driver, and take her to the meeting place.'

'She won't wait long for us,' Georgia said. 'Tink is in too bad a state. Let's hope she keeps her head.'

'What are we waiting for? Let's go,' Banham said grabbing his coat and looking at Alison.

'Where to?'

'The Aviary Estate. We'll get a TIU team in a van following.' He looked over to Stephanie. 'Get on to that, Sergeant Green, please.'

'Sir.'

'TIU will trace the call when Zhang rings, and get his location. We also need a CO19 gun team. Sgt Can you get onto them pronto. Zhang will be armed, I have no doubt, and I'm taking no chances. Stephanie, let me know when

227

they are on standby.'

'Sir.'

'I don't think we should all go over there to the Aviary,' Georgia said to Banham. 'Zhang might be nearer than we think.'

He glared at her. 'Last I knew, I was in charge around here.'

'OK, so we wait here for the feds,' Alysha told Lox and Panther. 'Call Karen back in.'

Lox opened the door to bring Karen back in to the room with them. She turned back within a second.

'She ain't there,' Lox shrieked in panic, rushing into the bedroom and looking out the open window that led onto the balcony. 'She's climbed out the window.'

Alysha and Panther looked at each other and both belted out the front door, closely followed by Lox. They ran along the walkway and turned onto the large stairwell. All stopped in their tracks. Karen was running down the stairs and wailing loudly.

Alysha called out to her. 'Karen, stop, please. It's OK.'

The girls all dashed to the bottom of the stairs and Alysha put comforting arms around her.

'Why did you run away like that? Alysha asked her. 'It's dangerous around here at the moment; you gotta stay wiv us.'

Karen shook her head. 'Zhang wants to kill me, don't 'e?'

Alysha and Panther and Lox made eye contact. Panther answered. ''E wants to kill us all actually, but 'e ain't gonna get the chance, 'cos we ain't gonna let 'im. We're gonna look after you, but you can't just run off. You gotta stick wiv us.'

'Is 'e gonna kill Tink?'

'No,' Alysha told her. ''Cos we got help, see, and

228

we're gonna outsmart 'im. We's all gonna meet 'im, but when we do, he'll have a big surprise, put it that way.'

Karen's eyes widened in interest, but she asked nothing else.

'I think we'll have a fizzy drink while we wait, and a jam sandwich,' Lox said, helping Karen up and linking their arm as they made their way back to the flat.

It all went up very quickly. No one had seen anything. Rook block, where Karen lived, was the ideal target for a warning. There was only one fed there, and he wasn't in sight at the time. It would also blow the forensic investigation away – not that they had left any traces, but you never know these days, this was the chance to make completely sure. All of the neighbours had been evacuated when all the feds had moved in. Not that it mattered, most of the neighbours were already half-dead anyway.

The newspaper was soaked in petrol and quickly pushed through the letterbox, catching fire as soon as the lighter flame touched it, and then they legged it. It wasn't raining either, so that was a big plus. There was a wind and that would help if the flames took the building up, it might take more than just this one. These girls were going to heed this warning; they would learn not to mess with the big boys. If they really thought that pussies could run this territory, then they were having a laugh. What was all that shit about community centres and opportunities? That had gone up in smoke too, like the rest of the shit they spouted. Now they were learning what really happened when you messed with the major players. And very soon the Aviary Estate, with its rich pickings, would be under their rule.

* * *

229

Alysha, Panther, Lox and Karen got a call from a neighbour in the flat two floors down. She could smell burning, she said, and was worried that the Hardys' flat was on fire. Alysha told her to call the fire brigade, and she would too. Within minutes they could hear the brigade on its way. Alysha decided not to mention it to Karen, at the moment the girl had enough to frighten her. She called Georgia to warn her, and told her she suspected the Chinese or Peckham boys might be around.

'Wait for us in the car park,' Georgia told her.

Georgia and Stephanie were following the TIU van at the time. Alison had gone on ahead to get Karen, the plan was to bring her to the station or keep her away from what was happening.

Georgia rang the news through to Banham. 'Sir, I hear there is a fire on the Rook block. I don't know how bad it is. Fire engines are on way. I'm thinking of Alison, she's afraid of fire because of what happened on that case a few years back. Shall we tell her turn round and go back to the station?'

'No, I'll deal with it,' Banham said. 'Get to the estate car park, pick up those girls and wait for me there. Is there any news on Zhang or his whereabouts yet?'

'No, sir, Alysha said he hasn't called back. But they could be responsible for the fire, in which case they could be on the estate.'

As Alison turned onto the main road leading to the estate, fire engines with sirens blaring were overtaking her car, and uniformed police cars, their blue lights spinning and flashing, were following. She slammed her foot on the brakes as she noticed the flames. It looked like an exploding fountain of burning colour shooting out from the window of the building. The area around, too, was black with the smoke. She was having a *déjà vu*.

She had taken a year off work on compassionate leave when her friend and colleague was burnt alive in an arson attack. Banham had persuaded her back to work. She had thought she was ready to return. But every time there was a fire involved in a crime, she lost her nerve again. Right now, she wasn't able to drive any further. That fire was where she was heading – the Aviary Estate.

She turned the engine off, she could go no further. She rang Banham.

'Go back, sweetheart,' he told her. 'Just go back to the station.'

Banham carried on and pulled into the car park on the opposite side of the estate. He was there and waiting, as Georgia and Stephanie and the TIU van drew in behind him.

Alysha, Panther, Lox and Karen were all there waiting. Karen was now shaking as she watched the fire rage around her mother's flat. The four girls climbed into the TIU van, and Banham and Stephanie and Georgia followed them.

'What do you know about the fire?' Georgia asked Alysha, fully knowing the answer. 'Is it an arson attack again?'

Alysha shrugged. 'We set fire to Ray Maxted's Porsche.'

She noticed of the angry look on Banham's face. 'So this'll be retaliation, will it?'

'We thought he had Tink,' Panther said. 'We had to get into his flat to get her.' She glared back at Banham. 'You weren't doing much to help. Tink could be dead as we speak. I ain't apologising.'

'Or it could be the Zhangs?' Georgia asked. 'George Zhang could already be here. Maybe he's just playing games with you. Maybe he thought Karen was in the flat

231

and decided to smoke her out.'

Karen's eyes widened in terror.

'There are three fire engines here,' Stephanie said, trying to keep matters calm. 'It'll be under control very soon.'

'Ring Zhang's number,' Banham said to Alysha. 'Tell him you've got what he wants. Ask him for an address.'

Stephanie turned to Karen. 'The fire brigade will keep us informed on the fire. Don't worry, everything will get put out,' she told her. 'There are no residents in the next flats. We vacated them this morning.'

'You must keep him talking,' Banham told Alysha, nodding to the TIU manager to tune into the call.

Alysha rang the last number that Zhang had rung from. He picked up within seconds.

'Have you got her?'

Alysha looked at Georgia, and then Banham. Both were nodding their heads. 'Yes. She's with me.'

'Bring her to the warehouse, by Katharine Docks. You know the one I mean.'

Banham shook his head and turned his finger in a circular movement as a signal for Alysha to keep him talking.

'Where will Tink be?'

'With me.'

'How many of yous going?'

'That's for me to know, and you to wonder.'

'No,' Alysha said watching Banham, who was still circling his finger for her to keep talking. 'You and I both know I can't trust your word. I need to know I am gonna get Tink, and that she is OK.' Banham was nodding his head and fluttering his fingers still, urging her to keep Zhang on the line. TIU hadn't got the location yet.

'Put her on,' Alysha said, 'So I know she is still there and OK.' She watched as Banham still signalled for more time. 'Let me talk to Tink,' Alysha all but shouted.

'I don't take orders from you, cunt,' came the reply.

'It's not an order. I need to know you'll keep your end of the bargain. I need to know Tink –'

'Then do as you're fucking told, and get a fucking move on.' The line went dead.

'Did you get it? Did you trace the call?' Lox shouted anxiously to the TIU technician.

Lionel and his assistant were both shaking their heads, disappointment written over their faces. 'We needed twenty more seconds,' Lionel said.

'Well, we know the phone's on,' Stephanie said to Lionel. 'And you've got the number. Trace its whereabouts,' she said.

'Or do we go to the warehouse, without Karen, and try and get Tink that way?' Lox asked Banham.

'In all probability he won't have Tink there,' Banham told her. 'And my guess is he isn't there anyway. He turned back to Lionel. 'How long will it take to trace that number's locality?

'He's just turned the phone off,' came a shout from Bruce, the other technical assistant. 'He knows what he's doing.'

'Let's hope Tink is still OK, and that she's there with him,' Georgia said.

'She is, I spoke to her my ...' Alysha said, and then her voice trailed off. She looked at Lox and Panther. 'You mean ...'

Banham turned to Stephanie. 'I want every available officer on this, now, tell everyone to stop whatever they are doing and get onto this. Put them all on standby, near St Katharine Docks. The whole team. He won't be far from there.'

Alysha looked at Lox, and then Panther, and then over to Georgia, and then back to Banham. 'I ain't letting you play wiv Tink's life,' she said solemnly. 'Time is everything for our Tink. And he won't hesitate, he'll just kill 'er if he thinks you're on board.'

'I'm afraid I am making this decision,' Banham said firmly. 'Everyone get in the cars. Karen and Alysha with me.' He turned to Stephanie. 'Give the gun team the address, and let's get going.'

Chapter Nineteen

Georgia helped Karen into the passenger seat at the front, beside Banham, leaving Alysha, Panther and Lox to share the back.

'I need to be in the front,' Panther told Banham after settling in the back. 'I get claustro-whatsits, in the back of a motor. It takes me back to me tomming days, I'm –'

'I'm not listening,' Banham said loudly, at the same time turning the police radio up to full.

Alysha's mind was fully on Tink. Had she done the right thing, or had she put her best friend's life in danger? She turned and watched Georgia and Stephanie climb into their car behind, then Stephanie gun the engine and turn, in one, then roar out of the car park, speeding up the road.

Banham was the exact opposite, he was being cautious. Alysha watched him check his mirror to make sure the TIU van was close on his heels. She knew he needed to keep them close by so, if Zhang rang, he could pull up quickly and get Alysha and her phone into TIU to get a trace on the call. Alysha was frighteningly aware how much danger she had put Tink in. DCI Banham was going to make sure there was a CO19 gun unit in place, and a fleet of unmarked CID cars too, before he drove to Zhang's meeting place. Alysha wondered if Banham truly knew how dangerous the EIBs were. They were cold-blooded killers; but then, she also knew she couldn't take them on alone.

She looked back as they drove out of the estate. She

could see fire officers aiming heavy water jets at the flames, which were now leaping and jumping from all sides of the Rook block in the heavy wind. She thought of the pain Tink must have endured as flames shrivelled the skin on her body, and wondered if their dream of a crime-free estate was even worth it. The feds didn't care; they only used the girls for the information they wanted. Alysha knew, only too well, that for every Alley Cat there were a hundred others from some gang or other, all ready to kill or maim the ACs in order to move in and sell drugs on the Aviary, just so those same gang members could buy anything they thought they needed to gain respect on the streets. How she wished she and Tink and Panther and Lox lived somewhere else, or even in another time.

Stephanie kept her eyes and attention on the traffic as she drove at speed, swerving in and out of cars along the main road, her blue light flashing and shrieking above her, hurrying and aiding her way to get to St Katharine Docks in record time.

'After all those girls have tried to do,' Georgia said, shaking her head and half speaking out loud as she watched the cars pulling into the side of the road to allow them access. 'It took hard work and guts to build that estate back, and now its burning again.'

'It's a tough world around here,' Stephanie told her, keeping her eyes on the road as she swung around a keep left sign, on its right hand side. 'In case you hadn't noticed.'

'They've had it tougher than most,' Georgia argued. 'Four sixteen- and seventeen-year-old girls, making an effort to clean up their own estate, and give residents chances and keep them safe. They should be given medals. All the DCI seems to give them is a hard time.'

'Remember the rules, ma'am,' Stephanie told her,

briefly flicking her a glance. 'We don't get emotionally involved.'

'I'm not.'

Stephanie flicked her a knowing glance. 'If you say so.'

'Did you get a negotiator,' Banham's voice came through the radio at that moment.

'I didn't manage that, sir,' Stephanie told him.

'Right, so I'll do it,' he told her. 'When you get to St Katharine, give us your exact location, but make sure you stay right out of sight, until I tell you we are approaching.

'Will do.'

'And keep me informed when CO19 are in place, and how many other pool cars are around, and where.'

'Will do, sir.'

The noise of Karen's continual pressing of buttons on her mobile, as she played Candy Crush, was making Panther's nerves worse.

'D'you have to play with that now?' Panther snapped at Karen. 'My nerves are doing somersaults in case anything happens to Tink. That continuous clicking is driving me mental. Can you put it away just for a bit?'

Karen shrugged, then clicked a few more times. 'Sorry,' she said giggling, and then frowning, as she put her phone in her pocket.

Alysha shook her head at Panther. 'Be nice,' she whispered. 'She's lost everything.'

Stephanie's mobile chirped a rendition of 'Stayin' Alive'. She pulled her phone from her pocket and threw the phone to Georgia.

Georgia checked the caller ID. 'It's TDC Hank Peacock,' she told Stephanie as she pressed the green button to answer.

'I hope this is good news,' Georgia said to him. 'And, important.'

Banham had only gone a few roads out of the estate, when he pulled over. The TIU van pulled over behind him.

He looked back at Alysha.

'No call,' she said. 'He's gone very quiet. I hope he don't know what we're doing.'

'You're going to ring Jo Zhang again,' Banham told her. 'Tell him you've got what he wants, and insist you speak to Tink.' He opened the driver's door and got out and opened the back door to let Alysha out. 'You three stay here,' he told Panther, Lox and Karen. 'We won't be more than a few minutes. I'm locking you in.'

Before Panther had the time to argue her claustrophobia problem, he had clicked his car key to locking mode, and was guiding Alysha into the back of the TIU van which had parked up behind him.

'Go ahead, ring that last number,' he told her as Lionel the TIU technician was putting earphones over his ears and connecting a jack plug to an amplifier ready to record the conversation.

'Keep him talking this time, as long as you can,' Banham added. 'If I've got a CO19 team at St Katharine Docks, I want to make sure they can get George Zhang in their eye line.'

'It's ringing,' Alysha said after pressing the redial.

Zhang picked up. Alysha looked at Banham.

Banham nodded back, signalling her to start talking and keep going.

'I'm ringing to tell you I'm doin' what you said,' she said keeping her voice completely calm. 'I've got Karen, like you asked, and I'm on my way over in a cab. I've got Panth and Lox with us. I'm being straight and giving it you on a plate. But I don't trust you. I wanna know Tink is safe.'

'She's here.'

'I only got your word for that. I wanna talk to her so I know for sure, an' she tells me you ain't hurt her.'

'You have spoken to her. I've got her, that's all you need to know.'

'No it ain't. I need to know from her that all is fine, not from you, so put her on and then I'll deliver as you ask.'

'You'll get to talk to her when you give me Karen Hardy.'

'I ain't giving you no one till I know my mate is still OK. Just let me talk to her. Just quickly, that's all I ask.'

'I'm not a patient man.'

Alysha raised her voice and the steel she was made of came through in that moment. 'And I ain't lettin' you play wiv my mate's life. So, just put her on, and then I'm on my way, and you can have Karen.'

'When I see Karen Hardy, you see Tink.'

'I ain't asking to see her, I'm asking to talk to her.'

'Not until I know you have Karen.'

Alysha looked at Banham. He turned his finger around and around in a motion that she knew meant the TIU unit needed more time to trace the call.

'You're def in Katharine Docks?'

'I told you I was.'

'Whereabouts? By The Brewers pub, are you near there?' she asked, now trying to get her nervous brain to think clearly and make conversation.'

'Yes.'

'Give me an exact location, I got a cab fare to pay, an' I gotta tell him where to go?

There was a loud sigh. Zhang raised his voice. 'Katharine Docks. Bring her to there.'

'I ain't bringing her, till I hear Tink speak to me,' she said. 'Just put her on, an' we got a deal.'

239

He hung up.

Banham looked at Lionel who shook his head and pulled the earphones off. Banham threw his hands in the air.

'Well, sort of good, ma'am,' Hank Peacock said to Georgia. 'And bad, depending on which way you look at it. 'I've been sitting here re- reading the forensic reports and studying those pictures that we have on the case.'

'Yes, and?'

'Well, I've had the photo of Karen Hardy blown up, like Sergeant Green and you told me. I think you wanted to get the registration of the car the girl was leaning into.'

'Did you get it?'

'No, it's not clear, but I can see by the front that the car is a Porsche. And it's red. It suddenly occurred to me that it was a red Porsche that was torched this morning down in Peckham, the one belonging to Ray Maxted.'

'That's interesting. Can you see her face clearly enough to read an expression?

'No, ma'am, unfortunately it's not that clear, but she is leaning in over the car, and then there's a photo of her in it. And that territory, just outside Waters Lane, is known to be pimped by the Zhangs these days,' Hank added.

'So, if it is Maxted's Porsche, why was Maxted talking to Karen Hardy and why was she in his car, and on EIB territory? Georgia spoke out loud. 'And not his lieutenants either, but Maxted himself. Surely he didn't fancy her? And did she even know it was EIB territory?

'Perhaps Zhang made her whore for him, to pay some of the debt, and that's why Larry stabbed him.'

'But the girls said themselves she didn't make any money at it, and she did it to help her mum.'

Stephanie was still weaving in and out of traffic at speed, although she was listening. 'Blow up the photo again,' she shouted. 'Blow it up from all directions. See if you can get any more that way.'

'Did you get that? Georgia asked him.

'Yes, ma'am.'

'Make it a priority and get straight back to me.'

'There's something else, ma'am.'

'What?'

'There's more here from Forensics. It appears the knife that was found in Waters Lane was definitely the one that stabbed Veronica Andrew.'

'Yes?'

'It's exactly the same shape and size as the knife that delivered the fatal wound that punctured Ji Zhang's lung, it is definitely the one that Larry Hardy used to kill him. They already said it was a possibility it is the same one that was used on Veronica Andrews, but now they say it's only a one in a hundred chance that it isn't.'

Stephanie slammed her breaks on. She looked at Georgia.' You aren't telling me Larry Hardy was working with the RIPs, are you?' she said.

'A lot of knives are very similar in size and shape, depending on where it was bought. The knife we have recovered isn't *that* unusual, but it does have that distinctive double prong.'

'And it does have Martin Baxter's DNA on it,' Georgia pointed out.

'Then how did it get from Larry Hardy to Martin Baxter?' Stephanie said. 'Unless Larry Hardy stabbed Ji Zhang for the RIPs, to pay off his mother's debts. Martin Baxter hid the knife and then used it on Veronica Andrews. Which is why Larry was hanged when he went on remand.'

Georgia nodded. 'Sounds very feasible.'

* * *

241

Alysha jumped when her phone rang again. They had just climbed out of the TIU van and were about to get back in Banham's car. She read the caller ID and turned the phone so Banham could see it was Zhang ringing back.

Banham nodded for her to answer it, immediately steering her back into the TIU van as she clicked *Answer*. Then a loud scream came through her phone.

Alysha recognised the scream, 'You bastard, you cunt and fucker. If you hurt her I swear I'll –'

'Oh, dear,' Zhang said calmly. 'She's got a very pink ear.'

'You bastard, if you …'

He'd hung up, again. Alysha kicked the door to the TIU van, and started shouting.

'I ain't playing nice guys with you lot. Let them girls out of your car. I've decided we ain't risking Tink wiv you lot. We're doing this on our own.'

'Alysha, calm down,' Banham told her. 'You'll never get Tink on your own. We have a skilled team with us, so calm down and we'll do our job. We will get her back and I promise he'll get what he deserves for this.'

She calmed down but shook her head. 'If 'e even gets a sniff the feds are around, 'e'll kill Tink, you know that, don't you. 'E's already hurting her, an' I ain't risking that. So this is goodbye, an' do what you like, but let my girls out of your car.'

Banham stood in front of her. 'This is a police matter, Alysha, and I know what I'm doing.'

'Like fuck you do, get out of my way.'

'Alysha, calm down. If I have to do this without you, I will, but it'll be a lot less dangerous for Tink if you help.'

'Fuck you, how would you feel if someone hurt someone you love?'

There was silence in the TIU van. The team all knew Banham's history.

'I do know how that feels,' he said calmly. He took a deep breath as the memory of his murdered first wife and their tiny baby flooded into his mind. 'And I assure you I will look after all of you. We have a gun unit in place, and a team of first-class detectives. I will not let you attempt to sort this out on your own. He could kill you all.'

Banham's phone rang at that moment, and Georgia updated him on Hank Peacock's news.

'Send a couple of detectives and a team of uniform back-up with them, over to Peckham to re-arrest Ray Maxted, and bring him in for further questioning.

Georgia looked at Stephanie, who was listening. She winked at her. 'Delighted,' she said jovially.

Banham took Alysha's arm. 'Just before you get back in the car,' he said, reminding her that it was going ahead as he planned, 'DI Johnson has photographic proof that Karen has been talking to Ray Maxted. We also know she has been working the streets on Zhang's patch. Do you have any idea why she would have been talking to Maxted?'

Alysha frowned. 'What? I dunno. I didn't even know she knew who he was. She's stupid, we all know that.'

'Is it possible he could have been her mother's supplier?'

'Yeah, he coulda been, as well as Zhang. They both coulda been. Lisa owed corn to everybody. So anyone who would supply to her, she'd have it. Which is why she got her family in such a mess.'

Alysha frowned again, and the thought occurred to her that when Karen was playing a game on her phone just now, the background music was Marley music. Lox had said there were Marley posters all over Maxted's flat in Peckham. But then, everyone loved Bob Marley…

She shrugged. 'Dunno. D'you want me to ask her?'

'Not yet.'

Alysha's phone then flashed a text. It was from Zhang. It read, "*Crane Street, number three. Be there and bring K, or pick up your friend's body within the hour.*"

Alysha stared at the message. Banham took the phone from her hand and read the text. He then handed the phone to Lionel.

'This phone may still be on if he just sent that text. See if you can get an exact location for it.' He reached out and pulled a stool from the side of the van. 'Sit down,' he told Alysha, gently. 'We're going to make sure he isn't sending us on a wild goose chase.'

Alysha was glad to sit down. She wanted to think. Karen was dangerous, not because she was a bad girl but because she couldn't help it, she did and said stupid things, she didn't have enough capacity to do things right, and that made her a liability. Still, she was an Aviary resident, she had lost her family, and the Alley Cats were going to look after her, because that was what they did.

A few minutes past, during that few minutes, veins of worry were creeping through Alysha's brain. Karen was stupid enough to befriend both Zhang and Maxted. *Had* her mother used Karen to get her much-needed drugs?

Trainee Detective Constable Hank Peacock looked at the blown-up photos. He'd had enlarged them from every conceivable angle. The close-up of Karen showed her smiling as she leaned over the open car window into Ray Maxted's Porsche. The one of Maxted showed he had a wad of notes in his hand. Maxted was buying Karen for sex? Or was he paying her to help her mother? Forensics were ninety-nine per cent sure that the knife Tink was stabbed with was the same as the one that Ji Zhang had been killed with. So how did it get from the school to

Maxted? He had to have an RIP member in the school. Yet the RIPs were in a completely different postcode, so it had to be Larry Hardy.

Hank phoned his information through to Georgia, who then phoned it through to Banham.

'Larry had to be involved in the RIP gang, and probably was doing it to help his mother,' he told his DCI.

The waving of Lionel's hand took Banham's attention at that moment. 'I'll call you back,' Banham said as he clicked off.

'Phone is on, and we got a location,' Lionel told him. 'It's near St Katharine Docks. We are trying to get in as close as we can. Can you give me another minute?'

'Ring him again,' Banham told Alysha, handing her back her phone. 'Keep him talking and don't let him hang up this time.'

Alysha noticed herself shaking as Zhang picked up the call. 'Now what?' he snapped.

At that same second Lionel lifted his two thumbs in the air, and peeled the earphones away from his ears to let them know he had finished the job, he could confirm the location.

Alysha clammed up and didn't speak.

There was a few seconds where everyone was looking at Alysha. She held the phone in her ear and everyone could hear the officious tone of George Zhang shouting, 'What, what is it? Why the call?'

Banham reached over and put a reassuring hand on Alysha's shoulder, he gently put the phone back to her ear and gave her an encouraging nod.

That did it; she found her voice, even though it was weak and tiny. 'Just to let you know I got the text, we'll be there very soon,' she said gaining confidence as she spoke. 'Have Tink ready. Don't you dare hurt her again. We'll be there in a few minutes.'

She hung up and looked at Lionel. 'Have you def got the address?' she asked him.

'It's number three, Crane Street.'

Banham was on his phone now. He was briefing the CO19 gun unit. 'We'll be with you in under fifteen minutes,' he said finally before he hung up.

He turned to Alysha. 'You'll have Tink back within the hour,' he told her with a gentle wink. 'Let's go.'

Chapter Twenty

'We're gonna bring Tink home,' Alysha said trying to sound upbeat, as she squeezed into the back of Banham's blue Ford pool car with Panther and Lox. 'Bastard's just rang again. We got the exact address now, and a lot of back-up from feds, so it's gonna be OK.' She turned to Karen who had turned to her and was grinning happily. 'You gotta do is exactly as we tell you, and when we tell you, have you got that?'

'Yeah,' Karen nodded, then turned to look at Lox and a puzzled look spread across her face.

'It's OK,' Lox told her patting her hand which was balanced on the back of her seat. 'It's gonna be fine, you just do as they tell you.'

'What? Do what the feds tell me?' Karen's voice became aggressive. She was getting agitated.

'Yeah, the feds have had to be involved,' Alysha said trying to reassure her.

'But you're safe, an' that's all you need to know, 'cos we're looking after you,' Panther told her.

'Us Alley Cats, we're a team. We help each other,' Karen said in a sing-song manner, her agitation still clear, as she turned her head from Lox to Panther.

Alysha raised her voice and her hand. 'We gotta get Tink back and safe, that's what matters,' she said firmly, in an attempt to keep Karen quiet. Alysha flicked a concerned glance to Panther. Lox leaned in and stroked Karen's hand again.

'It's OK,' Lox told her. 'The wankers won't hurt you. We promise we won't let them.'

Then Karen burst out laughing. 'What, you think you can take on them Chinese?' she said to her.

Now Banham had turned to listen.

'We've got back-up, so we can,' Alysha told her. We got the feds waiting and a CO19 gun team. It's gonna be OK.' Alysha turned to Banham. 'Can we go, let's do this?'

Karen turned to reach for the door handle, but Banham clicked the central locking into place to stop her.

'Calm down, Karen,' Lox said as Panther said, 'It's OK, keep it cool will ya?'

'I ain't goin wiv any feds,' Karen said defiantly. 'I got my own plans.'

Banham gunned the engine and pulled out into the road.

Alysha lowered her eyes and took a deep breath. She flicked a concerned look at Lox and Panther. 'What's the problem, Karen?' she asked her. 'Has this got anyfing to do wiv Ray Maxted?'

Karen's hand flew in the air. 'What, you jealous or somefing?' she shouted with such aggression that it took all three girls, and Banham, by surprise. He braked immediately and pulled over.

'Jesus, Karen?' Alysha said, clicking her tongue against her teeth, and looking at Banham, and then back to Karen. 'Has Maxted got to you? Have you been talking to him?'

'He loves me,' Karen shouted back, stunning them all into a shocked silence. 'An' I love him.'

'If this weren't serious, it would be funny,' Panther said.

The three girls turned to look at each other, then Banham said calmly, 'What are you saying, Karen?'

Karen put her finger in her mouth and became agitated as she realised all eyes were on her.

'You were working the streets for him?' Lox said to her. 'We knew about that. Did he make you? Or was it 'cos he said he loved you?'

Karen's cheeks had turned flushed with excitement, she couldn't keep still. She started bouncing around in her seat. ''E loves me, 'e's gonna marry me.' Then she became angry, as quickly as she had become excited. 'An' you're all jealous,' she shouted.

Alysha looked at Banham and then raised her voice. 'Tell me 'e don't know 'bout this,' she said, trying to control her urge to grab the girl and hit out at her as she thought of the danger that Tink was in.

'I texted him,' Karen boasted. 'Told him we was going to Katharine Docks. The RIPs are going there. They're gonna kill everyone.'

Panther grabbed Karen's hand, as Lox leaned over and wrestled the phone from her pocket. She quickly scrolled through the messages. Then looked up. 'She weren't playing Candy fucking Crush,' Lox told them. 'It says here, *Katharine Docks*, and he's texted back, *On way with crew.*'

Banham turned the engine back on and hit the accelerator. At the next traffic lights he called through to Georgia. 'We've got the thumbs up on the address, he told her. 'It's number three, Crane Street.'

'OK. We're at the Docks,' Georgia said calmly. 'We'll be at address in two minutes, I know where it is. We'll stay out of sight until you tell us to go in.'

Karen was now starting to struggle, and trying to get the door open. 'Let me outta here.' She screamed. 'Let me out. I wanna get out.' She attempted to fight Panther who had reached over and was holding her down with one large hand, but quickly realising she was no match for

Panther, she started to cry like a baby.

'Don't hurt me,' she whimpered.

'OK. But keep still. You can't get out. Got that?'

Karen nodded. Panther released her grip. Karen started howling.

'Let her play Candy Crush,' Lox said throwing Karen's phone back. 'Don't cry, Karen. It's OK.' Lox turned back to Panther who was shaking her head about returning the phone.

'Don't give her the phone,' Panther said.

'It'll keep her occupied,' Lox argued. 'And she can't do no more damage. The RIPs are on their way to the Dock.'

Banham put his foot on the accelerator. His mind was now on the fact he had a gang war, and a vulnerable highly injured girl to get out and keep alive.

Alysha too had her mind on Tink's welfare. She would leave dealing with Karen till later. Tink needed her. She knew Tink should be back in hospital, not taking another beating. She turned away and looked out of the window to hide the anger that was building inside her.

Then the voice of Ray Maxted rang through the car. Neither Lox nor Panther had noticed Karen stab one digit into her phone. The digit that dialled Maxted's mobile.

'Baby doll,' he said, obviously knowing it was Karen on the other end.

In the second that it took Alysha and Lox and Panther to register what Karen had done and to lean in and grab the phone back, Karen had screamed out. 'Crane Street, number three. I'm prisoner 'ere,' but Panther had her large brown hand over Karen's mouth, and her other hand wrestled the phone. Lox took it and shut it off.

'Stupid cow,' Panther said to her, slapping her across the back of the head. 'Now we're in the shit.'

Alysha's temper boiled over. She leaned in and

grabbed Karen by the front of her dungarees. 'Did you know it was Maxted who hurt our Tink?'

'Alysha, sit down.' It was the voice of Banham. 'Now.'

Alysha ignored him. She raised her voice. 'Did you know he was gonna burn my sister, you fucker,' she shouted, banging her knee several times into the back of Karen's chair.

'I said, sit back down,' Banham kept his eyes on the road, his foot on the accelerator and his voice calm. 'This will all be sorted. Now sit down before you could cause an accident.'

Alysha did as she was told. Tink's life was at stake. Sorting out Karen could wait.

'Ray loves me,' Karen shouted as Alysha turned back round and settled back in her seat. 'He'll be there an' he'll shoot you all. He's got more guns than you'll ever know 'bout.'

Banham slammed his foot on the brake and pulled over again. He rang Georgia and relayed the news. He said he had been told that the RIP gang were on their way and were armed, so to make sure CO19 were in place before any police went anywhere near Crane Street.

'She's bloody unbelievable,' Alysha said, shaking her head.

'You've been selling information to the feds,' Karen shouted back at her.

'Shut your mouth,' Panther warned.

Karen laughed. 'I told Ray 'bout you being a grass, an' he's gonna kill yous all.'

'You told him that?' Alysha shouted. She was very angry, but now she was also afraid. Every gang member in London knew only too well, it didn't matter what gang you were in, the penalty for grassing to the feds was a death sentence. And any and every gang member would happily do the honours and take you out. No one talked to the feds without paying the punishment. And now, thanks to Karen, the only thing the Alley Cats' futures held was a bullet in each of their heads. Every gang member around London would be after their blood. If they got Tink out of this alive, sooner, rather than later, they would all be pushing up daisies.

'I don't believe you told Maxted that we was informing,' Panther said trying to get the truth from her, as Banham gunned the engine again and drove at break neck speed through the traffic. 'That ain't true, anyhow.'

'I never needed to tell him nothing, he already knew,' Karen shouted back. 'Ray's really clever. He's been watching you, since you stole all their guns and drugs an' hid them at my mum's. He was worried for me, so he watched you. He knows all 'bout you.'

Alysha watched Banham him pull a recorder from his pocket and switch it to *On*. Either way, she knew she was done.

'So why didn't he get the gear back then, from your place. If he's so fucking clever,' Lox asked, digging Karen hard in the shoulder.

'We was gonna let you sell them all, do all the work for it, an' then raid you for the money,' Karen laughed.

'I don't sell drugs, or ammo,' Alysha said firmly, without even a glance in the very silent Banham's direction. 'I ban 'em from the Aviary. Them drugs were EIB drugs, Ray stole 'em from the Chinese, and tried to bring 'em on my territory to sell 'em to our young 'uns, so we confiscated them from 'im. We never gave them to the feds 'cos we knew how badly your mum was in debt, and the corn from them would have paid her debts off for her.'

Karen didn't answer so Alysha carried on talking. She knew that Banham was recording the conversation, and wanted to get the truth on record. 'Your mum was in debt

252

out of her depth. We took the gear to yours, to help her, to keep her dealers from hurting her, or you, or Larry. We hid them at yours, so she would have something to offer if they came after her. When we'd all got enough to pay off her debts, we were handing them to the police; it was the security that your family needed to keep your mum from getting you all hurt. We was trying to help you, Karen.' She looked at Banham. His face gave nothing away, but his recording machine was flashing its light, and she knew now, whatever happened, however this went, her and the Alley Cats were finished, they would pay a high price for trying to right the wrongs on the Aviary Estate.

Karen was still increasingly agitated. 'You stole the gear from Ray,' she shouted back. 'He'll get you. He'll kill you.'

'The gear was on our territory. The RIPs came on and tried to give brown and other Class A gear to our young 'uns. 'She spoke in an open and even tone, and then turned to Banham and opened up. 'The RIP gang hid that gear on the Aviary, and we caught them doing it. We have spent the last two years trying to stop all that, and make the estate clean, and keep the kids from getting into all that shit. And on they come, large as fucking life, going to hand out free heroin and coke, 'cos they stole it from the Zhangs and it was easy come, easy go. So they decided to use it to ruin our kids again, after all we'd done to stop all that. No one understands what it's like living on the Aviary. We'd worked to rebuild it. It was starting to do good things, and those Chinese fuckers burnt it all down. All our hard work.'

Banham didn't answer. His stony face said it all. Alysha shrugged.

'Council wouldn't give us another grant, an' we saw an opportunity to get some money for the Hardys, and the next rebuild,' she said, now deciding to tell him how it

253

really was. 'You said you'd talk to the council for us, but you didn't, no one did. We knew we had to rebuild the community centre an' the kid's play area, an' the judo club an' dancing classes if we was to keep our kids out of trouble an' crime, an' we was desperate to do that.'

Banham still said nothing. The green light still flashed on the recorder.

'We had to keep drugs away from the kids too,' she said. 'So, we took 'em.' She turned to Karen. 'We decided to sell the drugs and guns to help your mum with her debts, and try and persuade her to go into rehab, we would have paid for her, and then used the rest to rebuild the community centre. Loads of residents were gonna help this time, so it wouldn't 'ave been as 'ard.' She turned back to Karen. 'We wanted to help your mum, which is why I got Larry to hide the gear in your flat.' She looked at Banham again. He was shaking his head to let her know she had let him down, big time.

'By the time I had thought it out, I knew I shouldn't have hidden the gear, that I should have given it to feds, but it was all too late. Larry had shanked Zhang for threatening your mum and everything was standing on its head.' She put her hands to her head. 'We had just tried to help you all, but it all went wrong.'

Karen was silent for a moment, then she said, 'Ray told me you'd taken all his clothes and driven him into EIB territory and chucked him out of the car, naked.'

'He deserved a lot worse,' Lox snapped back.

Karen turned to Banham. 'You should lock her up!' she shouted.

Alysha caught Banham's eye. Through all this he had remained silent, but his recorder was running, and she was fully aware that she had admitted to a very serious crime. There was no going back: police informant or not, she was in very big trouble.

'I did what I did,' she said quietly.

Karen laughed. 'My mum owed money to Ray, so I shot her,' she blurted out, immediately silencing everyone in the car.

'What?' Lox said, after a quiet few seconds.

'Ray gimme a gun, and sent one of his gang to get it and the gloves I had to wear. He came on a bike.'

'You shot your mum?' Alysha repeated loudly. She was genuinely shocked, but couldn't have guessed what Karen was about to say next.

'Yeah.'

'Because she owed Ray Maxted money?'

'And 'cos she found out that it was me what shanked Ji Zhang, and it weren't Larry.'

'*You* shanked Ji Zhang? Panther said, turning her horrified face to Alysha.

'It wasn't Larry, it was you?' Alysha repeated. 'You shanked Zhang's brother? Why, for fuck's sake, Karen, why?'

Karen giggled. The sound was unusual; a sound, perhaps, that one would associate with madness.

'You shanked Ji Zhang? And then you told Maxted where Zhang's stash was in your flat, and then you shot your mum,' Alysha repeated, scratching her forehead and shaking her head.

Karen shrieked with laughter. She seemed to be getting a little more hysterical the more she spoke. 'And I set the flat on fire.'

Alysha looked at Panther and then back to Banham. 'You burned the Rook block?' Alysha was shaking her head.

'An' I burned Tink's shop, and that fucker of a Community Hall,' Karen shouted, proudly. 'An' I set fire to the kid's playground after Tink spent the weekend building it and painting it all fucking pretty.'

255

'But why? Why, Karen?' Alysha half cried as she turned to Lox and Panther. 'After all our work? After all we done for you. Why d'you do that, Karen? We was trying to help you. We wanted you to have a chance, and your mum to go to rehab. An' we wanted the kids on the estate to have choices. We wanted to prove to everyone that said if you come from an estate like ours you either die young, or spend your life in prison. We wanted a future for the next generation of kids. We tried so hard,' Alysha was nearly crying now. 'We was having sports and cards for the pensioners an' dance and music and stuff. It was gonna be so good. Fings were gonna be fun on the Aviary, it was new beginnings. Everything was gonna be different. No one was gonna be bullied or live in fear, not ever again, 'cos the ACs would sort their corner, always be there for our residents, old or young.'

'An' she fucked all that,' Lox spat at her.

Karen came back at her. 'What makes you fink you can be different? Who the fuck you think you are?'

'Why did you burn your own home an' *our* estate, Karen?' Panther asked her in a calm voice.

'It ain't your estate, it's Ray's. An' it got in his way. I weren't gonna let them listen to you lot, to go and do stupid stuff like sing and dance and play fuckin' table tennis. So I burnt it all.' She started to laugh again but was stopped as Panther lifted her large brown hand and slapped her hard in the face.

Lox immediately joined in, yanking Karen's hair so hard it nearly came out. 'You fucking little bitch!' she shouted.

Then all the girls were on Karen, punching and pulling her hair and slapping out at her. 'You stupid fucking cow,' they were shouting.

Banham stopped the car. He turned quickly, and leaning over from his seat, he quickly pulled the girls apart. 'Stop it. Stop it!' he shouted. 'This isn't your job. It's ours.

'Karen Hardy, I'm arresting you for the murders of Ji Zhang and Lisa Hardy, and for the arson attacks on the Aviary Estate. You don't have to say anything, but anything you do say may be taken down and used in evidence, do you understand?'

'Fuck off.'

'Please, we gotta help Tink,' Alysha said, her voice now merely a whisper. 'An' we need her to do it.' She raised her voice. 'You are gonna come wiv us, Karen, and you are gonna help us get Tink safe, do you hear me?'

'An' I fuckin 'ope Zhang kills you in the process,' Panther spat at Karen.

'Can we get going?' Alysha said. Her eyes were dry but the weight of her heart was becoming too much to bear. All she had done was try to stop others on the estate having to go through what she had as a desperate, lonely and hungry child. She pushed her own thoughts from her mind and concentrated on Tink. 'Tink's life's at stake here,' she said to Banham.

'We'll get her,' Banham said. 'But you have to know, you are all under arrest too.'

Alysha nodded. 'I know. 'But not Tink, don't include 'er, she ain't part of all this.'

'Georgia is getting the riot police on standby, too,' he told her. 'We'll go as soon as that's in hand.' He looked at Alysha, and shook his head. 'Why?' he said shaking his head raising his eyes to heaven. 'That's a custodial sentence for you, you know that don't you, and you know we can't help you.'

Alysha nodded. 'I know,' she said. 'I was desperate. It were all my idea, leave the others out of this.'

'Not me,' Panther said. 'I was with you, Queen. I'm as guilty as you are.'

257

Lox opened her mouth to say the same, but Alysha smacked her knee with her own. 'Not Lox, she weren't with us then.' She mouthed to Lox, 'Don't, Tink needs you.'

At the same moment Alysha's phone rang. It was Zhang. She picked up.

'We're waiting.'

'We're on our way. We got what you want, but we're in traffic.' She hung up.

It seemed like an age before Banham's phone rang with the news that the riot police were a few roads from Crane Street. CO19 was in position on the roof of all the buildings in sight of the warehouse and were standing by, and the whole of Georgia's team of detectives were in place. She also told him that cars packed with known RIP gang members from Peckham had been spotted speeding into the area, and that Ray Maxted had just passed her on a motorbike, and turned off the main road and was heading for Crane Street.

'Remember Tink's safety is our priority,' he told Georgia, so do nothing until we get there.'

Banham then gunned his engine and pulled out into the traffic, his foot flooring the accelerator as the speed dial left seventy and touched eighty miles an hour along the middle of the busy main road.

'We'll get done for speeding,' Panther shouted.

'They'll have to catch us first,' Banham told her. 'Ray Maxted seems to have arrived in Crane Street. We need to arrest him before Zhang kills him.'

'With luck they'll kill each other,' Lox shouted over the roar of the engine.

258

Chapter Twenty-one

They hit St Katharine Docks in under twenty minutes. Georgia was on the radio shouting directions of where every officer, or unit was, as Banham screeched into the side road near Crane Street. He pulled up beside her and wound his window down.

'The whole area is locked down,' Georgia told him. 'Uniform teams are on the outskirts of surrounding streets in cars and meat wagons, all ready to go in and arrest when called. Our team are in unmarked cars lined along adjoining streets, and the CO19 gun unit is on the rooves of the houses opposite the warehouse in Crane Street.'

Before Banham had the chance to ask if they knew for sure Tink was in there, and still alive, Georgia said, 'We know Tink is in there.' She glanced at Alysha as she added, 'We heard her scream.' The concern in her tone was evident.

'Let's move,' Banham said speaking in the flat tone he used when he was hiding his own feelings.

'There's yet another gang trying to get through into the roads west of Crane Street, but vans of riot officers are holding them back as we speak,' Georgia added. 'I'm told they are mainly Chinese.'

'RIP gang are in the area too, so let's move it,' Banham said gunning the car into action. 'Keep pinned to the radio. He then said to Alysha.

'I'm going to drive into Crane Street. I want you to get

259

out of the car, knock on number three, which is a warehouse, and ask to see Tink. CO19 are covering you. You are very safe, even a hint that Zhang is armed and they'll shoot.'

'What if Tink is with him?' Alysha asked.

'The team have perfect aim, Banham assured her. 'If he so much as shows any sign of holding a knife or gun, CO19 will take him out, and Tink will be safe.'

''K,' Alysha nodded, putting her hand on the door to open it.

'Good luck, Queen,' Lox said softly to her.

'She don't need it. We'll have Tink home and safe 'fore you can say nuffink,' Panther told Lox, winking at Alysha at the same time. Karen opened her mouth to argue but Panther snaked her big hand around the girl's neck, covering her mouth.

'We ain't interested,' she told her. 'So fucking button it.'

'If he tells you to go in the building, you say "no". Are you very clear on that?' Banham told her firmly.

Alysha nodded.

'If we can't see you, we can't protect you. You tell him you have Karen. She's out here, in the waiting taxi, and they must bring Tink out to you. When we have Tink safely in this car, then we'll move in and arrest Zhang.'

Alysha flicked a glance at Panther and Lox, and then nodded.

'Once we see Tink, we take over,' Banham told her. 'That is a clear order. You are to move away and leave things to us. Have you got that?'

'He'll ask to see Karen first,' Panther pointed out.

Banham nodded his agreement to that. 'So he can. Alysha will point to her in the front of the car, and you and Lox will make sure she doesn't get out.' He looked at Karen. 'And you are to sit tight, do you hear me?'

'Ray'll sort you all out,' Karen said, curling her lip as she spoke to Banham. 'He'll shoot you all.'

'Shut up!' Lox told her in a raised voice.

'Ray'll get you!' she shrieked back.

'Shh! Keep it down,' Banham told them. 'You don't know who is around, watching. I'm just the cab driver. So from now on, you just ignore me.'

Karen opened her mouth to shout again, but Panther covered it again with her hand. 'Don't make me smack you,' she said to her, landing her a small slap on the side of the head anyway. ''Cos that's just a starter.'

Karen retorted with a bite at Panther's wrist.

'You little bitch,' Panther told her, landing her a harder smack.

'Shut up,' Banham said sternly as he pinned his eyes around the street they were approaching.

'What if Maxted is around?' Alysha asked him.

'Riot police are under orders to stop any person, or any car, going up Crane Street, once we go in there. Anyone trying to break through the riot officers will be arrested. Any sign of a gun or any kind of weapon and they'll be arrested at best, shot at worst. So no, no chance, and so far it's all under control. He turned into Crane Street, pulled up, and pulled on the handbrake. OK, let's go and get Veronica.'

''K,' Alysha said taking a deep breath. 'And I hope all this'll be taken into consideration when we're in court, charged with concealing firearms and Class A gear.'

'Yes, it will,' Banham nodded solemnly. 'But you are still under arrest.'

'You'll be dead by then,' Karen said in a raised voice. 'Ray knows you're a grass. 'E'll shoot you as soon as 'e sees me.'

'Shut up!' Banham, Alysha, Lox and Panther all said in unison.

Banham relayed the message to CO19, via his radio, that they were now in Crane St.

Jim, the chief officer in this CO19 team confirmed they were in place, and standing by.

'Not a sound,' Banham said in a half-whisper as he nodded to Alysha.

Alysha was cautious as she climbed out of the car. She couldn't see any CO19 on the roofs, but had been around the police long enough to know they knew how to be invisible. Seeing Georgia Johnson standing at the end of the road was reassuring though. She and Georgia had had their spats but Alysha had known her a long while now, and was astute enough to know that deep down Georgia had a soft spot for her and the other three informants, and would run to help her out if anyone went too far.

She had to take a deep breath because the thought of anything happening to Tink right now filled her with more emotion than she could deal with. She couldn't get tearful, that was the last thing anyone needed, so she sniffed hard, looked away from Georgia and ignored her thoughts of her own father, who had only ever used her to make money for himself. Her mother had died long ago, or maybe she had left, Alysha wasn't sure, as she'd never known her, and her father wouldn't talk about it. Her real sister had died years ago, so the Alley Cats had become her family, and she was going to fight with all her strength to keep them safe. Right now, she had to get Tink back to hospital then she would worry about being under arrest.

She flicked another glance at Georgia Johnson. The feds weren't as bad as everyone made out. They just didn't have a clue what it took to survive if you lived on the Aviary. It wasn't their fault either, they'd all had proper dinners and parents who cooked for them while they went to school, they hadn't had to steal or sell drugs to eat. They were just doing their job. She was going to jail, she knew she couldn't save herself from that, but she could save Tink, and that was exactly what she was going to do now.

'Zhang!' she shouted as she approached the door to the old warehouse. 'Zhang, I'm 'ere. Come out, and bring Tink wiv you. I've got what you want. It's out in the street waiting for you.'

There was no answer. After another minute of excruciating silence, she shouted, 'Zhang, I ain't giving you what you want, till I see Tink, and see she's OK.'

She hadn't expected this was going to be easy, but then she hadn't expected Ray Maxted to open the door, holding Tink like a body shield in front of him. He held a gun too, the nozzle of which was boring into Tink's temple. This really took her by surprise. She had to think quickly. The anger and upset she felt as she looked at her friend, burnt and bleeding, welled up so quickly that she nearly sprang at Maxted and attacked him. The only thing that stopped her was the fact that the bastard was holding a gun to the side of Tink's head. Tink's dyed pink hair was completely gone on the side of her skull that the gun bore into; in its place was red, raw, and blistered skin. Her eyes were closed. Alysha didn't even know if she was unconscious or dead.

Alysha held her arms out to Tink. At the same time she studied her closely. The girl's arm was broken, it dangled like a broken puppet's string by her side. It didn't take much to see that she had taken another beating.

If only Alysha had had her much-loved cricket ball in her hand she would have leapt at Maxted and broken his jaw in a heartbeat.

'Did you do this to her, you bastard?' she shouted at him.

'You set my car on fire,' Maxted snarled back, shaking

Tink as she fell in and out of consciousness, and sneering, reminding Alysha of a twisted alligator. 'So I set your friend on fire.' His thumb slid to the trigger on his gun, then he pulled the safety catch away so just the slightest amount of pressure from his finger would send a bullet soaring through Tink's head. Alysha was wondering why the CO19 hadn't shot him. They obviously couldn't get a clear shot with Tink falling and moving and unable to stand still as he held her.

'Stop,' Alysha shouted in panic. 'I got Karen,' she told him, 'CO19 are aimed at you. If you shoot Tink they'll shoot you.'

He looked up and around for the CO19 crew. 'You're lying,' he said. 'Ain't no gun team here.'

'Tink don't deserve this,' she pleaded, wishing with all her might that CO19 would just shoot the bastard and she could watch him squirm and die. 'She ain't nothing to do wiv your car. She was in 'ospital at the time. I set your car on fire 'cos you burned Tink and our community centre. Well, Karen done the burning of the centre actually. But you know that, 'cos you told her to.' She turned her back briefly and pointed to the car full of girls. 'She's over there in the cab.' Tink's good arm lifted momentarily and only a fraction, and then, just as Alysha was about to tell her everything was going to be all right, it fell to Tink's side again as the girl lost consciousness. Alysha took a deep breath. 'Give me Tink,' she almost cried. 'I gotta get her help, she's in a bad way.'

Maxted pulled Tink back as Alysha reached to take her. 'I don't want Karen Hardy,' he said with a shrug and indifference in his tone.

'Ain't she your girl?'

'What, you think I'd hump that lump?'

Alysha was watching every move that Tink didn't make, and was becoming seriously worried. Tink was unconscious. She needed help, and quickly.

'Look, I don't give a pig's fuck who you're humping,' she said. 'I'm here, as agreed, to seal the deal, and get Tink. So where's Zhang, or 'ave you killed 'im?'

'He's tied up in the back with a few of his puny crew,' Maxted told her. 'A few of them are dead.'

Banham had got out of the car at that moment, and had started walking toward them. Maxted stared at Banham then turned back to Alysha.

'He's a fed,' he said to her, aiming the gun at Banham.

'Don't be stupid,' Banham said, lifting his hand to stop CO19 taking Maxted out. He walked closer to Maxted, but stopped a few feet behind Alysha. He indicated to Tink. 'Let her go.'

'Fuck off.' 'Maxted pushed the gun hard into the side of Tink's head. 'I'm out of here, and I'm taking her with me.'

'You're going nowhere,' Banham told him. 'There are a team of armed CO19 officers on the roof above, and opposite. The only reason you are still alive is because I have been telling them to hold off. Right now all their rifles are aimed at your head. One move of that gun and you are a dead man.'

Maxted laughed. 'I ain't swallowing that one.'

'Take a look around the roof.'

Ray looked up. The CO19 officers had now moved further in and stood in full view, rifles aimed at Maxted.

'Where's Zhang, Maxted?' This was the voice of Georgia. She too had now moved from the corner of the road and was standing next to Banham.

Alysha knew she was wearing a bulletproof vest, and was armed, which meant she was prepared for what might be about to happen, and was there to protect Banham. Alysha also knew that Banham wasn't wearing protection. He wouldn't have had time to put any on. He was in danger of being shot, as was she, and Tink's life was very much in question at this second.

'Where's Zhang?' Georgia asked again with more urgency in her tone.

'I've no idea.'

'Drop your gun and hand Tink to us,' she said. 'At the moment you are facing a charge of possessing firearms, and possessing and selling Class A drugs. That in itself is bad enough. If you don't let her go, then you're facing a further charge of kidnap. Don't make this any worse for yourself.'

Maxted didn't move, nor did his gun.

Alysha was watching Tink. Every minute was vital to saving her life, that she could see.

'What is it you want, if you don't want Karen?' Alysha asked him.

'I want a helicopter. I'm going back to Jamaica.'

'He says he's killed some of Zhang's crew,' Alysha said to Banham, not caring now that she was grassing in front of one the most prominent gang leaders in London.

'What are you –?' Georgia's question was interrupted by the voice of the riot police coming over her radio. Another gang had broken through their barriers, they were telling her. There were about a hundred of them, and they were now within yards of Crane Street, the message warned. Word had reached them that Maxted had broken into the warehouse and had taken hostages, and had hurt some of their fellow gang members. But no one had mentioned hearing any shots. So what had become of Zhang?

'Back in the car,' Georgia ordered Alysha. 'Move,' she shouted as Alysha stood her ground next to Tink. Georgia turned back to Maxted. 'Quickly, give me Tink.'

But there wasn't time. All attention was taken by the two ambulances that were parked at the end of Crane

Street. Bricks had started flying and were hitting the vans, as well as the paramedics, who had been anxiously standing by, waiting with a stretcher to help Tink.

One of the female paramedics, waiting by the van's open doors, fell over after catching a brick to the side of her head. Within seconds, over a hundred EIBs charged into Crane Street, followed by riot police, vans, and officers with dogs. Messages for urgent back-up were being desperately shouted into all the police radio systems.

In the hysteria, Panther and Lox, who had been ordered to stay inside the car, had decided enough was enough. Lox opened the car door and jumped out to go and help Alysha and Tink, then, as Panther followed, Karen took the opportunity to leap out of the passenger door, shouting to Ray as she ran, and heading toward him.

Charlie Zhang, Yin Zhang's brother, was at the front of the rioting EIBs and saw her first. Before anyone had the chance to take in what was happening, he had pulled a handgun and fired.

The shot landed in the back of her head. Karen was dead before she hit the ground.

As that happened, he put his hand in the air. 'Mission accomplished,' he shouted to large gang.

'Drop the gun.' It was the voice of Jim Baker, the leader of the CO19 unit. 'Drop the gun *now* or we'll shoot,' he ordered.

A crowd of uniformed police and plain clothes officers hovered nearby, none daring to step too far into the line of fire.

Charlie Zhang was surprised and dropped the gun. Then everything happened at once.

Ray Maxted fired into the Chinese mob. The shot woke Tink up. Alysha threw herself around Tink and as retaliation shots rang through the air from the EIBs, Lox and Panther were legging it over to protect Alysha and Tink. Lox caught a shot in the top of her leg and toppled forward. Panther threw herself over Lox to protect her.

Baker fired, deliberately missing Maxted but making enough of an impact for him to drop his gun. Panther was near enough to reach over and grab it, and before anyone could stop her, she had turned and shot the Chinese EIB gang member who had shot Lox. Banham was beyond furious. he gripped Panther by her arm and forced the gun from her, but the EIB soldier was now lying on the ground squirming in agony.

'It was self-defence,' she shouted as Georgia shouted up to Baker to stop CO19 shooting Panther. They had been under orders to shoot at anyone who fired a gun.

The CO19 team were now off the roofs and all rifles were pointed at the mob, who, on seeing the team with their rifles pointed at them, all dropped their weapons and threw their hands in the air.

More police were now speeding in, their blue-lit vehicles shrieking their warnings, followed by more sirens screaming from arresting meat wagons and more police cars. Uniformed officers were then out of their cars and rounding up the mob and all were being rounded into the vans of prisoners, to be driven away to the station for charging officially.

As Maxted was handcuffed, a paramedic was attaching oxygen to Tink and laying her carefully on the stretcher. A body bag was in a waiting forensic car and Karen was taken away.

Banham then led another team of uniformed officers behind the CO19 team, into the warehouse. CO19 had their guns raised in front of their chests, ready to fire if necessary, as they shouted ordered anyone inside to drop their weapons and put hands in the air. The RIP members that were there all obeyed, and they too were arrested, taken out, and loaded into more vans. Some had to wait at the side of the road while more vans were ordered.

Inside, the police found George Zhang. He had been beaten unconscious, saving him the embarrassment of being arrested in public.

Alysha and Panther were now tending to Lox as the paramedics urgently lifted Tink into the waiting ambulance.

Lox was then picked up in one of the paramedics' arms and placed on the bench opposite her.

As Panther and Alysha went to climb into the back of the ambulance, Banham stepped in their path and stopped them. 'No,' he said noticing the look of question on Georgia's face. 'They are under arrest for the theft of Class A drugs and firearms.'

'What?'

'Make sure the Zhangs and Maxted's lot are in separate vans, for Chrissake,' Banham said to Stephanie.

Police vans were still roaring in and filling up with arrested rioting gang members. Others were being frisked. First they were pushed against walls, hands in the air, while weapon after weapon was confiscated and then the culprits arrested.

Banham had to keep warning the uniformed officers to search them all, in case of incidents in the arresting vans.

Panther and Alysha settled on a nearby wall. Georgia and Stephanie walked up and joined them.

'You've been arrested for that haul in Lisa Hardy's flat,' Georgia said to them. Then she shook her head in disappointment. 'Why? I trusted you.' She let out a large sigh. 'I believed in you, all of you, and I tried to help you. I can't pretend I'm not bitterly disappointed. You lied to me.'

'It weren't like that,' Alysha said, turning her head,

unable to face Georgia.

'Don't bother,' Panther said. 'She don't get it. Feds don't, they never will, and how could we expect them to?'

Georgia ignored this. 'You've really let me down,' she said, 'but worst of all, you have let yourselves down. All this about rebuilding the estate, and making it into something, and giving the youngsters and yourselves chances for the future.'

'The council wouldn't help us, and you wouldn't talk to them. We only confiscated drugs that was brought on our patch. It was to stop them being sold to our young 'uns, and we was trying to 'elp Lisa,' Alysha said.

'And now you are looking at custodial sentences for doing so,' Georgia said, raising her voice and glaring at Alysha. Alysha turned away again.

Georgia calmed down and spoke evenly. 'I will do what I can, and speak for you, but it won't count for much. She shook her head. 'Believe it, you are all going to jail, and for a long stretch.'

'As long as Tink survives,' Alysha said quietly, turning her eyes away, which were full of sadness. Then she turned back to Georgia. 'Keep her out of this. It weren't her, she knew nothing 'bout this,' she lied.

'Get in the car with Stephanie,' Georgia said. 'You are both under arrest.'

'An' it weren't Lox neither,' Panther said looking at Alysha. 'It were just me and Lysh that handled and hid them drugs and guns, we never told Tink nor Lox. We know we done wrong, but we was trying to help the Hardys. Lisa was in big trouble with her debts. We wanted to stop her getting killed.'

'Now look where that led you,' Stephanie said evenly.'

'I did say if you live where we come from it's early death, the streets, or jail,' Alysha reminded her. 'There are no choices,' she added, following Stephanie to the police

270

car. 'We're just stupid enough to think we could change things and do something for the kids and the future.'

'At least we tried,' Panther agreed.

'And failed,' Alysha added.

'It's better to have loved an' lost than never to have loved at all, didn't someone famous say that,' Panther said. 'And we achieved stuff.' Then she shrugged, 'OK, so half the Aviary's been torched, but we've got plans to build it back it up. The council weren't helping, and we weren't gonna let that stop us,' she looked at Georgia. 'We busted two big gangs today for you, I hope you'll take that on board.'

'Yes, you did, and you nearly got yourself and your friends killed doing it,' Georgia answered, then noticing Alysha's sad face, she added, 'I'll make sure the CPS knows all that you have done for the police.'

'Not *all* we done,' Panther argued. 'They'll crucify us inside if they know we informed for you, you know that, don't you.'

'Yes. I'm aware of that,' Georgia told her.

'Putting us in prison won't help no one,' Alysha told her. 'We're the good guys. The Robin Hoods, no, the *robbin'* hoods is better, 'cos as Lox says, we stand up to the bad guys.' She shrugged as she got in the car and Stephanie passed her the back seatbelt. 'You'll always have gang feuds,' she told them. 'It's like we said, once a baron from a territory goes down, another two rise up, and they war each other till one of them wins the territory, and it all starts over again. Feds know fuck all.'

'Is that right?' Georgia said, sliding into the passenger seat.

'You need us out there on the streets,' Panther told her.

'Is that right too?' Georgia said again.

'Yeah, it is right,' Panther argued back. 'You *do* need us out there on the streets. We're better for grassing, 'cos at least we know what's going on. And believe it or not, we are honest.'

'And them gangs will get us if we're inside prison, but outside we stand a chance.'

Georgia and Stephanie made eye contact.

'Those gangs will scatter,' Stephanie said. 'Neither Zhang nor Maxted will get bail. They'll both go down for very long custodials. You'll be OK.'

'Look what happened to Larry Hardy,' Alysha reminded them. 'It's easier to get you in jail than anywhere.'

'We'll keep our eyes on you,' Stephanie said. 'Even in prison.'

Alysha shook her head and looked to Panther. 'Whatever,' she said with a dismissive shrug. 'Told you, if you come from where we come from you don't get a chance of getting old. It's drugs, being shot, or suicide, or you rot in prison.' She looked at Panther again and shook her head. 'That's why we tried so 'ard to make changes and make a difference. Wish we 'ad managed them changes, 'cos that would 'ave been worth dying for.'

Georgia made eye contact with Stephanie again.

272

Chapter Twenty-two
One month later

Georgia was looking very serious as she walked out of her office and headed to Stephanie's desk. 'Guv'nor wants us,' she told her sergeant.

'Both of us? Now what are we supposed to have done?' Stephanie said, putting her spoon back in the yoghurt pot she was eating from and wiping traces of the pink goo from the sides of her mouth.

Georgia frowned, then lifted the pot and carefully examined it. 'This says *low fat*,' she said inquisitively.

'And? Your point?'

'Whenever you eat anything that says *low fat* on the container, it means you're having a new affair.' She looked around at the detectives in the room, and as no one was taking any notice, she moved in on Stephanie, lowered her voice and said, 'so who is it, and why don't I know about it?'

'Nothing to tell,' Stephanie shrugged. 'Just a possibility,' she added lifting both her hands in the air in a defensive gesture. She then got up from her desk and careful to keep her voice down, she spoke confidentially 'It isn't anyone new, it's someone I've had before, and got bored with, but am getting interested in again.' She then turned and headed in the direction of the DCI's office, and stood outside waiting for Georgia to catch her up. When she did, Steph lowered her voice and whispered, 'There was a clue in that.' She lifted her hand to knock on

Banham's door, but Georgia grabbed it and stopped her.

'Every man you've bedded since your marriage split up sixteen years ago, you've got bored with and moved on from,' Georgia reminded her. 'So not much of a clue there. I need another one. Does he work in the department?'

'Sort of.'

'What kind of an answer's that?'

'All you're getting, for now.'

'Jesus!' Georgia's eyes widened. 'It's not the DCI is it?'

Stephanie burst out laughing. 'I wish! But no, he's getting married soon, and he's far too straight-laced to have a bloody good fling before he signs his life away.'

'Are you coming in?'

Georgia and Stephanie both took a deep breath. It was the voice of Banham from inside his door.

'Hope he didn't hear,' Georgia whispered as she knocked and walked in. 'You asked to see us both, guv.'

'Yes.' Banham was sitting behind his desk. Beside him, making them look like an old married couple already, sat Alison Grainger. 'Just a couple of updates for you both,' he said. 'Sit down,' he pointed to the two seats he had put out for them. 'You know Alison and I are getting married in two weeks?'

'Yes, yes, we're looking forward to it,' Georgia said politely.

'And something you don't know, Georgia,' Banham continued, 'but Stephanie does.'

Georgia turned to look at Stephanie. Normally they told each other everything.

'I told Stephanie to keep it to herself for now. I wanted to be the one to tell you,' Banham added quickly. 'Alison will be leaving us. She has decided that, for now, she will take a career break.'

Georgia was secretly relieved, but merely nodded politely and made no comment.

'So that leaves a vacancy in the department for a new DI,' he explained.

Georgia turned slowly again to Stephanie, but Banham shook his head. 'As we know, Stephanie has passed her DI exams and both her boards, and is fully qualified for the post.' Banham looked at Stephanie as he spoke. 'I offered the place to her, but regrettably, she turned it down.'

'I don't want the extra hours or the responsibility,' Stephanie said. 'The kids are at university and I want to be on hand for them.' She smiled and then added, 'And have a little extra time for myself.'

'That's fair enough,' Banham said. He turned back to Georgia. Then the penny dropped for Georgia. DI David Dawes was coming back. He was known as a 'gangs expert', and had been called in for difficult gang feud cases on two previous occasions. Stephanie had bedded him and then got bored, and dropped him. Georgia couldn't bear him, she found him a boring know-all, a little squirt with a paid-for education, rich parents, and an expensive, but bad, haircut. She sighed inwardly. Working with him was going to be worse than babysitting Alison Grainger. She held her breath as Banham confirmed what she had already guessed.

'I have offered the job to DI David Dawes,' he said joyfully, 'and, he has accepted. He will be coming over to start next week, giving us a week of handovers before,' he looked at Alison, who up until now had said nothing, 'before we get married.'

'He's a first-class detective and very experienced as well as knowledgeable with all the gangs in and around London,' Alison said, looking Georgia in the eye. 'He has been in the force all his working life, and was made up to a DI post very quickly.'

Georgia stopped herself saying that was because his father was an ex-police commander.

'So, I'm sure you've got a lot to learn from him,' Alison continued, making Georgia bite down on her tongue even further.

'He really is an expert on London gangs,' Banham added.

He thinks he is, Georgia thought, but didn't say it. She nodded. 'Will that be all, sir?'

'No,' Banham said. 'I also wanted to say thank you for speaking up for our informants in court. They got lighter custodials because of the speech you gave.' He looked her in the eye. 'Georgia, I know you're upset they've gone to prison, and I know you feel the system could have done more to support them, but the bottom line is they committed a serious crime and they are answerable to the law like everyone else.'

'I'm not arguing they committed the crime, guv. I'm worried for their safety in the young offender institution.' She swallowed down the lump she felt forming in her throat.' If word gets out that they were snouting for us, they'll be watching their backs twenty-four hours a day. You know yourself the price of informing around these gangs is death.'

'I am assured they will be under constant surveillance in there, Banham told her. 'And we have managed to keep the two of them together.' Georgia was aware he was watching her carefully. 'No one will want to take on our Panther,' he told her, the side of his sensitive blue eyes crinkling as he smiled at the thought. 'She will more than look after herself in there, and Alysha too. Tink and Lox weren't involved, so they aren't in the equation.'

'I am confident that no harm will come to them,' Alison added.

Georgia glared at her, and just managed to say nothing. She then turned back to Banham. 'I was going to ask about Tink,' she said to him. 'She will be coming out of hospital in the next few days. Lox is already out, and living alone in the flat on the Aviary. What about their safety? And what about the Aviary, and the state of that, the council have yet again refused …'

'DI Johnson,' Alison butted in, 'you have allowed yourself to get far too involved with those girls, and the problems of the Aviary Estate. Veronica Andrew will be fine. If she and Alice Baker … Lox, hadn't been injured, they would be in front of a judge too, and probably should have been. Personally, I believe they are as guilty as the other two.'

'Tink has paid a very high price,' Georgia said, just stopping herself telling Alison that this had happened because the police had reneged on their promise to push the council for another grant for rebuilding the estate. She shook her head. What was the point? Alison didn't have a clue.

Stephanie obviously saw the storm brewing and jumped in on Georgia's side. 'They are young, very young girls, none have had parental guidance, they have survived and they had started to make remarkable changes to make it easier for their kids in the future. They needed more money to make good. No one would help them and all their hard work building and expanding the estate had been burned to the ground. An opportunity presented itself to make quick money. Yes, it was illegal, and stupid, a big mistake, but it was too big a temptation. Tink lost her shop, she had been teaching kids there were other ways to survive. She nearly died because of those drugs. It wasn't those girls that brought them onto the estate, it was Maxted's gang and the Zhangs.'

'They're behind bars, too,' Alison reminded her.

277

Stephanie nodded. 'And Lox took a bullet that just missed an artery, and Alysha and Panther are paying the price for their stupidity.'

'That isn't our problem.'

'I'd argue that partly it is,' Georgia argued. 'We promised we'd try and get another grant from the council for them.'

'Which we did, and our request was turned down,' Banham said sharply, now jumping to Alison's defence.

'So that's it, is it?' Georgia heard herself raise her voice. 'We just leave them now, do we?' She stared defiantly at him. 'Lox and Tink up there, both badly injured, and Alysha and Panther in constant danger of being murdered in prison. Lox and Tink are still our informants, they're back on the payroll. We have a duty to protect them.'

'You will need to take that up with DI Dawes,' Alison told her dismissively. 'He will be in charge of informants budgeting, and estate patrols, when he gets here. Personally I think they should come off the payroll permanently. They have proved themselves to be deceitful.'

Georgia and Stephanie turned to each other, but as Georgia opened her mouth to argue Banham spoke.

'That's it, then, I think, for now,' he said with a dismissive nod. 'Thank you, Georgia, Stephanie.'

Summer, Lox, and Amber were waiting as Tink limped slowly out of the hospital ward. The hair on the side of her scalp had started to grow back in tiny tufts, and was covered in strong-smelling bright orange cream to keep the pink and blistered skin underneath it protected. Her scalp was still raw in places, but, as she pointed out, she was at least colour-coordinated – the bare burnt skin matched the pink hair on the other side of her head, although that had also been growing, and an inch of ginger roots were now peeping through.

She had been given a sling to help speed up the healing process for her badly broken arm and shoulder. Her left arm was resting in that while her right hand held the crutch that she leaned on as she limped along the corridor to meet them. The knife wounds that had been inflicted in her stomach had been stitched, so leaning on the crutch was fine; it was the straightening after that made things difficult. The knife wounds where she had been stabbed in her calves and thighs by the Zhangs, like pins in a map, were also covered in stitches. The knife had pierced deeply into the top of her thigh, which was already burned and blistered, so the doctors feared the damage and her limp might be permanent. However, she had survived, they told her, and for that everyone was delighted.

She limped, very slowly, out of the hospital exit doors and squinted as the early spring sun pierced her eyes. A month inside the hospital, two weeks of it in intensive care, and her eyes had to adjust to the daylight.

'Wayne's got the car just over there,' Amber told her. 'Can you manage OK?'

'Easy-peasy,' Tink nodded and lifted her crutch. 'Didn't want it at first, but now I'm glad I've got it.' 'They can't have me for carrying an offensive weapon and it may come in handy,' she laughed. 'I might push it up George Zhang's arse.'

'You won't get the chance,' Summer told her. 'Maxted and the Zhangs never got bail. They're all looking at *very* long custodials, and their lieutenants are goin' down with them. We are safe. No one is threatening the Aviary at the minute.'

'Mind you, it's in a shitty state,' Amber added, taking a position on the other side of Tink, opposite Lox as they all walked at a snail's pace over to Wayne's car.

Wayne was standing in front of his battered Nissan, his rear door open, and his cap tipped down in a jest of a chauffeur.

'Let me help you in, madam,' he said with a grin.

'Lysh and Panth were refused bail too, then,' Tink said to Lox, as they settled into the back of the car together. 'S'gonna be a sorry old sight back at the flat.'

Lox put her arm very carefully around Tink. 'But it ain't for ever,' she said, trying to sound bright. 'And we gotta get on and get stuff done so they got something good to come out to.'

'You won't be alone,' Summer told her. 'I am only a few blocks away, and Amber and Wayne are on the next block. We'll get through this. All the Alley Cats will be there for you.'

'There won't be no more Alley Cats, though, will there? Not now we ain't got a community hall, no shops and no grant. We ain't gonna touch nothing illegal again, so we can't get no money to make a better tomorrow, so that ain't gonna happen.'

'Don't give up, Tink,' Lox and Summer said together.

'We done so much, and we only stole them drugs and guns to help the Hardys out of their debt. Big mistake that was too.'

'We'll build it up again,' Summer assured her. We've got a good seventy Alley Cats out there, and together we can do it. We'll tom double time, an' give special offers if we have to.'

Tink shook her head. 'Won't be the same without Lysh and Panth,' she said sadly.

'Georgia Johnson says they'll do about three years, and that's taking into consideration that she's given them character references and stuff,' Lox told her.

'Well, they gotta have somefing to come back to. Can't have a burnt out estate,' Summer added.

'Why not, that's what we grew up wiv? Look at the mess we made trying to make it better for the next generation.'

'Yeah, but look at what we achieved,' Lox said looking at Summer, as she tried desperately to pull Tink out of her depression. 'We got Zhang's lot and Maxted all banged to rights, they ain't gonna do no harm to no one's kids no more.'

'Weren't them though, was it, that killed everyone, it was mad Karen Hardy, and we tried to 'elp her. It was trying to 'elp her and her mum from being done in that got Lysh and Panth banged up.'

'Well, Karen ain't gonna do no harm to no one no more,' Amber said.

'What you gotta do, Tink,' Wayne piped up as he pulled up at a red traffic light, 'is get stronger and better. You got a lot of injuries, and you need to rest up for a good month or so. After that you'll feel better in yourself. See, yous all dark and depressed right now, and understandable too, you been to hell and back, but you gonna get better and then your head'll be OK, and you can make plans again. Till then you need to just rest up.'

'Council refused another grant,' Tink shrugged picking at a scab on her knee with an un-manicured nail. 'So no plans to be made. We can't get no corn, 'cos we can't sell nothing illegal, and we got no shops to sell anything legal in, an' I can't do hair 'n' stuff wiv my arm, so end of.'

Lox moved in closer and hugged her friend very gently. 'You can still teach hair and nails an' stuff, from the flat,' she offered. 'When you're stronger. And you can do people's hair an' stuff when you're better, home to home like. That's what you got your qualification for, and that's what you're so good at, and that'll get you some corn and will give you somefink to do.'

Tink tried to shrug again, but winced in pain. 'We'll

281

see,' she said pulling her hand away from the scab she had been picking at.

'Yeah, just concentrate on getting stronger for a bit, an' we'll be there whenever you need us,' Wayne said again.

Due to the circumstances of the case and the fact Georgia had spoken so highly of the two girls, the judge said he was showing leniency due to the fact that they had contributed so much to their community. Panther and Alysha were each given sentences of five years and sent to a young offender institution. When it came to the Zhangs, Ray Maxted, and Maxted's lieutenants, the judge made it quite clear he was showing no leniency. All were given life sentences with the recommendation that there was no consideration of parole for at least fifteen years. Their fellow gang members all received considerable sentences, and all were sent to separate prisons.

Tink was getting stronger, and doing as Lox told her, resting up a lot, so she and Lox could make the weekly journey to see Alysha and Panther. Wayne had offered his services as a taxi driver, adding that no one knew the way to the young offenders' unit better than him. After a lot of encouragement from Amber, and Lox and the rest of the Alley Cats, he too was making a new start for himself after coming out of prison. He was now going straight and was planning to become a cab driver.

Tink didn't want to take his time when he could be earning. If she agreed to let him drive her to see Alysha and Panther once a week, she said, then she was determined to pay her way, so when she got better she planned to put up an advert at the edge of the estate, telling neighbours and residents that although her shop had been burnt down, she would be taking clients in her flat on the thirteenth floor.

Lox encouraged and worked with her constantly on her physio. Both their legs were getting better from walking the thirteen flights of stairs every day, albeit very slowly. And Tink was working hard on the arm physio as she was so keen to get back to doing hair. She could use both hands and one arm fully, which meant if Lox washed the client's hair, Tink could sit in a chair and do the tinting, colouring, and cutting while seated.

They were expecting a client at three o'clock on this Thursday afternoon, so when the bell rang at half past two, they were both a little surprised, then nervous.

Lox told Tink to stay sitting and not to come out of the room.

She put her cup back on the table and her plate of biscuits beside it and made her way over to the window, then moved the curtain slightly, to peep around it. At first she didn't recognise the man that stood at her door, and then she realised that she did.

Adam Cambridge had a generous and kind face. He looked even better in person than the man she saw every week on television, talking about his rise from rags to riches and how he wanted to encourage others to do the same. She had to pinch herself to make sure it was actually him on their doorstep and she wasn't dreaming.

'Who is it?' Tink whispered.

'Adam Cambridge,' came the reply.

'Yeah, and my dad was a bishop,' Tink joked back.

Lox giggled and went to the door.

'Still smells of smoke up here, and yesterday's cabbage,' Adam said as Lox opened the door and stood staring at him, speechless and blushing.

'Can I come in?' he asked her.

Lox opened the door and he stepped inside, and then she showed him through to the lounge.

Tink was tidying her bag of hair rollers. She looked up and stared at him, and then she turned to Lox. Before she could say anything his arm went out to shake hands, but then noticing she was resting one of hers on the table, and obviously couldn't stretch it out completely, he quickly brought it back.

'Hello, Veronica. I'm Adam Cambridge.'

'I know who you are.'

He turned to Lox. 'Alice – or would you prefer Lox?' he asked, turning to the other girl, 'wrote to me and I have been following your story in the paper.

'It's Tink actually, my name is Tink, not Veronica,' Tink said. 'And my sister is Lox. Are you on your own?' she asked him, suddenly becoming nervous, and frowning at Lox.

'I've got my secretary and my solicitor in the car. I didn't ask them to come up, I wanted to wait to see what you said.'

Tink frowned again.

'I can ask them to come up if you want,' he continued.

'What for?' Tink asked, frowning, confused.

He picked up his phone and spoke quickly to someone asking them to join him, then clicked his phone shut, slipping it into the inside pocket of his silk suit. 'It's all right,' he assured, smiling at Tink. 'I know all about you, and what's happened to you.' He turned to Lox again. 'Lox here wrote to me, and asked for my help. I front a television programme on business advice and investment.'

Tink nodded, remembering then that Lox had indeed mentioned she might write to Adam. They were curled up together watching the television at the time, and Adam had been on, talking about investing in projects.

'The letter interested me,' he told Tink. He was looking around at the peeling wallpaper and the sofa that dipped so badly in the middle it looked more like a banana. 'I have been to this estate many times since. I read what happened to your community hall and shops. I also read about the Rook block being burned out yet again recently, and the children being in dire need of a play area and things to do. Now I hear that Alysha, and … Panther, is it? … are in prison for drug and firearms offences. I also understand that their crimes were not for personal profit but to help the children rebuild their estate.'

'It's a long story,' Tink said.

'Yes, and I know what happened to you, too. I'm so sorry.'

Tink frowned. 'That wasn't in the papers.'

'No, Lox has been keeping me informed, and I am following your story.'

There was another knock on the door. 'May I?' he asked walking to open the door to his secretary and team of advisors, and inviting them in.

Tink turned to Lox but before she could say anything, a very well-dressed man and woman walked into the room.

'Lesley and Glenda, my legal advisor and PA,' Adam said. 'We have all followed your journey, and we want to tell you that we admire you, very much,' he added. 'All of you, for what you have been trying to do to this estate. I was born around here. It's a place close to my heart. I am a self-made man. I made my money on my own.'

'I don't like to be rude,' Tink said. 'But I've got a customer coming to get her hair done in a minute, and it takes me a while to set up.'

'I'll come to the point, then,' he said, half-smiling at Tink's bluntness. 'I am here to offer you a proposition. I would like to invest in this estate. Help you to build your shops, community hall, and children's playground back up. I too, would like to see somewhere for the kids to have clubs, and sports and music and local shops. I remember the same problems in my time: bored and depressed children. That spells disaster.'

'That's what we wanted,' Tink said. 'But lots of –'

'Obviously, I will make it legal, and I'll take a small percentage,' he interrupted. 'That's what I do. I'm an investor. I invest in businesses.'

Tink and Lox turned to each other, both too surprised to speak.

'Also, I would like to help your friends. I would offer them my legal advisor.' He indicated the man standing next to him carrying a laptop.

'Lesley Grant,' he said.

Tink looked at the laptop he was carrying. 'You shouldn't carry that round here,' she laughed. 'Lots of tea leaves on this estate. The kids are out of control again. You could get mugged.'

Adam smiled.

'She's serious,' Lox said. 'I hope you gave the young 'uns downstairs some money to look after your car. 'Cos if you didn't it won't have any wheels on it when you go back.'

Adam smiled again. 'Lesley would like to put in an appeal on your friends' behalf,' he told them. 'See if we can get their sentences reduced. After all, as your friend said, what your friends did was wrong, very wrong, but you only took the firearms and drugs to prevent them causing harm around London, and you thought you could sell them to help the underprivileged around here. Then, when you had them, you hid them because you didn't know what to do with them.'

'That isn't quite what happened,' Tink said. 'But why do you care?'

'I care about this estate. I care about the future of it, and I see it as an investment,' he said plainly. 'And that's the business I'm in, investing in things.'

286

'*Can* you get their sentences reduced?' Lox asked, turning to Adam's legal advisor.

'I'm going to try, if you'll agree to let me,' Lesley said. 'First thing I would like you to do is to start an association. I thought we'd call it "Funds not guns". We will get you a lot of media attention, talking about what you did, and why weapons and drugs don't pay.'

'That'll just piss a lot of people off in Youth Offenders,' Tink argued.

'I disagree. I think it will help your friends. And while all that's going on, we will be investing, and applying for backers, and starting the rebuilding of your community area and shops. In a couple of years I think you'll see a flourishing estate. If you accept my help.'

'We'll have to run it past the others when I visit,' Lox told him.

'Of course,' Adam told her. 'But I think you'll find opportunities like my offer don't come along every day.'

'So you are going to repair *all* the damage on the estate?' Tink questioned.

'Every bit of it, and build some very good buildings for activities that will be fun and profitable. We'll get media backing and feature you and your friends as a reason not to use drugs or weapons.

'And all the while we'll be appealing for reduced sentences for them,' Lesley added.

'Sounds too good to be true,' Tink said, turning to Lox.

'If you have a dream, it truly can happen,' Adam Cambridge told her, with another of his half-smiles. 'But you must never give up, no matter what life throws at you,' he added.

Two Months Later

Georgia and Stephanie were having lunch when DI Dawes walked into Georgia's office without knocking. 'Have you heard what's happening on the Aviary Estate?' he asked them.

Georgia looked up. 'Yes, of course I have. Work has started already. The kids' playground is up and running and there hasn't been any trouble there since it started.'

Dawes nodded. 'Yes, all since I came back on board,' he said smugly. 'I was in a meeting about it the other night. All the big bods were congratulating me on the work I've put in on that troubled estate in the short time I've been here.' He turned, beaming, to Stephanie. 'It's all looking good for me and for my next promotion.'

Georgia turned to Stephanie, who hadn't batted an eyelid.

'It was one of the reasons I took the job here,' he continued. 'No one else could sort that estate out and I knew I could. I merely told them we were showing a no tolerance policy down there. Any drug or firearm or knife found on the premises and they would be in front of a judge. Courts are showing no tolerance either; it was jail for carrying weapons or any amounts of drugs, no matter how insignificant. And that's done it.'

'If you say so,' Stephanie said.

'I suspect it has more to do with the fact that our informants enabled us to capture the RIP and EIB gang leaders, and that most of their soldiers are locked away

289

too and won't be seeing daylight in a long, long while,' Georgia told him. 'No one down there to cause trouble now, and with the playground nearly up and running the kids are happy, and won't be out on the streets.'

'Whatever,' he shrugged. 'I'm Chief Investigating Officer on anything that happens down there, so I get to take all the glory.'

'You'll have so little to do, then,' Stephanie said with a grin and a wink at Georgia. 'Seeing that it's all sorted down there, for now. So, how about I cook you supper tonight?'

Georgia just managed to stop herself saying she hoped it choked him.

A sample from

BEHIND YOU!

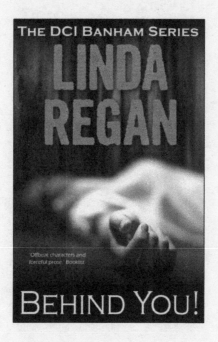

Prologue

'Are you enjoying yourselves?'

'YES!' the audience shouted.

'Oh no you're not,' the Ugly Sisters shouted back, goading the studio audience to join in.

'OH YES WE ARE!' came the animated response.

The smaller of the two over-dressed pantomime dames jumped up and down on the spot, squealing like a spoiled child. 'Oh no you're not!'

The response was even louder. 'OH YES WE ARE!'

'Blimey.' Lottie Banham pointed to the television screen. 'I'm sure that's Roy Hudd, but who's the thin one? I know his voice.' She looked over to her brother, suddenly aware he wasn't watching. 'Paul? Sorry, are you hating this? There's a rerun of three old comedies after.'

Her brother shook his head. 'Not at all, I'm enjoying watching the kids enjoy it.'

The children giggled and shouted at the screen, as if they were in the live audience. Lottie and eight-year-old Bobby still wore paper hats from their Boxing Day lunch; little Madeleine modelled a glittering tiara which matched the pink fairy outfit, complete with fluorescent wings and sparkly pink ballet pumps that Paul had bought her for Christmas.

'I can't believe how big they're getting,' he added.

Bobby screwed his face up and Madeleine giggled. A smile spread across Paul's face.

'Actually,' he said to his sister, 'I was just about to go

anyway. I've got some things to do, and I'm on call so I should check in with the station.'

Lottie gave her brother a knowing look. 'Are you meeting Alison?' she asked.

'No, as I said, I'm on call.'

'Shame,' Lottie replied. 'I approve of Alison, she's good for you. And she really likes you.'

'Alison is my sergeant, and that's as far as it goes, OK?'

'You fancy her,' Madeleine chipped in, her uncle's love life suddenly more interesting than the pantomime. 'Bobby told me you did.'

'I'd just like to see you happy again,' Lottie said.

Banham stood up, lifted his niece from the sofa and held her high in the air. 'I think I'll put you on top of the Christmas tree. You look more like a fairy than the fairy that's up there.'

Madeleine squealed and giggled, spitting chocolate over the front of Banham's denim shirt. He pulled a handkerchief from his trouser pocket and wiped the chocolate from her chin. 'You're much prettier than Cinderella,' he said, 'even with chocolate all over your face. And one day I'll bet you'll marry a handsome prince and live happily ever after.'

She giggled again and he put her back on the sofa gently and carefully. 'Watch the pantomime,' he told her. 'You can tell me about Prince Charming later.'

'Oh, stay and watch it with us,' Lottie pleaded, 'and then I'll make us all turkey sarnies and fill you a doggy bag to take home, 'cos if you haven't got a date, I'll bet you've no food in the house.'

Banham picked up the sparkling shoe and carefully put it back on Madeleine's foot. He caught Bobby looking dolefully at him. 'What?' he asked him.

'I like Alison,' Bobby said. 'She's good at football.'

'Ah, but she's not better than me,' Banham told him. He nodded at the television. 'It's Brian Murphy,' he said to his sister.

'Who?'

'The other Ugly Sister. It's Brian Murphy, from *George and Mildred*.'

Alison Grainger had just put the word *TREE* on the Scrabble board. She scribbled down her score and looked up to see her father putting his letters either side of the R.

She frowned and shook her head. 'No, you can't have *MURDER*, Dad. It's not Christmassy.'

He looked indignantly at her from the other side of the onyx coffee table, but she didn't give him time to argue.

'We agreed only words with a Christmas theme,' she said quietly. 'Murder has nothing to do with Christmas.'

'Yes it has,' he said gruffly. 'You're a detective sergeant in the Murder Division, and you're on call, and it's Christmas.'

Alison looked at her mother, but there was no support to be had.

'If there's a murder it'll ruin our Christmas,' her father argued. 'Because you'll have to go and solve it, and your mother and I will be left here alone.' He nodded his head. 'So it has everything to do with our Christmas.'

Alison shook her head. 'No, that wouldn't wash in court.'

'We're not in court, Alison,' he said, raising his voice. 'Tell her, Beryl. This is my house, and it's Christmas, and we're having a friendly game of Scrabble.'

'Let him have it,' her mother said anxiously. 'It's only a game, Alison.'

'That's double points too,' her father said, stabbing his large finger at the scoresheet.

'No, it's cheating,' Alison said firmly. 'What's the

point of playing Christmas Scrabble if we can cheat?'

There was a silence.

'OK, fine by me,' Alison said at last, throwing her hands in the air and standing up. 'Absolutely fine. It's your go, Mum. I'm going to make some coffee. Do you want some?'

'I'll make it,' her mother said, starting to get up.

'No,' Alison told her. 'It's your go; put a Christmas word down.'

'I can't, I've got mainly vowels,' Beryl Grainger said apologetically. 'I'll miss this turn and make the coffee. You go again, Alison.'

'I can't go either,' Alison said. 'I haven't got any vowels.' She threw the pen down. 'Oh, let's call it a day. You win, Dad.'

There was another silence.

'What is it? What's getting to you?' Gerald asked his daughter.

Alison took a deep breath and put her hands to her eyes. 'Nothing. Sorry, Dad. I've been busy lately. I'm tired, that's all, and it's making me a bit snappy. Sorry. Carry on, I'll change my letters and miss my go.'

Gerald carefully studied his new letters for a few moments, then put six of them down on the board under the last R in *MURDER*. They spelled *ROMANCE*.

'Romance happens at Christmas,' he said innocently.

Banham closed his front door behind him and threw his keys on to the table by the door. He walked into the kitchen and put Lottie's doggy bags on an empty shelf, then opened the fridge and took out a can of lager. As he straightened up the photo on the wall made him catch his breath: a young blonde woman, proudly holding a new baby. He stared at it, then turned away and walked into the lounge, but too late; the memory was back. He looked around the bare room, imagining the Christmas they would have had if Diane and Elizabeth were still here. Elizabeth would have been eleven – just a few years older than his beautiful niece Madeleine. Diane would have cooked the family dinner, and together they would have watched Elizabeth tearing her presents open. The memory invaded him: his adored eleven-month-old daughter, her tiny head bloody and unrecognisable on her bunny blanket. Diane, only inches away, covered in congealing blood from multiple stab wounds as she reached out to save her baby. Ten years, one week, and around one hour ago – but their killer had never been brought to justice. And he hadn't been there for his wife and child when they needed him most.

He knew Lottie was right; his life had to move on, and Alison was right for him. But when he had tried to get close to her, the memories and guilt came back and he couldn't go through with it.

He popped the lager and took a long gulp. He should have rung her, but he hadn't known what to say after shying off at the last minute with the feeble excuse that business and pleasure didn't mix. She was furious, but he just couldn't admit the truth.

He would keep his appointment with the counsellor this time; it was his new year's resolution. If the counselling worked, maybe they could try again. The Phil Collins CD that Alison had bought him for Christmas lay on the coffee table. He slipped it into his stereo and pressed 'play'. 'A Groovy Kind of Love' filled the air. He flopped into an armchair and closed his eyes.

Then the phone rang.

More From Linda Regan

Guts For Garters
DI Johnson Series

Behind You
DCI Banham Series

For more information about **Linda Regan**
and other **Accent Press** titles
please visit

www.accentpress.co.uk